She'll trap his outlaw's heart with love's most dangerous secrets...

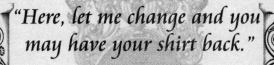

"Here, let me change and you may have your shirt back."

"It's not necessary—"

But she'd flitted into the next room.

Will stood, ill-at-ease. The corner of his eye caught movement in the other room. She stood with her back to him, struggling to take off his shirt with one hand. She lifted the hem. The sight of that curving indentation where her waist met her hips threatened to bring him to his knees.

Will knew he should look away, but he lacked the ability to do so. The blood had left his brain. Again.

She pushed one arm through the sleeve and then winced as the upward movement shot pain through the injured shoulder. She stood for a moment, her head down.

His feet moved forward. He told himself he was being kind.

Maybe he was.

By Cathy Maxwell

Cathy Maxwell

THE SEDUCTION OF SCANDAL

AVON

An Imprint of HarperCollinsPublishers

AVON BOOKS
An Imprint of HarperCollins*Publishers*
10 East 53rd Street
New York, New York 10022-5299

Copyright © 2011 by Catherine Maxwell, Inc.
ISBN 978-0-06-177212-2
K.I.S.S. and Teal is a trademark of the Ovarian Cancer National Alliance
www.avonromance.com

First Avon Books mass market printing: September 2011

Avon Trademark Reg. U.S. Pat. Off. and in Other Countries, Marca Registrada, Hecho en U.S.A.
HarperCollins® is a registered trademark of HarperCollins Publishers.

Printed in the U.S.A.

10 9 8 7 6 5 4 3 2 1

For Olathe, Kansas . . .
where I have my roots.

Prologue

Cease to think that the decrees of the gods can be changed by prayers.

Virgil

1810

Nestled between Liddell Water and Kielder Forest, Ferris Parish was located on a piece of land that jutted boldly into Scotland, although only the wealthy took pride in English roots.

The rest were descended from reivers, those brazen border raiders who had crossed the line between Scotland and England with impunity, rustling livestock, kissing women, and wrecking havoc in the name of justice or good fun, which-ever term fit their purpose at the moment—until the first earl of Bossley had taken control. He'd battled the raiders, offered protection to his people, and brought peace to a land rich in bounty.

And the parish had prospered.

But that had been almost two hundred years ago, and times had changed. The crofters were no longer bold, and the current earl of Bossley far from just.

He'd left for school when still a lad and had never returned, preferring to seek out the world. Few remembered him. He'd been away from the parish for too long.

But upon his father's death and his inheritance, the earl finally came home, and they discovered he had become a hard man.

A greedy, ambitious one.

His word ruled as law in a way his father and father's father would not have condoned. His coffers grew rich off the assessments he charged his crofters. He expected payments for duty, for privilege, for protection . . . although it was from him the people needed protecting.

Only a fool refused to pay—and the earl's power grew stronger.

* * *

The storm finally drove him to seek shelter.

He'd pressed on through the wind and rain, knowing that as one of Bossley's men he would be an unwelcome guest. But lightning struck too close. To ride on would be madness.

He turned back, his horse anxiously moving toward the nearest cottage. It was the miller's home, a fine stone building with quarters for the family on one side of the mill house and shelter for the animals on the other. The light in the window beckoned him closer.

Rain poured off the brim of his hat as he dismounted and trudged under the roof of the stalls. He didn't bother to unsaddle his horse because he knew he would not be asked to stay. Two miserable cows and a goat stood huddled together, staring morosely out at the evening's gloom.

There was no fodder. Fodder cost money.

His gelding snorted his disappointment. "Wait until we reach your own stall," he said to pacify the horse, then took off running through the rain toward the house's front door.

To his surprise, it was cracked open.

"Hello?" He pushed upon the door.

It swung to reveal a tableau of several men

crowded into the room. They stood over the miller's body. Seth was his name. Seth Pearson.

His wife was weeping. She was pregnant, and the two children they already had, both no older than five, buried their faces in her skirts.

Joshua Gowan, the village blacksmith, was bending over Pearson's body. The men's coats were wet, as if they'd just come in from the rain as well. Water dripped from their boots onto the floor and the air smelled of wet wool, home-baked bread, and blood.

The first impression was that Pearson was dead, but a low moan belied that thought. The man lived . . . but why was he on the ground?

And then he noticed Pearson's legs. They were bent at an unnatural angle, blood seeping through his stockings and staining the floor-boards.

Pearson's wife's eyes went alive with anger when she caught sight of him gaping at her husband's legs. "What do you want? Haven't you done enough? We have no money. You've taken it all, or has Lord Bossley sent you here to check his man Porledge's handiwork—"

"Sarah," Gowan ordered, his voice sharp. "Be still."

"How can I be still?" she demanded, her voice

sounding as if it came from the very bowels of her soul. "My husband has been ruined. Destroyed. Seth can't work like this. And he stands at the door as if he knows nothing. Take a look. See what has been done! What the devil has wrought—?"

"Take her out of here," Gowan ground out, "and the children, too." The order was swiftly carried out by one of the two other men in the room. Broxter was his name, and the other, who stayed with Gowan, was McBride.

"Hold Seth down," Gowan told McBride. "Be ready." Without wasting a movement, Gowan grabbed one of the injured legs and yanked the shattered bone in place.

Pearson shrieked in agony—

And the man fled his post by the door, unable to witness more.

His stomach churned with a bile he could no longer contain. He stumbled out into the rain, bending over and heaving as if his body wished to rid him of his doubts. Lightning shook the world but he no longer feared God.

What sort of man destroyed another for money? How much more could a simple miller give?

He'd pretended he hadn't known what was happening. Fealty to the title dictated he do so—

and there was personal loyalty as well—but he had reached the breaking point.

The rain started to let up. He wiped his mouth with the back of his gloved hand as he walked to retrieve his horse, shame in his shoulders, his heart, his soul.

How could he go on? And even if he was posted some other place, how could he ignore what he knew?

The miller, a man as young as himself, was ruined. If he could not walk, he could not earn a livelihood.

Simon Porledge was well known. He was a bully boy the earl often used to inflict his will. Simon probably hadn't even thought twice about breaking the miller's legs. His lord Bossley's orders were all that mattered. Why, even now, the henchman was probably slaking his thirst down the road at the Old Buck, a public house.

The man threw the bridle over his horse's head, his movement curt in his disgust over his own powerlessness.

The earl of Bossley yearned to rise to the highest ranks of this country. They spoke of him someday leading his party and being named prime minister—and thanks to the money he stole from his crofters, he had power.

No one would stop him. In the rich, glittering world of politics and London, no one cared about a miller's family.

But he did.

He started to pull himself up in the saddle but then realized the leather was still damp. There were empty flour sacks close at hand. He grabbed one, ready to wipe down the saddle seat, and that was when an idea—so daring, so shocking—was born.

He could not challenge Bossley. He had responsibilities, loyalties . . . but what if no one knew it was him? What if he was disguised?

Stories from his childhood of a bold reiver named Black Thorn rose in his memory. The Thorn was a legend. He'd terrorized the countryside hiding his identity behind a mask.

Holding the flour sack up to his own face, a plan formed in his mind.

" 'Twas the miller's own fault," Simon Porledge muttered to himself as he tromped through the wet woods on his way to Lord Bossley's manor. His words ended upon a burp from drinking too much ale.

He didn't like having to be firm. Made him angry. That had been the case at the miller's.

Pearson should have kept his mouth shut, paid the price, and not given Simon any reason to lose his temper.

Bossley would not be pleased with him for lingering over a drink, or two, or four . . . but Simon had needed to wait out the storm somewhere, and the pub had been as good a place as any.

The paltry sum of coins he'd beaten out of the miller weighed heavy in his purse. Being his lordship's strong arm was not an easy job on the conscience, although Simon liked being on the side of the strong instead of that of the weak.

'Twas a dark hole he'd dug for himself, and he had no choice but to continue to jump to the earl's command. He feared the price of disloyalty—

Something, someone moved onto the path before him. A shadow. A bulky shape blacker than the night.

Porledge stopped short and squinted his eyes, disbelieving what he was seeing. It was the drink. Made him fanciful . . . and then the moon drifted out from behind a cloud, silhouetting the figure of a man on a black horse with pawing feet. He had no face but two dark holes where eyes should be.

"Simon Porledge?" a deep, netherworld voice demanded.

"Who's asking?" Simon dared to say.

"One who knows what evil you have practiced this night."

Porledge's heart slammed his chest. His knees, his hands, his whole body began to shake. The drink, he reminded himself. He'd had too much. This thing before him could not be real.

But in case it was, Simon took a step back. "I've done nothing. I've been nowhere."

The devil's horse moved forward. "You've been to the miller's house. Lay the money you stole from him on the ground and be gone."

"I didn't steal money. It's an assessment. 'Tis owed to Lord Bossley."

"Not any longer. Do as I say, Porledge, or I shall see you . . . to . . . *hell*."

With those words the specter lifted his arm. He wielded a cudgel that seemed as huge and formidable as one of the forest's mighty firs.

"You don't understand," Porledge protested, on the verge of tears, torn between two fears. "I dinna do it for myself. It's Lord Bossley. He makes the demands."

"Leave the money."

"*Be damned to you*," Porledge shouted and took off running, moving so fast that he churned the damp earth with his booted feet.

Porledge heard the horse leap at the chase. Hooves pounded at his heels. He felt the sweep of the cudgel. It grazed off his shoulder. This was no ghost, no play of drink and imagination. This man was real. His threat was real.

Porledge did what any prudent man would. He pulled the leather purse holding the miller's paltry payment out of his pocket and tossed it over his shoulder. But he didn't stop running. It was a good half hour before he realized he was no longer being chased.

And then he realized he must make his report to Lord Bossley.

A day later, Porledge's body was found facedown beneath the old stone bridge over Liddell Water.

In the midnight sanctuary of Holy Name Church, a man crawled on his knees to the altar. The guilt of Porledge's death weighed on his soul.

Dear Jesus, dear God, forgive me. He repeated the words, begging for solace. . . .

The response was Divine silence.

As it should have been.

Because he knew he would not stop.

He could not. The battle had been joined, and either he or the powerful Lord Bossley would win.

Chapter One

1811

She wouldn't have to marry Lord Freddie Sherwin.

Lady Corinne Justine Rosemont, youngest daughter of the seventh duke and duchess of Banfield, yearned to kick her heels up in joy, but there was no time for celebration. She had to reach the guest room her parents shared before Freddie stopped her.

The wide hall of the earl of Bossley's cavernous country estate was the perfect place for a sprint. Freddie's frantic *"Corinne"* only spurred her to run faster with little more than a glance over her shoulder.

He'd just come out of her bedroom. His face was flushed, his shirt hanging out over his dress evening breeches. "*Stop, please,*" he urged as he tucked himself in.

Her response was to give a quick knock on her parents' door. Without waiting for admittance, she turned the handle and threw herself inside. Slamming the door shut, she faced her parents and announced, "I will *not*, can *not*, *should* not marry Freddie Sherwin."

Her father sat in a chair beside the desk so that he could make best use of the reading lamp as he perused his paper. He did not look up or acknowledge her declaration other than to turn the page and frown at some article that obviously displeased him.

Nor did her mother respond. She was giving herself a critical eye in the dressing table's looking glass, her maid lingering behind her with a hare's-foot and powder. Circling her finger in the air around her face, the duchess commanded, "A bit more here, Delora. The weather in the north always brings the ruddy to my skin. I so detest that. Makes me look like a scullery maid."

Delora, dressed in Banfield's ducal colors of

green and white, immediately applied more powder to the duchess's flawless skin. People said Corinne was a replica of her mother at a younger age: slender figure, blonde hair so pale it could have been white, cornflower blue eyes. Her mother's figure had filled out through childbearing and age, but she was still a handsome woman . . . and a vain one. "And pin this feather down closer to my ear. I hate the idea of it flopping."

The maid dropped the hare's-foot to move the diamond clip holding a vibrant blue ostrich feather to the place where the duchess wished.

Corinne placed her hands on her hips in disbelief. "Did you not hear me? I said I should not marry Freddie. I *must* cry off."

Her father still ignored her, but her mother answered with a distracted air. "Oh, please, Corinne, you have been carrying on this way for the past three months. The wedding is in four weeks. It's too late to cry off. Can't be done. Will not be done." She smoothed out a stray eyebrow hair before adding with a bored sigh at having to state anything so obvious, "Besides, we are the guests of honor at dinner this evening. It would be *de trop* to join the guests waiting for us and announce over the dinner Lord and Lady

Bossley prepared especially for our pleasure that the wedding is off. Rude, actually. Very rude."

"But you don't understand," Corinne crowed in triumph. She'd expected her parents to refuse her demands. After all, they had been doing so ever since they'd decided she was to marry Freddie. "I just stumbled upon Lord Sherwin in a compromising way with *my maid* in *my* bed. I suppose he was whiling away the time before dinner . . . but his position was rude, actually. Very rude." She couldn't refrain from mimicking her mother. This was such a sweet, brilliant moment.

Now she had her father's attention. He lifted his nose out of his paper. "Say what?"

"Freddie was in *all his glory,*" Corinne happily informed her sire, glee overtaking righteous indignation. "He has the whitest buttocks. One can't miss them."

Oh, how she had come to despise this man who would be her husband. He was selfish, had a lazy intellect, and adored feeling superior to others.

She'd once caught him cheating at cards, a crime for which she was certain her father would have let her cry off, but it was not to be. Freddie had laughed away her objections, pointing out they'd been playing a "friendly" game. Her father, who was usually a stickler about cheating in any form—including those times when she and he played piquet—had agreed.

However, tumbling around in bed with his future wife's maid must have ranked above cheating. Corinne dived into her report. "Remember, I was just here and Mother suggested I might need a heavier shawl, so I returned to my room and that is when I caught him in the act. Oh, my eyes." She threw her hands over her eyes to dramatize her agony. "I would pluck them out if it would erase the memory."

Actually, opening the door and seeing Freddie's bare bum had made her burst into laughter.

"I did suggest you send Delora," her mother reminded her. She'd sat back in the dressing table chair to appear as if she'd been listening . . . although she did slide another glance at herself in the mirror. "I didn't think you should return to your room yourself. That's why we have servants. If you'd listened to me, you wouldn't be so distressed—"

"Or have found him cavorting—" Corinne liked the sound of that word. She had to repeat it. "Yes, *cavorting* with my maid if I hadn't gone myself." She couldn't suppress the grin any longer. "And I am most happy I did, because I can't possibly marry him—"

"Is this the French maid?" her father interrupted to ask her mother.

"Yes," the duchess answered. "The one Corinne insisted she must have. I warned her that you mustn't trust the French. We are at war with them . . . but she would not listen."

"Warned me?" Corinne repeated. "That Freddie would seduce her?"

"*She* probably seduced him," the duke said with a sniff, reopening his paper. "Her Grace is right about the French. Can't be trusted. Sack her."

"Delora," the duchess said, "go tell Sybil to pack her things—"

"*No*, wait," Corinne protested. "I like Sybil, and we should hear her side of the story." The maid was the child of impoverished émigrés. Corinne had met Sybil when the girl had been working as a menial in a dress salon. In a burst of sympathy over the young woman's plight—because after all, if Corinne, a duke's daughter, had been French, such could have been her fate, and she would not have enjoyed being a dressmaker's assistant—she'd offered the girl a position.

In truth, Sybil *wasn't* the best maid. She was haughtier than Corinne's grandmother, the dowager duchess, and often helped herself to creams, potions, and clothes as if she didn't think Corinne would miss them. Furthermore, a good maid would not have been taking liberties with her mistress's betrothed, but this was not the direction Corinne wanted the conversation to take. Sybil was welcome to Freddie—once Corinne cried off.

"We must hold Freddie accountable," Corinne informed her parents. "I do not want a husband who cavorts"—oh, she adored that word—"when my back is turned. Especially in my bed. I will not sleep there this night. I can't." She tried to sound weak, defenseless. "My sensibilities—"

"Oh, posh," her mother interjected. "If you were Belinda," she said, referring to Corinne's older, married sister, "you would be carrying on, swooning and in tears, but you are made of sterner stuff, Corinne. So much like your father. We shall have the sheets changed and you can sleep there very well—"

"I don't want my *sheets* changed. I want my *betrothed* changed," Corinne said, dropping all pretense at weakness. "I *don't* like him, I don't *like* him, I don't like *him*."

"So you have told us several times," her father said. He'd reburied his head in his paper, and Corinne knew she must take action.

She crossed to him and slammed her hand upon the paper. "Then why won't you listen to me, Papa? What have I done that is so terrible that you would wish me married to the most annoying man in England? He slurps his soup. He talks over everyone. He believes himself the most handsome, the most clever, the wittiest—" She groaned her dislike. "He has no appreciation for anyone but himself."

The duke had not liked having his paper slapped. A militant gleam came to his eye, a promise of a reckoning. He put the paper aside and stood.

Perhaps Corinne had gone too far—*no, she hadn't*. She was desperate.

She stood her ground. "The sight of Freddie's naked bottom has not endeared him to me. If anything, the sight has made me realize I don't want to see the other side of him naked."

"Then you will have to consummate your marriage in the dark," the duke informed her.

"Please, Papa." She softened her voice, begging him. "Let me cry off—"

"A moment," her mother said, a warning. "Listening ears," she reminded them. She looked to her maid. "Delora, please go downstairs and inform the butler that we will join the company momentarily."

"I don't want to join them at all," Corinne declared. "I want to leave, *now*, this minute."

The maid practically ran from the room, both to carry out Her Grace's wishes, but also because Delora valued her position in the household. Her wide eyes said she'd heard more than enough and was truly shocked.

As the door opened and closed, Corinne caught a glimpse of Freddie hovering in the hallway. Her parents noticed him as well.

"He is such a dunderhead," Corinne murmured.

"And you have no one to blame for this state of affairs but yourself," her father answered. "I gave you your lead to choose a husband who was suitable. You did not. You had hundreds of suitors, and not one met your exacting standards."

"I'm a duke's daughter. Is it wrong to expect the best?"

Her father leaned forward so he could look her in the eye. "The best? How many offers have you had, Corinne? How much interest? And yet you have given every one of those men the cold shoulder. There had to have been at least one good man in the lot."

"Is it wrong to want to meet a man who has substance?" she asked, guilt edging her words.

"Freddie has substance. His father's money accounts are full of substance," her father answered.

"I'm not talking about money—although I know you believe I should," she added quickly to stave off another old argument between them. "Papa, I look at your generation and see men who are leaders and scholars. The men of my age have more hair than wit. They spend more time primping in front of their mirrors than I do. Their idea of substance is writing terrible poetry about the lobe of a woman's ear or placing outlandish wagers on silliness like seeing whose rig can reach Newmarket first."

"Sherwin doesn't write poetry," her mother chimed in.

"We should be thankful for that small favor," Corinne said.

"I attempted to find a husband of my generation for you," her father pointed out, "and you refused them."

"They were old."

"*I'm* old," the duke said, his exasperation clear. "But do you understand, my daughter, that at one time all the men my age whom you admire were silly young men like Sherwin?"

"I am not attempting to be difficult," Corinne pleaded.

"Well, you are very good at it," her mother announced tartly.

"I just want someone whom I can respect, who is young and handsome, and listens to what I have to say and wants to be with me not because I'm a duke's daughter but because he admires *me,* the person that is me. One who relishes my opinions and my passion and my silliness—"

"And your obstinacy," her father tagged on.

Corinne ignored him. The man she wanted was there. She knew it. She believed it. But she hadn't found him. "Life has to mean more than endless parties because you are bored with your marriage," she whispered, knowing she was describing her parents' marriage, and those of her brothers and sisters. "There must be more to life than what we have now."

"There isn't," her father said. "Life is about obligations. I've taught you that since you were knee high."

"And I've listened, Your Grace," Corinne answered. "I have helped with the parish poor, served charities. I've tried to be good."

"It's not about the poor." He crumpled his paper and tossed it aside. "The poor are the poor. They will always be there—poor. We are *not* poor. We marry for advantage to keep from being poor. Your obligation to this family, the name Banfield, is to marry the man I've chosen for you. Sherwin is remarkably well-heeled."

"I don't want to marry Freddie." Corinne sensed where this was going, but she would not budge.

Her father wouldn't either. "Our bloodline goes back to before the Conqueror to Rolfe the Great and we shall carry forward as stewards of this sacred trust delivered to us by our ancestors. I'm done with coddling you, Corinne. Sherwin may be an oaf, you might not like the look of his naked buttocks—and I'm not certain I blame you—but the earldom of Bossley is one of the richest in England. His father is not only wealthy but clever. And he is certainly a powerful ally."

"Because money is everything." Corinne hated this discussion.

"*Yes*," her father said, punching the air with one finger for emphasis. "It's a new world we have now, my daughter, and Lord Bossley is a man of our times. He lets nothing stand in the way of what he wants. And I want that man's power and influence for my own purpose. I want his wealth for my descendants."

"Which will include his son's bastards," Corinne couldn't keep from saying. "Because if Freddie pokes all the maids, his descendants shall populate the county."

"*Corinne,*" her mother chastised, but her father didn't bat an eye.

"You are naive about the ways of men. We are what we are. Perhaps *you* are what they call you: the Ice Maiden."

Corinne hated the nickname—especially since she feared it was true. She'd yet to meet that man who made her wish to toss aside her God-given sense. She'd never once felt giddy or silly or flush or any of the other things women claimed men did to them. She liked strong, practical men.

"I believe that the right man shall be everything I desire," Corinne said, silently praying it was true. "And I believe he will find in me the same. We shall mean those vows we make."

"You are betrothed to the right man for *my* purposes," her father said. "I don't care if you don't like Sherwin. I'm not overly fond of him myself. Yes, I believe he has disgraced himself with your maid. A gentleman is always discreet. However, the die has been cast, Corinne. My duchess is right. It is too late to cry off. You shall marry Sherwin in London four weeks hence and you shall go downstairs, greet his relations and friends, and be everything I expect of you."

His words settled in her stomach like stones. She was trapped. If only she could run away . . .

She bowed her head, no longer able to meet his eye. "I won't like him. I can't."

"You don't have to like him," her mother commiserated. "Your sister doesn't like her husband, but she has a very generous lover in Lord Hammond."

Corinne felt herself flinch. "I don't want a lover. I want a life that makes sense."

"This life *does* make sense," her father said, "for those in our class. It is what we do."

He didn't wait for her response but turned to the door. "Duchess?" He offered his arm.

Her mother tucked her hand in the crook of his elbow, giving herself one last glance in the looking glass. Both of them appeared regal and certain of their place in the world.

Corinne wished she could be like them . . . and she didn't understand why she wasn't. Her three brothers and her sister never questioned "what we do."

The duke opened the door. Freddie lingered on the other side of the hall. He'd put his time waiting for them to good use. His evening wear was in impeccable order, the brown waves of his hair once again in place, his expression composed.

Welcoming even . . . although there was a hint of worry about his eyes.

He was considered the catch of the Season. Even her own cousin had been calf-eyed in love with him. And Corinne had to wonder why she was able to so clearly see his faults, while everyone else appeared blind to them.

"I'm here to escort you downstairs, Your Grace," Freddie said.

"Very well," her father answered, accepting his due. He started for the stairs, but then stopped. "Sherwin?"

"Yes, Your Grace?"

"You will never again upset my daughter in that manner."

"I'm sorry, Your Grace, I do not understand to what manner you refer."

A glint of anger appeared in her father's eye. His gaze met Corinne's.

Her mother stood quietly, studying the crown molding.

Let me cry off, Corinne silently begged her father. *Please*.

His answer was to look away. "Don't be a 'dunderhead,' Sherwin," he said and started down the stairs, his wife on his arm.

Freddie had won—again.

Corinne's chest tightened with anger and disappointment.

The dunderhead didn't even bother to hide a smirk.

"Lady Corinne?" he said, offering his arm. "Shall we join the guests gathered to meet my soon-to-be bride?"

She couldn't cry off, but she didn't have to be obedient.

Corinne stomped on the toe of his thin leather evening shoes with all the might she could muster.

Freddie yelped and jumped back, his lower lip jutting into a pout, his brows lowering in anger.

"I'm not afraid of you," she informed him and turned to sail down the stairs, head high—

Her arm was rudely yanked back. She stumbled, almost fell. Freddie held fast and pushed her against the wall. The suddenness of his attack caught her off guard.

He leaned his body against hers. He was taller, stronger, heavier. "I don't mind a show of spirit," he said, his breath hot against her cheek. "In fact, I like it." He released her before she could gather her wits to retaliate.

Corinne had to use the wall for balance. Her first reaction was to double her fists and give him a roundhouse punch, much like she'd witnessed her brothers throwing at each other when they'd been playing rough, but she caught herself in time.

It would not be good for the company below stairs to catch her brawling with Freddie. Such an act would fuel gossip for years.

No, she had to be wiser, think ahead of him.

He walked to the top of the stairs. "Lady Corinne?" he said, offering a gentlemanly sweep of his hand to indicate he waited for her to descend first.

Corinne wanted to wipe the grin off his face, and she would. When he reached for her arm as she passed him, she jerked it away.

But he caught up with her downstairs and took her elbow right before she entered the reception room, where thirty of his friends, relatives, and neighbors waited to make her acquaintance.

"Now you've become interesting," he murmured, lifting her gloved hand to his lips and pulling her into the room to the sound of applause and good wishes.

Corinne had no choice but to don a smile and follow his lead—for now.

Chapter Two

Dinner was an endless affair.

In the reception room, during introductions, Freddie plastered himself to Corinne's side, taking her gloved hand whenever he deemed it acceptable, daring her to pull away, to make a scene, to risk scandal.

The company consisted of Lord and Lady Bossley's relatives and neighbors. It was the sort of dinner party that had to be done to introduce a new couple, although few of these guests would be invited to the wedding. That honor would go to important people. London people. And Corinne could see why. This was a hodgepodge group, and they behaved as if they barely knew each other.

Bossley's side—the Sherwins—was light on family. The only one in attendance from his people was an Aunt Minerva, who had a distressing amount of hair on her ancient chin and who had promptly fallen asleep after meeting Corinne.

Lady Bossley's side was represented by the young and charming couple Lord and Lady Landsdowne, and her sister, the gregarious Dame Janet, and her husband, a Sir Somebody or Other—Corinne didn't catch his name—who was such an old roué that he wore a bagwig and light blue silk evening clothes, and sported a patch of a prancing horse on his cheek. It had been ages since Corinne had seen someone in powder and patch, and she noted a faint air of camphor about his person.

Freddie had inherited his looks from his father. Lord Bossley was handsome in a rugged way. He'd obviously spent a great deal of his life in the sun and had the squint lines around his eyes to prove it. He was of medium height with generous, albeit distinguished, touches of silver in his thick brown hair to mark his sixty some years of age.

To meet him and his son, one would assume they were the most pleasant of people. Smiles always lurked on their faces, but Corinne knew that pleasantness was a mask Freddie wore and suspected it was the same with the father. A man didn't grow as powerful as Lord Bossley without a measure of ruthlessness.

She'd said as much to her parents. They had argued that her love of reading made her fanciful and she should turn to a higher quality of literature instead of novels pertaining to romance and adventure. Corinne had disagreed. She believed there was a great deal of truth to be found in fiction, and certainly few characters were as mysterious as she found Lord Bossley. She'd barely been able to discover anything about him.

Apparently, after finishing his university studies, he'd set out to tour the world, ending up on the island colony of Barbados, where he'd lived for close to fourteen years. Upon the death of his father a little over twenty-six years ago, he'd returned to claim the title. Since that time, he'd become an Important Personage. He'd taken a modest inheritance and turned it into a fortune. Everyone quoted him. Everyone curried his favor and turned to him for financial advice.

Corinne's uncle was Banker Montross, another famed and shrewd investor. She'd asked him recently what he thought of Lord Bossley. His gaze had narrowed at her as if he'd been surprised and appreciative of her question. "He's a tough customer in gentleman's dress," he'd answered. "I know because the same could be said of me. We both go after what we want, but I'm honest."

"And he's not?" Corinne had prodded.

"I've found no proof of chicanery," her uncle had answered. "But sometimes when a man is overscrupulous, it's a sign he is hiding something. Of course, I haven't been able to sniff anything out, bad or good, and I tried. The mystery to me is his life in Barbados. Granted it is a world away, but I've found no one from there who remembers him. They'd heard of him, but he didn't seem to be a part of society there. Not like he is here."

"He was a very young man then," Corinne had pointed out.

"I don't like mystery," her uncle had countered. "And I didn't want my daughter to marry his son." His only child, Abigail, had been in love with Freddie since they'd been children. She was now married to a stellar gentleman, and from what Corinne could see, her uncle was pleased with the match.

Of course, Corinne had duly reported this conversation to her father, who'd ignored her concerns. The duke's position was that everyone knew Bossley here and had known him for a good two decades and more. Besides, who cared about society on some island colony?

Who, indeed? A glance around the reception room told Corinne that everyone fawned over his lordship, including his wife, who had a habit of echoing the end of his sentences.

In contrast to her husband, Lady Bossley wasn't interesting at all. She was a good fifteen years younger than her lord and was as plump and pretty as they come. Her passion was rings, and she sported one on every finger whether her hands were gloved or not. Of course she'd been a grand heiress at the time of her debut into Society. Rumor had it Bossley had scooped her up into marriage before anyone had known his name.

As the ranking guests of honor, Corinne's parents had places at the head of the dining table beside Lord and Lady Bossley. Corinne was supposed to sit on her father's left, with Freddie on her mother's right.

Taking advantage of the confusion of settling twenty guests—including the chaos of what seemed to be a footman to service each individual—Corinne switched her place with that of the local squire's wife, Mrs. Rhys-Morton. It wasn't polite, and it was incredibly nervy of her, but Corinne felt she had to have space between Freddie, her parents, and herself.

Mrs. Rhys-Morton was beside herself to realize her dinner companion was a duke and that once the guests sat, it would be awkward to make a change. Corinne knew Lord Bossley had noticed what she'd done. He smiled. She smiled back. She sensed he was not pleased.

Freddie, who'd already polished off one bottle of wine while they'd been in the receiving room, was more interested in having his glass filled than where his betrothed was sitting. He was angry with her and apparently was showing her that anger by diving headfirst into his cups. The thought wandered through Corinne's mind that perhaps he was afraid that her father or even she herself might say something to *his* father about the maid.

She rejected the idea. Lord Bossley, dressed in elegant evening attire, didn't give the impression he cared overmuch about servants, and he certainly doted on his son. This was his heir apparent. He didn't see Freddie the way she did. He was indulgent, even when Freddie burped.

The dinner table setting was spectacular. Her

parents were known for their entertainments, but they did not possess the means to display the wealth shown by Lord Bossley. The glasses were crystal, the plates were trimmed in gold, and the silverware was heavy and solid. And everything, from the serving dishes to the braid on the footmen's livery, sparkled in the light of hundreds of candles.

Lord Bossley was in complete control of the evening. Whenever he had a story to tell, conversation stopped. Men and women would lean over their plates to hear what he had to say. Well, everyone save for Aunt Minerva, who'd nodded off over her soup.

Both Aunt Minerva and Dame Janet were seated at the low end of the table. It was apparent that Dame Janet had been placed there so that she could talk all she wished and not disturb anyone important. However, she fought that edict by sending very loud salvos of opinion up the table.

The chair between the two women, the one at the very end, was empty, and perhaps, given Dame Janet's talkativeness and Aunt Minerva's snores, that was a good thing.

The charming Lord Landsdowne sat on Corinne's right, while a very handsome—*truly*

very handsome—gentleman in a red military
jacket covered with badges and medals sat to
her left. He had the look of a young war god.
Corinne was not surprised that Freddie had overlooked introducing her to *him* earlier.

"I'm Major John Ashcroft, commander of the
local militia," he said in way of introduction.

"Lady Corinne," she said, finding herself suddenly shy. He had the most amazing blue eyes.
They went well with the dimple in his chin and
his curling black hair.

Corinne wasn't one to have her head turned
by a gentleman—except if the gentleman's looks
were exceptional . . . and Major Ashcroft fell
into that category. She was also pleased to tweak
Freddie's arrogant pride in any way she could.

So she turned flirtatious, and Major Ashcroft
kept the conversation flowing between her and
the other women seated around him. He didn't
have much competition. Lord Landsdowne was
involved in the political conversation going on
between the duke and Lord Bossley, and, across
from Corinne, Squire Rhys-Morton was busy
shoveling his supper into his mouth. His wife
chided him a time or two, but, given his girth,
the man obviously had a robust appetite.

The squire's wife leaned around Lord Landsdowne to say to Corinne, "You are so lucky, my lady, to have snagged Lord Sherwin. He is very much the catch. Tell me, how did the two of you first meet?"

That question.

Everyone romantic asked it. Usually, Corinne breezily answered they'd met through their parents. After all, she'd known of Freddie a long, long time. At least as far back as when she'd been thirteen and Abigail had been so mad for him.

But before she could speak, Freddie boozily jumped in. "Allow me to tell."

"I prefer to answer," Corinne argued. "She directed the question at me—"

"They called her the Unattainable," Freddie declared as if she hadn't spoken. With an opening like that one, even Dame Janet went silent. "But I knew that with enough charm, her defenses could be breached. She was just waiting for the right man."

Corinne gained a new respect for Freddie's drinking ability. He might have been in his cups, but his mind was shrewder than it was when he was sober. She gripped the handle of her fork. He spoke rubbish, but she could smile because she was picturing how he would yelp if she jabbed his nose with the tines.

"And what charms did you use?" Mrs. Rhys-Morton demanded with excited anticipation.

Freddie continued with some nonsense about wooing and buying flowers and being gallant. He left out his father's visit to her father and what she was certain had been a discussion of money. For whatever reason, Lord Bossley had insisted he wanted her for his son and was willing to pay for the honor.

Her papa might claim he was doing his duty toward her, but he hadn't been anxious to rid his hands of her until Freddie's offer.

And if Freddie had ever purchased one posy for her, she was at a loss to remember it.

She wondered what the table would say if she told the story of his bedding her maid and how incredibly white his backside was?

Corinne pushed her uneaten lobster around her plate. Was it too much to ask for a husband she could respect and admire? For a man who thought of something else besides his own leisure? His own interests? His own pleasure?

"Is the dinner not to your liking, my lady?" Major Ashcroft asked.

"The dinner is lovely, Major, thank you," she murmured and tried to take a bite.

"Don't force yourself," he responded, and she

had the urge to throw herself into his noble arms with her tale of woe. Why couldn't she have been marrying *him*? Why Freddie?

Major Ashcroft was the sort Corinne felt she could respect. After all, he had medals to prove his courage and his loyalty. He was the sort of man who would rescue damsels in distress and slay Freddie-dragons.

And then his gaze dropped to the decollete of her gown. It was a bold perusal . . . much like the sort of look Freddie gave her when he thought she wasn't looking.

Did men think women *wanted* to be ogled?

She tucked her napkin into her bodice and he looked away, aware that she had caught his leer—

"And *that*," Freddie said on a note of victory, "is why Lady Corinne is called the Ice Maiden."

Everyone at the table turned to look at Corinne to see what Freddie was talking about. He'd noticed what had been happening and had used her action against Major Ashcroft's roving eyes to his advantage. Heat rushed up her neck, staining her cheeks. Major Ashcroft had the good grace to be equally uncomfortable.

Before any more could be said, the dining room door opened. Without introduction or preamble, a tall man, close to Freddie in age, entered the room. He was dressed in black but not evening wear. The toes of his shoes were scuffed, and his thick, dark hair was in need of a barber.

"So good of you to finally join us, Will," Lord Bossley said in greeting, his annoyance clear.

"Sorry. So sorry I'm late." Will went straight for the chair at the foot of the table between the evening's two most undesirable guests, Dame Janet and Aunt Minerva. He had a lean, wiry frame with broad shoulders that hunched a bit, as if he tried not to attract attention. Dark brows gave him a distracted, earnest air, and the shadow of his beard emphasized his jaw. Corinne wondered if he'd been too busy to shave or if he had simply forgotten.

He wasn't an unattractive man in spite of being rumpled, and there was an air of intelligence about him.

"Your Graces," Lord Bossley said with an air of long-suffering, "may I introduce you to my foster son, the Reverend Mr. William Norwich."

Reverend? Foster son? Corinne caught herself staring in surprise. The man didn't look any kin to Lord Bossley or particularly reverent.

"Will," Lord Bossley said, "your preaching

bands?" He tapped the place on his chest beneath his throat to show what he meant. "If you won't dress for the evening, at least dress properly."

Reverend Norwich reached up to his neck as if surprised the symbol of his calling wasn't there. "They blow every which way," Reverend Norwich said as his fingers found the string that tied them and turned it around so that the two rectangles of white material that served in place of a neck cloth—and as the brand of his service to the Church—could be seen.

"You'd forget your head if it wasn't attached, Will," Freddie said as he lifted his wine goblet to his mouth.

"I fear you are right," Reverend Norwich answered with perfect pleasantness in Freddie's direction. A footman placed his dinner before him. He nodded his appreciation and said, "I missed grace. I'm so sorry. One moment, please." He bowed his head.

No one had said grace before the group had eaten. Corinne wondered if this was a mild rebuke or an earnest belief. She'd met more than her share of posturing pastors. The Church was as political as anything else in England. Of course, all those men shaved.

After a silent moment, Reverend Norwich

picked up his fork and tucked in as if he hadn't eaten in a week.

"Foster son?" The duke of Banfield asked the question Corinne had wondered. For some reason, Reverend Norwich tickled her memory. Had they met before? She was certain she hadn't known Freddie had a foster brother. Or had she?

"I brought Will home from Barbados," Lord Bossley said. He'd finished his dinner and now sat back in his chair, at ease to entertain. "I found him living on the streets, no more than nigh high and begging for any crust of bread he could find. I couldn't leave him there. He was all of three. Big eyes and big belly. You know how they are when they are starving. 'Course, by the way he is gobbling his dinner, he's still starving."

Corinne noticed Mr. Norwich slowed his eating.

"How good-hearted of you," the duchess was saying.

"A white child on the streets of that island would have been prey for so many evils," Lord Bossley declared, accepting her praise. "I did what I felt I was obligated to do for my fellow men. Over the years, I've paid for Will's education, gave him the curacy at Holy Name

Church right here in Ferris. And he is thankful I have, aren't you, Will?"

The Reverend Norwich had been busy buttering his bread, as if he'd been trying to ignore being the topic of conversation. However now, as if on cue, he looked up. "Yes, my lord," he answered, his tone soft, dutiful. He knew what was expected of him and did it . . . and then his gaze met Corinne's.

For a second, he stared as if shocked to see her. His butter knife stopped moving.

"Do you remember her, Will?" Freddie asked as if he'd been anticipating the moment the two of them met.

He did. Anger appeared in Mr. Norwich's eyes, censure—and she didn't understand why.

If they had met before, she had no recollection. Disconcerted, Corinne picked up her fork. She'd been staring at the clergyman as hard as he'd been looking at her. "Remember me, my lord?" she said, directing the comment to Freddie. "I don't remember you talking about a foster brother or being introduced to him. When would we have met?"

"His name hasn't come up in conversation," Freddie answered blithely. "Will and I live two very different lives. However," he added as if warming to the topic, "you did meet. Years ago at one of Lady Mayhew's routs," he explained to the table at large. "Will asked Lady Corinne to dance."

Lady Mayhew's parties had been for the younger set, those who had not yet been introduced to Society, to teach them the social graces. Corinne had to have been fifteen, perhaps sixteen. She slid a glance in Reverend Norwich's direction. He focused on his eating.

"Still don't remember him, do you?" Freddie said in a teasing whisper.

"It's unimportant, Lord Sherwin," Mr. Norwich said from his end of the table.

"Oh, come, Will. You can't still have your nose out of joint after all these years," Freddie commented. "That would be silly. And you won't mind my sharing the tale?" Without waiting permission, he launched into it. "It all happened back in our days at Oxford. I was a first-year student. Will, of course, is four years older, but when we were out and about, he caught sight of the Ice Maiden—"

There he was, using that name again. If Corinne had harbored any doubts about her determination not to marry Freddie, he'd dispelled them over dinner.

"—and he was smitten," Freddie finished.

Everyone made *ooh*ing sounds. Corinne studied the food left on her plate, once again uncomfortable with Freddie's making her the topic of conversation.

"So," Freddie continued, "my friends and I heard Lady Corinne would be at Lady Mayhew's affair, and since they always need gentlemen for those events, we volunteered ourselves and Will. Will who rarely went out. Who preferred books to women."

"What happened?" Lady Landsdowne asked . . . a question Corinne wondered as well.

"He asked her to dance," Freddie said. "Do you remember?" He directed the question to Corinne.

She looked up, glanced at Reverend Norwich, and shook her head. "I fear not."

"Well, you were shy, and the other girls whispered because Will is—*was*," Freddie corrected himself, "nothing more than a seminary student and without title. Your face was brilliant red as he led you to the dance floor."

Suddenly Corinne remembered. It was an incident she'd wanted to forget. "That was seven years ago," she murmured, embarrassed by his observation that she had been reluctant to accept the invitation to dance.

"Yes, about that time," Freddie agreed. "Anyway, Will tripped. He has big feet," he informed his audience. "And as he went down, he pulled both Lady Corinne and a maid carrying full punch cups to the reception table. What a mess. And the laughter? I can still here it now. Can't you, Will?"

The memory of the afternoon returned to Corinne. It had been one of the most embarrassing moments of her youth. She'd been infatuated with the Marquis of Dinsmore's son and had been forced to leave the party, her dress ruined. She'd hated being the center of attention, the mark of laughter for the mean-spirited and small-minded. She'd learned a lesson that day and consequently kept her distance when out and about. Hence the name the Ice Maiden.

But she'd forgotten the identity of the young man who had started this chain of events. She'd barely remembered what he looked like.

She *did* remember how he had not apologized for his clumsiness. He'd risen from the floor, helped her up, and had then walked right out the door without speaking two words, leaving her to stand alone in her ruined dress.

"We were young, Lord Sherwin," Corinne told Freddie. "We'd laugh those things off now."

"Will doesn't," Freddie said. Corinne couldn't stop herself from sliding a glance in the clergyman's direction. He was eating his meal with the air of a man at peace—but he wasn't. She could feel the tension, and it was directed toward her.

He did not like her.

His attitude made her angry. How silly of him to bear a grudge against her for what had happened years ago. What sort of prig was he?

"I can understand why he wouldn't," Major Ashcroft said. "I would be furious with myself for having missed the opportunity to dance with one as lovely as Lady Corinne."

For his gallantry, Corinne gifted him with her most dazzling smile, and she noticed that both Freddie and the reverend frowned a response.

They were both prigs.

"I say, is anyone else traveling home this evening besides the squire and I?" Mrs. Rhys-Morton asked.

Several people nodded that they were. "Be careful," she warned.

"Careful of what?" the duke of Banfield asked.

"Nothing really," Lord Bossley was quick to answer.

"Nothing?" Dame Janet shouted out. "What of our highwayman, the Thorn?"

"The Thorn?" the duke of Banfield repeated, turning to his host.

Lord Bossley laughed dismissively. "We have a highwayman lurking around these parts. He's more of a pest. Major Ashcroft and his men will capture him soon, won't you, Major?"

"Absolutely, my lord. My men have the roads well guarded, especially this evening."

"Does he also rob by day?" Lady Landsdowne asked. "My husband and I are staying the night, but we don't know when we shall leave on the morrow."

"Don't worry, coz," Freddie said, ending the sentence with another of his small burps, which he obviously thought no one would notice, for he never excused himself. "The man is a buffoon. He hasn't been seen in weeks."

"What is the story?" Lord Landsdowne pressed.

Lord Bossley released his breath with exasperation. "He's the usual. 'Stand and deliver' and all that. However, Ashcroft has done an excellent job of chasing him off."

"And we shall keep him away," the major assured everyone.

"I met him," Dame Janet's roué of a husband announced. "Robbed me. Took all I had in my pocket. I was quite frightened."

"Why?" Lady Landsdowne wanted to know. "I've never met a highwayman. This could be exciting," she said to her husband.

"I'd rather keep my money in my pocket," he responded.

"Sir Felix is correct. He is frightful," Mrs. Rhys-Morton assured her. "He robbed the squire. I've never seen my husband white-faced, but he was on that occasion."

"What does he look like?" Corinne's mother asked.

"That is the difficulty," Sir Felix informed her. "He wears a mask. It's a sack over his head with two holes cut out. You wouldn't find it scary just to see it laying on that table there, but on his head, he is most horrifying."

"It's his horse," Squire Rhys-Morton deigned to answer, wiping his mouth with his napkin and setting it aside, a sign he'd finally finished his meal. "The animal is as black as night. Solid black and the biggest beast I've ever laid my eyes on. His nostrils are red from his snorting and his hooves are sharp and ready to take a man out. Some think they are ghosts—"

"What swill," Lord Bossley declared.

"Ghosts of whom?" Corinne had to ask.

"The Black Thorn," Mrs. Rhys-Morton answered. "He was a reiver who plied his trade all through this area dressed just like this highwayman dresses. That is why the locals refer to him as the Thorn. They believe he has come back to life from the dead."

"Was the first Thorn captured?" Lady Landsdowne asked.

"Not according to the legend," Major Ashcroft answered.

"Let us not forget," Lord Bossley said, his voice overriding the others, "that our current Thorn is also a murderer. Ah, see, ladies, I thought that would change your romantic notions of him."

"Who did he murder?" Corinne wanted to know.

"Please, my lord," Lady Bossley said, "this is not a fit conversation for the dinner table."

"But we want to hear," Lady Landsdowne said.

Lord Bossley ignored his wife. "He is responsible for the murder of one Simon Porledge. A good man who often performed small errands for me and my steward."

"Why did he kill him?" the duke of Banfield asked.

"We surmise that the Thorn wanted to rob poor Porledge, who was known to drink whatever coin he had. When the highwayman found

Porledge did not have money, he exacted a revenge."

Shudders went around the table until Sir Felix chimed in, "He was gracious to me. Reminded me of robbers in my day. Gentlemen all."

"And on that note, perhaps the ladies should leave the men to their port," Lord Bossley said, a hint of tension in his voice.

"Yes, we must leave the men to their port," Lady Bossley echoed and rose, a signal for the female guests to join her in the reception room for tea before the warmth of the fire.

The men did not linger over drinks but quickly joined the women. Freddie was decidedly the worse for wear. He was now at the point of fixing brooding stares upon Corinne. She stayed close to her father, who was not one to stay up late.

The duke thanked the earl for an entertaining evening, laughingly warned those leaving to "beware the Thorn," and took up to his bed, Corinne and her mother accompanying him. Freddie had nodded off in a chair by the fire.

Corinne was happy to escape. However, once she was in her room, she regretted it.

For obvious reasons, her maid Sybil was no longer there. The bed was still mussed from the lovemaking. The sheets had not been changed, and no one had laid out Corinne's bedclothes.

Her parents were wrong if they thought she was going to make peace with being Freddie's wife. She walked over to the window. Her room overlooked the back garden. She could hear coaches pulling away. She wished she could go with one of them. A highwayman didn't frighten her half as much as Freddie did.

And if there was a way out, she vowed she would take it. She looked up at the full moon, wishing she'd been someplace else. *Anywhere* else.

A movement not far from the side of the house caught her attention.

Major Ashcroft stepped out of the night's shadows, dressed in a cape for travel. He signaled someone, and a moment later, a coach and pair, the torch lights lit for travel, pulled up in front of him. He returned inside.

Funny that the major hadn't mentioned he was traveling this evening. He didn't strike Corinne as the sort who would take a coach back to his command. He must have been planning to go some distance.

Curiosity bade her keep a vigil on the coach. The driver jumped down from the box. He was joined by an armed guard, but little else happened.

All became quiet.

Bored, Corinne turned back to her room. She wasn't going to sleep in *that* bed. She didn't even want to sleep in the room, but given the number of guests spending the night, she doubted if there was another one available.

She pulled two chairs together. They might work for a bed, at least for the night. She'd see about changing rooms in the morning.

Of course, what she really needed was a distraction. A book would be nice.

A glance around the room told her there wasn't one close at hand. However, Lord Bossley had a huge library. Certainly there was something she would enjoy on his shelves. She didn't worry overmuch about Freddie, because there still should be enough people up and about. She would definitely be locking her door after she returned.

Downstairs, Freddie was no longer asleep in the chair before the fire.

The sounds of the servants cleaning the dining room drifted toward her as she walked to the library. Her assumption that there would be more activity from the guests was proving incorrect.

Cautious now, Corinne went to the library.

Wood paneling and books deadened all sound
in the spacious, well-appointed room. A welcoming fire was in the grate and several lamps had
been lit. She went to the shelves, pulled down
a book, and immediately put it back. It was in
Greek. She moved along the shelves, taking another and finding it not to her liking either.

At last she came upon a book about botanicals
in Barbados. This might have been interesting.
Over the last summer, she'd discovered a passion
for gardening. She'd just opened the book when
she heard a footstep in the hall.

Fearing it could be Freddie, she started to close
the book, when a piece of paper fell out. Picking
it up and realizing it was a page from a record
of some sort, she tucked the paper back in the
book and shoved the volume back in its place
on the shelf. Deciding discretion was wiser than
bravado, she sought to hide her presence until
she knew who was coming.

Thick, heavy draperies framed the window,
any child's favorite hidey-hole, and Corinne took
advantage of them now. She pulled back the one
nearest the bookcase—and came face-to-face
with the Reverend Norwich.

Chapter Three

W hat are you doing here?" Corinne demanded in a furious whisper.

"Avoiding you," Mr. Norwich shot back. He
came out from behind the drapes, obviously embarrassed at having been caught.

Corinne didn't have time for discussion. Whoever was out in the hall was coming closer. She
took his place and let the draperies fall into place
just as she heard Lord Bossley's voice.

"Will, what are you doing in the library?" he
asked with mild surprise.

"Looking for that book on the Reformation,"
Reverend Norwich answered.

"Good heavens, why?" Lord Bossley said. "Sounds deadly dull."

"I have a question in my mind about it."

Corinne was feeling a bit silly standing behind the draperies now that she knew it was Lord Bossley and not Freddie who had alarmed her. But then, what could she do? To step out would be awkward . . . and a bit compromising, since the clergyman would appear to have been alone with her.

Apparently he thought the same, since he didn't give her up.

"The things you think about," Lord Bossley said to his foster son, sounding bemused. "Did you find the book?"

"Um, no, I think I may have already borrowed it and have it at the rectory."

"Ah, the location of a good number of my books," Lord Bossley pointed out.

"I'll bring them back, I will," Mr. Norwich promised.

"I await the day."

"Well, then," the reverend said, his voice moving away from Corinne. "I'll bid you good night?"

"Good night," Lord Bossley answered. "Take care riding home."

"You know Roman. I point him in the direction of his feed bucket and he goes."

"At a snail's pace. How old is that horse?" Lord Bossley wondered. "He has to be ancient."

"Seventeen, and still the best mount I've ever had."

"He's fortunate he has you. I would have shot him two years ago."

Corinne frowned. She was obsessively fond of animals, especially horses. She knew most didn't like feeding anything that couldn't earn its way, but she disliked the practice of tossing an animal aside as if it had no feelings or didn't deserve a reward for faithful service.

"He has good life in him," Mr. Norwich said.

"If you like riding swaybacked," his lordship observed.

"He could surprise you." This time his voice seemed to come from the doorway.

"I doubt it," was the dry rejoinder.

The reverend must have left then, because there was silence save for the movements of Lord Bossley at his desk. Corinne shifted her weight from one foot to the other, feeling very silly. A drawer was opened and closed. There was the scrape of metal. She longed to spy out the edge of the drape and see what was going on, but she didn't dare.

A moment later, she was happy she hadn't when she heard the library door close and Major Ashcroft's voice say, "A horse pulled up lame. We must change out the team if we are driving straight to London."

Lord Bossley swore softly. "I hate delays. Are the other teams set up along the road?"

"Yes, my lord. All arrangements have been made."

"This package must be delivered to Lord Tarrington by tomorrow noon. I do not want it left out of your sight."

"It will be delivered to his lordship. You have my word upon it."

But apparently that wasn't enough. "What about outriders?" Lord Bossley sounded anxious. Corinne wished she could see the package he wanted to have delivered.

"They aren't necessary. I will ride in the coach with one of my men. Two more will be up with the driver. I'm not worried about the Thorn, if that is what you are suggesting, my lord. My men are patrolling the road in this county and their presence is a better deterrent than any outriders. If the Thorn is still in the area and does manage to stop us, he will be shot. I'll fire the bullet myself."

"I don't want to lose this money to that bastard," Lord Bossley responded. "He's uncanny. He seems to know everything that is going on in the shire. And that old rake Felix can complain about being robbed, but what the Thorn wants is *this* shipment. For whatever reason, he has singled me out. Only one of these has made it through over the past six months. Williams is decidedly testy."

"I understand my mission, my lord. The Thorn is nothing more than an irritating black fly who has stumbled into what he knows not. I shall end him. It will be quick and ruthless. You have my word on that."

"I never forget a favor, Major."

"I merely serve, my lord . . . however, I pray you remember my service when your star rises."

"I shall. And now, you'd best be on the road if the ruse to make you and your men appear to be my departing guests is to be successful."

"The lads are changing the horses now," the major answered.

"Then go on with you. Godspeed, and don't fail me."

"I will not, my lord."

There was the sound of the officer leaving the room. A moment later, the butler came by to inform the earl that the last party of guests was leaving. "I'll be right there," Lord Bossley answered. "Hold them for me."

He took a moment more and then left the room, shutting the library door behind him.

Corinne didn't realize she'd been holding her breath until she released it. She stepped out from behind the draperies, her mind active with possibilities. Eavesdropping was wickedly rude but, in this case, enticing. Something was afoot. A grand mystery.

She thought she'd heard of Lord Tarrington before. She might even have met him. What was so important to deliver to him that Lord Bossley would go to such lengths?

Preoccupied with the puzzle of Lord Bossley's actions, she moved to the door and was startled when Freddie opened it. He grinned, as if he'd been looking for her.

"How nice to finally have a moment alone, my lady. I believe we need a little chat about how cold you were toward me over dinner. And how I shall not tolerate it again." He took a step into the room.

Corinne stood her ground. "Stop right there," she ordered, her voice low.

"Here?" Freddie asked, a teasing light in his

eyes and a madcap smile on his face. He took another step toward her. "Or here?"

He was so close that she could smell the sourness of his breath.

She forced herself to look up at him. She was a tall woman and almost looked him in the eye. "There are many who believe you are handsome," she said. "But in this moment, I find you the most disgusting, *ugliest* man of my acquaintance."

If her insult offended him, he hid it behind that insane smile. "I shall look forward to teaching you manners when you become my *wife*."

Corinne could scream in outrage over the title. "Why do you want me so much, especially knowing I have grown to detest you?"

Freddie shrugged. "I don't know. Perhaps it's the challenge. But I do want you, Corinne. To have what no one else has been able to claim. Everyone is already envious because you will be mine . . ." He leaned forward.

Realizing he meant to kiss her, she placed a hand against his chest. "We are not married yet," she reminded him.

"Why wait?" he mumbled and opened his mouth, his hands coming to her waist, where he grabbed her dress to hold her in place.

The only kisses Corinne had ever experienced had been pecks on the cheek from brothers and sisters, cousins, maiden aunts, and, occasionally, her parents. The closest she had allowed any gentleman, including Freddie, had been her gloved hand—and if he thought she was about to let his wide-open maw anyplace close to her body, he was wrong.

She jerked her head away. He laughed, moved closer. She had to escape. Her hand found the side table behind her and began searching for something she could hit him with. Then again, she knew he was prepared for her to pull away. What if she moved closer—

"Sorry, I didn't mean to interrupt," Reverend Norwich's voice said from the doorway.

The man was a godsend. His arrival gave her the time she needed to duck under Freddie's arm and escape. She brushed past the clergyman and walked out into the hall.

"Damn you, Will," she heard Freddie swear. She stopped, curious as to the reverend's response.

"I didn't know you would be wooing in the library," Reverend Norwich commented, unapologetic.

"Still, it must put the frost on it for you, having

lusted for her for so long and now knowing she will be mine."

"I didn't notice you were making headway," Mr. Norwich replied. Corinne doubled her fist and gave a glad little punch in the air that the foster brother had stood up for himself.

Freddie was a bully, and she did not like bullies.

Worse, she didn't like men who laid in wait for her. At Glenhoward, Freddie acted like the son of some medieval warlord who freely took any wench he pleased.

Corinne could go to her parents with her complaints again—but to what purpose? They were intent on handing her over to him on a silver platter.

How she wished she hadn't been there. . . .

The moment she had the thought, an idea struck her that was so daring, so outrageous that she almost refused it.

But it wouldn't go away.

What if she *wasn't* here? What if she disappeared? At least until after the wedding. It could not take place without her.

Where would she go?

Her sister Belinda might be of help. She could take her in. Or not.

Belinda's marriage wasn't a happy one. She *might* be sympathetic to Corinne's plight. At one time the sisters had been close, but over the past few years, they had drifted apart, and Belinda would certainly not like Corinne involving her in such a scandal, because a scandal it would be.

One didn't run away from any marriage, let alone a wedding to which everyone of importance had been invited.

Or did one?

Corinne thought of the scandals she knew about just over the past year. There had been a lady who had left her husband for her horse master. Another wife had gone off to the Continent with some rake. She couldn't recall hearing of any young woman of her age and rank running from marriage, but truly wasn't she just applying common sense? She hated embarrassing her family, but why wait until she was married to run away? Wouldn't that be an even *bigger* scandal?

Before she could change her mind, Corinne slipped into the dining room and found her way to the butler's pantry. There had to be a servant's door here leading to the outside and the side of the house where she'd seen Major Ashcroft's coach.

Corinne didn't have time to pack belongings, and she didn't want to do so. If she reasoned her plan out too much, she'd change her mind. There were too many pitfalls, too many questions— and yet the excitement suddenly flowing through her veins told her she was making the right decision.

In the end, it was deceptively simple.

She heard Major Ashcroft's voice in the kitchen. Apparently his men were eating the food remaining from dinner. She had to smile. That they had delayed their trip would not please Lord Bossley, but it suited her perfectly.

Finding a doorway was easy enough. She chose a servant's entrance. Several capes hung from pegs by the door, and she took a gray wool one to hide her muslin gown. Sneaking outside, keeping to the shadows, she approached the coach.

The lad holding the horses was occupied with the task. Corinne knew she could not sit in the cab. She moved to the boot, the storage compartment at the rear of the coach for luggage. When playing hiding games as a child, she'd often curled up in the boot of her father's coach, so she knew exactly how to fit herself in one.

The catch on the boot's latch opened too

quickly, a sign it might be loose or broken. She must beware it flying open or she'd be bounced out.

The boot was empty. Corinne tucked herself inside and pulled down the leather cover. Her hair had pins in it, and they scratched her scalp. She took off her gloves and began removing them. She'd keep them in her gloves so that she could make herself presentable once she reached London.

There were details she needed to work out. But the more she lay in the dark, the more plausible this opportunity became. If her sister would not help her, then she'd turn to a friend. Certainly someone could hide her for four weeks?

On the heels of that thought came the realization of how foolish she was being.

What was she doing? No one would hide her from her father or Lord Bossley.

If she was wise, she'd return to her room—

Her change of mind came too late. She heard voices outside the coach and realized Major Ashcroft and his men were ready to leave.

She held her breath, hoping no one opened the boot.

Someone must have started in her direction, but a man's voice said, "Don't put that bag in there unless you want to chance it falling out. The catch on the boot's lock doesn't hold."

There was a grunt of an answer, then Major Ashcroft ordered his men to take their places.

Corinne reached out to grab hold of the boot's cover.

With the shifting of weight in the cab of the coach, a snort from the horses, and a snap of the whip, they were off.

And Corinne had sealed her fate.

Doubt is the enemy of adventure.

Someone had once said such to Corinne, and she now discovered it true. If she'd had doubts before making her escape, she was assailed with them as the coach moved farther and farther away from the Bossley estate.

But she was not sorry.

With each turn of the wheels, she was standing up for herself. That was a heady emotion. She'd been told that after her wedding night, she would feel like a woman, presumably because the "deed" would have been done.

She felt like a woman *now*.

For too long, she'd yearned to be her own mistress, and she hadn't wanted to wait for marriage to be one. Of course, once news of her jilting Freddie Sherwin came to light, she'd never marry.

The idea threw her into a sullen mood. "Jilting" sounded much worse than "crying off."

Perhaps she wasn't doing the right thing?

And then she remembered Freddie being rough with her. Oh, yes, she had her pride, and before she was done with Freddie, everyone would know it.

But in the meantime, she had a very uncomfortable ride to London to endure. The dirt from the road filled the boot—?

The coach came to an abrupt halt, the horses snorting and whinnying. The force of the stop rolled Corinne toward the door. The latch on the boot came unhooked. She grabbed it just in time to close it without, hopefully, being seen.

"What is it?" Major Ashcroft barked.

"There's a tree across the road, sir," came the reply. "We must move it."

"Have your arms to the ready, men," the major ordered.

"Aye, sir," one of them responded.

Corinne's head began to pound from stress, road dirt, and fear. From the urgency in the major's voice, she could tell that he anticipated this might be an unusual situation.

The coach weighed to one side as the soldiers climbed down or out of it. It felt as if even the major had left the cab.

She couldn't stop herself from lifting the boot cover enough to peer outside. It was too dark for her to see anything but fog and night shapes. The air smelled of forest and damp ground.

"It may have just fell, sir," one of the soldiers said. "Trees in the forest do that. We appear to be alone."

"Then move the tree," the major snapped. "Come on, hurry with you now."

Corinne wished she'd had a view of what was happening. The horses seemed to stand quiet. She was certain the brake had been set and that someone stood at their head. Her imaginings of all that could go wrong were torturing her nerves—

The cab tilted, an ever so slight change of weight.

She caught her breath, wondering if she'd imagined it and then sensed movement in the cab, just on the other side of the wall from her.

Beyond the coach, the soldiers were shouting orders at each other and swearing when they weren't obeyed. Major Ashcroft sounded extremely frustrated.

There was a scuff sound against the wall. She smelled something start to burn.

The coach rocked to one side and the horses moved nervously just as Corinne heard the sound of a footstep on top of the coach.

She opened the boot, uncertain of what was happening but every sense warning her it was not something she would want—

A ball of flame exploded on the ground a mere three feet from the back of the coach. Hot licks of flame and sparks burst toward the sky.

The horses stamped and reared, causing the coach to rock precariously before the animals suddenly went screaming off without the coach. The soldiers shouted an alarm, trying to stop them. Obviously, the horses' traces had been cut.

Smoke filled the boot. Corinne could feel heat and knew the coach was not a safe place.

She didn't think, she reacted. She scrambled out of the boot just as whoever was on the roof threw another ball of flame.

Looking up, she saw the tall figure of a man and knew why they feared the Thorn. He had no face beneath his tricorne hat. Two dark holes served for eyes, but there was *nothing* else.

The cab of the coach was on fire, but he showed no fear of the smoke billowing around him.

"Ashcroft." The highwayman's voice was deep, commanding, chilling. "What is it you want me to say? 'Stand and deliver'? Don't worry. I already have what I want." He held up a small chest in his hand. "You left it in the coach."

Corinne had stepped back to see the Thorn better. She heard Major Ashcroft swear, knew he was coming for the highwayman.

The Thorn held another flaming ball of fire on a rope in his hand. He whirled it around and around his head before sending it flying toward the soldiers.

They ran before it hit the ground. They even dropped their weapons. Corinne caught a glimpse of them running into the forest and heard Major Ashcroft shouting orders for them to return.

The highwayman turned to the rear of the coach and whistled. From behind her, Corinne felt the sound of hooves before she heard them.

A midnight black charger with a foaming mouth, flaring nostrils, and red, red eyes came charging right through the smoke and the fog.

Corinne realized she stood right in the demon animal's path.

She did the only sensible thing she thought she could do—she went running for Major Ashcroft.

His face was contorted with rage. "You bloody bastard. It's time someone sent you to hell." He lifted his arm to aim the pistol in his hand, but then he noticed her movement. As if expecting an attack from another quarter, he turned and fired.

For a second, the world seemed to stop. Corinne was aware of the heat of the flames. She could sense the highwayman still standing on the coach roof. He'd been surprised by her presence as well.

And she believed she could see the bullet coming for her, but she had no time to move.

The pain of it seared her shoulder. She'd been shot.

She came to a dead halt. Took a step back.

"Lady Corinne?" Major Ashcroft said, as if he didn't believe his eyes.

Corinne looked up at him. "You shot me," she replied. It truly was an inane thing to say. She raised her hand to her shoulder, even as her knees buckled beneath her. *She'd been shot*. She started to faint. She never fainted. Ever. She struggled for a clear head.

The ground was damp beneath her shoulders, and she didn't remember lying down. She looked up to the sky. It was clear and covered with thousands of stars, and she realized she could die, but she would not now. She believed that.

Turning her head toward Major Ashcroft, she waited for him to come to her aid, but he backed away. His face in the firelight had gone pale with horror. He tossed down the weapon, turned, and started running toward the surrounding dark forest.

He was leaving her? *That* was not gallant.

The Thorn's horrible face appeared over her. His eyes in the shadows appeared to be two fathomless black holes. He'd lost his hat.

She wondered where his horse had gone. She had half expected to be trampled.

"What are you doing here?" he asked, his voice harsh. He'd lifted her head up.

"Have we met?" she murmured, feeling dreamy. The world was growing blurry around the edges, but she couldn't help noticing that his mask was really a flour sack. A silly, common flour sack.

"You little fool."

Her response was to reach up, grab the top of the flour sack, and rip it off his head before he knew what she was about.

Now she knew she must have been unwell. "This is so out of character," she whispered.

"Reverend by day, highwayman by night?"

It was her last thought before her conscious world went black.

Will Norwich frowned at the woman who had passed out in his arms and knew he had a problem. He glanced toward the woods.

Ashcroft and his men had disappeared, and if Lady Corinne died, it would be another death pinned to the Thorn's name. If she lived, and remembered pulling off his mask, it would be his death . . . at the end of a noose.

Behind him, the coach burned. Roman had tired of waiting for him to mount and started grazing along the side of the road.

Will removed a glove and placed his hand on her heart. It beat steadily, but even with the fire it was too dark to examine the wound clearly, and minutes mattered for such an injury. He had only one choice, and that was to take Lady Corinne with him.

Tearing his mask, he made a pad and bandage, which he loosely wrapped around her shoulder before giving a low whistle. Reluctantly, Roman pulled his nose away from eating and moved to join him.

Will found his hat on the ground. He used his

leg to slap off the dust before placing it on his head. He gathered Lady Corinne in his arms. For a slender woman, she seemed to weigh twenty stone as dead weight. He took a step toward the horse.

Roman shot Will a look as if to say he wasn't certain about this.

"I know," Will said, agreeing with the horse. "This isn't the wisest decision I've made, but I'm in a devil of a fix this time, Roman. A devil of a fix."

He draped Lady Corinne over the saddle. He picked up Roman's reins and started leading him into the forest.

Chapter Four

Corinne came awake with the sudden consciousness of a person startled by a dream.

Bright light hurt her eyes. She shut them quickly, trying to orient herself.

Her body felt battered and sore. She had the oddest images in her mind. Scarecrows chasing Major Ashcroft; Freddie kissing her; her parents *encouraging* him. She could recall faces, but not conversation. Not voices. There was the rushing melody of a nearby stream. The sound might have been part of her dream—but it was not a dream. It was real. There was a stream close at hand. The air was full of it.

Keeping still, she tried to remember where she was supposed to be. *Bossley's country estate.*

She wasn't there. She knew that.

Corinne attempted to open her eyes again, going slowly and letting them adjust to the light. A thatch roof came into focus. Ancient cobwebs hung from the rafters, their gentle movement in the air highlighted by a sunbeam streaming in from a hole in the thatch. Someone had best patch that hole or rain would pour in right where she was sleeping.

And what was she sleeping on? This wasn't one of the downy-soft mattresses to which she was accustomed. This bed was slung low and hard . . . like a cot.

Glancing around, she found herself in a small room bundled up warmly beneath a soft blue wool blanket and a quilt. There was no pane on the windows, and the morning's chill swirled around her nose and any other part of her body not tucked beneath the blankets.

A matter of more concern captured her attention—she wasn't naked, but she wasn't wearing the dress she'd had on for dinner.

Corinne moved to lift the blankets to see what she had on, and the motion sent a searing pain through her shoulder. Memory returned. She'd been shot. How could she have forgotten something like that?

There had been fire all around and a fiendish character, laughing and threatening her. She'd turned to Major Ashcroft for help and *he* had shot her.

Corinne frowned, remembering. Not intentionally. He'd been aiming for the Thorn and her presence had surprised him.

The flames, the frightened horses. All of it was clear to her again.

And what she was wearing now was a man's shirt over her petticoats. The material was sensible stuff, not the fine lawns and muslins that filled her closet.

She reached up and felt the line of a large shoulder bandage. That was where the bullet had entered. Corinne started to rise, needing to know more about where she was and why she was here. Furthermore, she had needs.

The world spun. She held herself still until it settled. She pushed back the bedclothes and put her bare feet over the edge of the cot. There, by the side of the rickety bed, was her bloodied dress—and a knife. She looked around for her shoes but didn't see them.

The hard dirt floor was cold beneath her toes

when she stood. Another wave of dizziness threatened, but she refused to give in to it. She was stronger than that. Her stomach rumbled from hunger, but this was no time to forage for food. She needed to leave. She didn't know how much danger she faced—

A horse snorted.

The image of a huge, black destrier with red nostrils and rolling eyes filled her mind. However, the munching sound following the snort told her that although the horse was close at hand, he was no threat to her. In fact, the ordinary sounds eased her tension—and then she remembered the horse's master. Fear vanished.

As if she'd conjured him, there came the sound of a man's exasperated release of breath.

He was in the other room.

She was not alone. *Good.* Because she had a few things she wanted to say to the Reverend Norwich. Pampering her wounded shoulder, she gathered his shirt around her and walked to the door.

Will couldn't light the fire. He'd started one in the night, but when he'd mistakenly fallen asleep, it had gone out. He needed to stave off the chill in the air. That could kill Lady Corinne as easily as any setback from the wound he'd dressed. She was lucky the ball had gone clean through.

He struck the flint again. The charred wool in his fingers refused to catch the spark. He could have thrown the tinderbox across the room. He didn't need this delay right now. The parish elders were paying a call in an hour's time to discuss much-needed improvements to the church's bell tower. The bell had a crack, and they hadn't been able to ring it as a call to service for over a year.

Furthermore, people expected to see him out and about in Ferris. He didn't need to be here playing nursemaid—not if he didn't want his secret identity discovered.

And that was another frustration. Will had to find a way to make the Thorn disappear. He needed his life back. He needed to not be hanged. . . .

The wool caught the spark. Praise the Lord. Now he just needed to deliver it to the kindling—

"Reverend Norwich," a sharp female voice said from behind him. "You have some explaining to do."

Surprised, Will burnt his fingers on the wool's tiny flame before dropping it into the kindling, where it gave a small wisp of smoke and went dead. All that struggle for nothing.

But now he did have a focus for all his frustrations.

He turned, ready to eat her up alive with his tongue. If it hadn't been for her foolishness, he wouldn't have had to spend the night traipsing back and forth fetching bandages, worrying if he was doing the right thing, worrying if she'd stay alive.

The tongue lashing he'd wanted to deliver evaporated from his mind at the sight of Lady Corinne standing in the narrow doorway between the two rooms wearing little more than one of his shirts.

Dear God. He leaned forward onto his knees. He remembered too clearly how soft her skin was and how full, how perfect, how luscious her breasts were.

It had been his penance to undress her, to keep his hands off of her.

And it didn't help his sorry state to have her standing there as proud and demanding as a Teutonic goddess. Her pale blonde hair caught the beams of sun coming in from the back room, creating a halo of light around her. That backlight also delineated the shape of her amazingly long legs, which could be seen clearly beneath the sheer, fine material of her petticoats.

Her feet were bare and as perfectly formed as the rest of her.

She was The One. The Incomparable.

The Unattainable . . . and whoever had christened her such had named her right. The lure of a siren mixed with the scorn of a harpy in the duke of Banfield's willful daughter.

Will came to his feet, needing his extra height to keep her, and his lust, at bay.

Her intelligent blue eyes swept his person. "You appear the worse for wear, Reverend."

He was conscious that he needed a shave. His beard was such that he looked quite vicious if he didn't keep it under control. And there were probably circles under his eyes that matched the weariness in his bones. Yesterday had been a very demanding day *before* he'd made an appearance at his foster father's dinner table. Certainly his hair must have been going every which way now.

In contrast, she appeared well rested and amazingly fresh and lovely.

"I needed to see to your welfare, my lady. You are lucky I discovered you injured on the side of the road on my way home last night." If there was a chance she didn't remember anything after being shot, Will was going to play it.

"And my undressing?"

"Necessary for attending your wound."

"So you didn't believe Major Ashcroft would return for me?"

There was an edge to her voice. "You remember," he said. He might as well lay it all on the table. He had to remember how willful she was, how bold. Dislike and distrust were good foils for lust.

"Not the undressing," she said. She crossed her arms as if protecting her breasts from view. The movement caused her to wince, but she bravely, stubbornly kept her hands where she'd placed them. "But I remember *everything* else."

"I feared you would." He tucked the flint and stone in his pocket. "So what happens now? Are you to go running to Freddie with your discovery of who I am? I don't believe so. There was a reason you were stowed away in that coach last night."

There, straight talk for straight talk—and it worked. A small frown appeared between her brows.

"You saw me?" she asked.

"You came from somewhere, and Ashcroft was

obviously surprised at your presence. I had been inside the coach, and you hadn't been there. I was very careful to ensure I'd accounted for everyone present."

She dropped her arms, reached up, and placed a hand on her left shoulder, as if the bit of pressure relieved the pain. "You truly are frightening as the Thorn."

"I try to be, my lady," he said. "Although you don't seem frightened now, and perhaps you should be."

She cocked her head at his warning, considered him, then shook her head. "You won't hurt me."

"Don't be so certain."

"You aren't frightening now," she answered. "That's not the sort of man you are. I don't think." She came into the room. "Why do you do it? Why are you robbing your foster father? And what did you take from him? What was so important it called for that many armed men?" Without waiting for answers, she said, "It wasn't me you were hiding from in the library, was it?"

"No, it was you." Granted, he'd planted himself behind the curtains to overhear the details of what Bossley had been about—he'd pulled that trick many times before and had picked up nuances of a meeting over brandy and port after dinner—but he would have avoided *her* as well if he'd known she was coming to the library.

He also had the pleasure of seeing his response throw off her imperial manner. "That wasn't kind."

"I didn't mean for it to be."

Her brows came together. "I have done nothing, Mr. Norwich, to earn this attitude from you."

"I'm certain it's different from the attitude you are usually accustomed to receiving from men, but I am not one of your lapdogs, my lady."

"I don't have lapdogs," she informed him briskly. "And you might be more effective as a man of faith if you didn't listen to gossip and rumors."

"Not rumors. Freddie is obviously besotted with you"—he ignored her sharp sound of denial and continued—"but you don't care for him. Tell me, my lady, why were you in the coach and not safely in your bed?"

"Freddie is the most unbesotted man I've ever met. But let us talk about *you*. Why do you rob from your own family?" she countered. "Or is that how you define a sterling character?"

Lady Corinne was no nitwit.

He'd spent years nursing his grudge against her. She was lovely to look at, but, he'd assured himself, she had to have been dull, like so many other beautiful women. A plaything. A filly to be married off to some Corinthian stud—although he'd never imagined Freddie a stud, and he didn't like thinking about it now.

So, Will tried taking command of the questioning again, this time letting go of some of his defensiveness. "What were you doing in the coach?" he asked.

"I was on my way to London?"

"You were jilting Freddie," Will hazarded and was rewarded for his guess by her disarming honesty.

"Yes, I'm crying off," she replied. "And in spite of my father's command, I must. Especially after what I caught Freddie doing last night."

"Kissing you?" He hadn't been pleased to catch her in his foster brother's arms . . . especially since he'd found himself wandering back to the library for a possible chance meeting with her.

"You call that a kiss?" she challenged. "I liken it more to being slobbered on by a cow's mouth. I was never so happy to see anyone in my life as I was you."

"And here I feared I was interrupting Freddie's wooing." He had to make the jab, even if his jealousy embarrassed him.

He earned a frown for his sarcasm, and her quick turn of mind. "Why are you masquerading as a highwayman?" she said.

"Money," he answered. It was the best answer and all she needed to know.

"I thought better of you," she allowed.

"I'm thankful, my lady. What an endorsement."

"You are rude."

It was a mild rebuke, but Will latched onto it as one more barrier between them. "Fortunately, your opinion does not matter with me. However, we are at an impasse. You can understand why I don't want anyone to know I'm the Thorn, and I don't think you want anyone to know you ran away last night."

"Do you believe Major Ashcroft will say anything?"

"I don't know."

She walked to the front doorway. There were no doors or windows to the cottage. Time had destroyed them. "Where are we?"

"It's an old reiver's haunt. You know of the reivers? The raiders who used to go back and forth between the Scottish and English border. If you look outside, you can see that this one whole wall is built into the hill and the rest is overgrown with bushes."

Lady Corinne didn't take his word for it but stepped outside. She looked around, then nodded, as if pleased. "How did you find it?" she asked.

"I came upon it by accident." He'd been hiding from soldiers one night and Roman had actually led him here.

She disappeared from his view. "Where's your horse?" she called. "And who is this old boy?"

He couldn't believe she'd walked off barefoot. He couldn't imagine one other genteel woman of his acquaintance doing such. Will walked to the door. She'd crossed to the lean-to built alongside of the house where Roman was stabled. She gave the gelding a scratch behind his ears, Roman's very favorite place to be scratched. The old boy groaned his pleasure.

"That's him. That's my noble steed," Will said, enjoying the moment her eyes widened in disbelief.

"This is not the charger I saw last night," she informed him.

"He most certainly is." Will walked over to the stable and reached inside to the shelf on the wall. He brought out a small tin. "Lamp blacking and ash. I mix it myself. I cover that blaze of his and that hind sock. He's the best part of

my disguise, aren't you, Roman?" He scratched
the horse's other ear and Roman was in heaven,
leaning his head down and forward to offer
better access to his itchy part. "No one would
believe this horse moves out the way he does.
And when we are on a tear, he acts as if he is
half his age and younger. What a great heart.
Of course he has to sleep it off."

"You appear as if you need to sleep it off as
well," she answered.

He dropped his hand. She found his looks not
to her liking? "Yes? Well, it was a busy night."

"Yes, it was. And now what do we do?"

She was so beautiful.

Will felt a bit dizzy every time he looked at her.
He didn't want to admire her. He didn't want her
around. She was a distraction.

"We both have secrets," she continued. She
was rubbing Roman's nose. She had long, graceful fingers. "I will not marry Freddie, but the
wedding is in four weeks."

"That's soon," he murmured, not interested
in discussing Freddie. He needed to leave. The
elders did not like it when he was late for meet-
ings.

"I need to hide here," she said.

It took a moment for her words to register,

but he didn't believe he'd understood correctly. *"What did you say?"*

"I need a hiding place for four weeks, and this is perfect." She stepped back, as if reevaluating the hut. "Once I miss my wedding date, my father won't be able to force me to marry. Why, the scandal will be huge. There is no way Freddie will want me after such humiliation."

"You can't stay here," Will said.

"I can. This is the perfect place."

"No." He started to saddle Roman.

"What else were you going to do with me?" she asked.

"I don't know. I was more concerned over ensuring you didn't die from your wound," He tightened the girth too quickly and Roman snorted.

"And I thank you for that," she said. "You did a fine job. My shoulder is sore, but I don't feel feverish."

"You were lucky the ball went through the fleshy part of your shoulder."

"I'm lucky you robbed that coach last night," she corrected. "Otherwise, I would be in London with nowhere to go."

"You didn't have anywhere to go? A plan? You didn't know what you were going to do after you reached London?" he demanded, turning in disbelief.

"I knew I wasn't going to marry Freddie, and that was all that mattered," she answered. "Sometimes a person must plunge into life if she is going to escape a fate worse than death."

"A fate worse than death?" he asked, confused. "What could be worse than death?"

"Becoming Lady Sherwin," she replied without missing a beat. "It would be a living death. I'd thought to go to my sister . . . but I wasn't certain she wouldn't turn me over to my parents. Certainly her husband would if she didn't hide me from him, which would have been a problem since the wedding is four weeks away. But here? I'm safe here. And best of all, you must protect me."

Suddenly, she turned pale. "Oh, dear, I need to sit. I'm feeling a bit weak."

Will took her arm and guided her back into the hut to a wobbly chair by the fire.

Lady Corinne recovered the moment she took her seat, like a queen attending her coronation. The woman was as healthy as a plow horse, he realized. She'd recover from her wound without difficulty.

She confirmed Will's assessment by saying,

"I'm also hungry. Famished. I didn't eat well last night. And I'll need clothes. I can't walk around like this. Food and clothes. Please don't be long at fetching both. Oh, and I don't like cheese. It upsets me—"

"Wait a moment," he said, realizing she was maneuvering these circumstances to her liking. "I'm not hiding you for four weeks."

She raised sympathetic blue eyes framed by the most impossibly long, dark lashes, and said, "You have no choice. You see, Reverend, I know who you are. There is a price on your head. It would be awkward if you sent me back to Freddie and I, not on purpose of course, revealed I know the Thorn's identity."

How had he ever for one second of his life been attracted to this woman?

She was manipulative. Like Delilah or Salome or Eve or hundreds of other women God in his masculine wisdom had warned men like him to beware.

And she had him. He was trapped.

Her silence for his silence, and food, and shelter, and clothing—and, oh yes, no cheese.

Without answering, he marched out of the hut, snatched up Roman's bridle, and finished tacking the horse.

She'd come to the door. "One more matter," she said. "Did you really murder a man?"

The accusation of Porledge's murder from anyone rubbed Will raw, but it was especially galling coming from her. "What do you think?" he snapped.

Clean eyes assessed him. She was an intelligent woman, far sharper than many he'd met. "Murderers don't carry wounded damsels around the countryside when they are in danger of being pursued by authorities," she answered. "I also think you aren't pleased with me, but this really is the best for both of us."

His answer was to climb into the saddle and ride off. He was late—very late—for his meeting with the elders, who would wonder where he'd been.

But as exasperated as he was with her, Will was pleased she didn't believe him capable of murder.

Lady Corinne had the ability to goad, challenge, and praise him.

Who said the devil wasn't a woman?

Corinne watched him ride off until his tall, dark figure was gone from view.

Only then did she slowly slide down the wall, exhausted from the encounter. Her shoulder had started to ache and she felt light-headed, but she also felt invigorated.

Reverend Norwich wasn't like any other man of her acquaintance. He would not be easy to handle.

He was also attractive. Very attractive.

She'd best be on her toes and keep her wits about her. He had a dangerous secret to hide, and as far as she could tell, she was the only one who knew the truth. Her sole protection was that he truly was an honorable man. He had saved her life last night, and she sensed he would guard her as long as she was under his care . . . which was where she planned to stay.

An honorable outlaw. Something more than money drove him to be the Thorn. Curiosity made her wonder. However, intuition warned her he was not the sort of man to play games—or give quarter.

Still, she found herself looking forward to when they met again.

Chapter Five

The gray stone walls of Holy Name Church had withstood every war and every sin England had been able to conjure. Built in Norman times, countless penitents had turned to her for refuge and forgiveness.

Will tried to remember that as he struggled with his own conscience. Many a night he had knelt for hours inside the church's cool darkness, begging for guidance.

He wanted to understand his purpose. Why was he here, half a world away from the land of his birth? Why did he feel such a connection to this place, to this village? Where was he supposed to go? Who was he supposed to be?

He was wise enough to know that many of
his questions stemmed from being an orphan.
His parents would always be a mystery to him.
He was a human island, untethered to heritage
and obligations of family, and yet he knew he
had a past.

There were times when he sensed he was supposed to know something, to realize significant
memories—and he couldn't.

He dreamed of his parents. Faceless creatures
conjured from his yearnings for roots, for blood-
lines, for commonalities and all the other traits
and understandings that connected one to lineage.

His solace was to turn to God. The heavenly
Father. He wanted to believe in Divine Guidance, but he received only silence.

Then again, that seemed to be God's univer-
sal response. Had Will not prayed for justice for
the crofters? He'd become the Thorn when he'd
no longer been able to stand aside and tolerate
God's silence.

And now, by tossing Lady Corinne—the Unattainable, the Ice Maiden—into Will's arms, his
heavenly Lord was playing a trick that would
have made any Eton schoolboy proud. Lady
Corinne . . . the most beautiful woman Will had
ever laid eyes upon.

God must have been laughing. He had to have been up in heaven with St. Peter and St. Paul, their three heads together with the same glee Freddie showed when he played a particularly nasty trick at Will's expense.

Will would have liked to prove himself stoic and completely immune to Lady Corinne's charms. He wanted to find fault, and he could. He hated being blackmailed. He hated being forced to do anything against his will. He disliked what she represented, an imperial upper class that thought more of their own pleasure than what was good for the country.

He also, now that his temper had abated a bit, couldn't wait to see her again.

What a pathetic creature he was.

The church was located on the far side of Ferris village. The rectory was set off from the church with the graveyard stretched between them. The location gave him the privacy he needed to come and go as he pleased.

Ferris itself was small. There was only one road in and out, and it was lined with a few cottages, a public house, and the blacksmith's forge. Most of the parish was spread out through the countryside.

Old Andrew the caretaker was raking the last

of winter's debris from the graves, and he nodded to Will as he rode up. Will gave a careless wave and headed to the run-in shed that served as Roman's stall. He unsaddled the horse, gave him water, stirred a mash of oats, and went hurrying to the rectory.

He'd not seen signs of the elders milling about the church, so he hoped he'd had a bit of luck and they were late. He needed to shave and to put on a shirt, since Lady Corinne was wearing his. Thank heavens for his parson's jacket and wool vest, which covered him from chest to hip. Otherwise he'd have looked decidedly odd.

However, when he opened the rectory's back kitchen door, he realized he had a visitor. The heavyset Squire Rhys-Morton sat at his kitchen table, his hat to one side, his hands clasped in front of him as if he'd been a schoolboy awaiting his tutor.

It was not unusual for parishioners to make free of the rectory. They often saw this dwelling, just like the church and himself, as their property. It was annoying, but what was a parson to do?

Except this visitor *was* a surprise. Squire Rhys-Morton only appeared in church at Christmastide and the Passion.

Knowing how close the squire was to the earl—and just how much the Thorn had stolen from his lordship last night—Will's guard came up. "Why, Squire, this is a surprise. How may I be of service?"

The squire leapt to his feet, acting as if he was embarrassed to have been caught there and almost knocking over the chair. He was a ruddy-faced man of middling height, whose unease turned to alarm as he took in the sight of Will.

His bushy brows rose to his hairline. "Good God, Reverend, you look as if you were set upon by thieves."

Will tried to smile. "It was a rough night. I'm called out at all hours. But enough about me. What brings you here, Squire? Although your presence is fortuitous. I have a meeting with the elders about a new bell for the tower. We could use your opinion." *And your money.*

"No, no, I don't want *anyone* to know I am here."

Now he had Will's full attention. "I beg your pardon?"

"I must talk to someone. If I don't, I think I may have a fit of apoplexy. I can't go on this way." He raked his fingers through his gray hair, pulling on it in his frustration. "And seeing that you are related in a sort of way to Lord Bossley, I thought it best to talk to you. I can trust you . . . I think."

Before the stunned Will could respond, the squire fell to his knees before him. "Forgive me, Father, for I have sinned."

This was the part of Will's calling that made him uneasy. Who was he to grant absolution? For the past four months and more, he'd been chalking up sins to St. Peter's list with an abandon that would have put his bishop in his grave if he'd known.

"Please, Squire Rhys-Morton. That's unnecessary." Will bent to help the heavier man up.

The squire turned to dead weight, refusing to move. He raised anguished eyes to Will. "I'm betraying my country, and I can't live with this on my conscience any longer."

Will froze. "Betraying your country?"

"Aye." There was fear in the squire's watery eyes. The man didn't look healthy. Will remembered he'd thought as much last night as the squire had shoveled food into his mouth, as if trying to avoid the company. Right now, his skin was pale and sweat beaded his forehead.

Sitting down in the chair the squire had just

vacated, Will feared the answer as he asked, "What do you mean?"

"I can't say this to just anyone," Squire Rhys-Morton whispered, glancing around them as if he was afraid someone might have been peeking in the window. "I *know* things. At first, it was just a lark. I'm not the most honest of men. I don't mind lining my coffers, and I can say that those crofters have cost me more in aggravation than they have in gain. I should double their rents."

"You did."

"Well, double that," the squire said without remorse.

"What is this about betrayal?" Will asked.

Such a strange conversation for an early morning. The sun pooled light on the brick tiled floor. From the open window came the sound of a whippoorwill calling his mate, the spring buzz of happy bees. This was not the place for talk of treason.

"I know you owe a debt to Lord Bossley," the squire said.

"I do," Will said perfunctorily. He was always reminded of it. Always had been; always would be.

"That's why I reason I could talk to you. You

won't go running with my tale, but I can remove it from my back."

"This involves Lord Bossley?"

Again, the squire shot a fearful glance over his shoulder. "You know Simon Porledge didn't run afoul of the Thorn."

Will knew that better than anyone . . . but he was surprised Rhys-Morton did. "He didn't?" He managed to keep his voice level.

The squire laid a finger to the side of his nose, a sign he was in "the know." "It wasn't him. Although he's been blamed for it. You don't cross Bossley."

"My foster father can be a hard man."

"And a greedy one."

"You said that, Squire. I didn't." The thought threaded through Will's mind that perhaps this was a test. That Bossley suspected his loyalty and had sent the florid squire to ask questions. "I'm not here for gossip."

"I'm not here *to* gossip," the squire answered, and there was enough fear in his voice to lead Will to believe him. He bore a great weight. Secrets or knowledge of evil could do that to a man. Will knew. He walked a fine line himself.

The squire reached for his hand, the supplicant pleading for mercy. "I don't want to end up like Porledge, but I can't keep this to myself any longer. Bossley is dealing with the French," he whispered. "They are helping him in his bid to become prime minister. Last night, he sent a shipment of money he'd received from the French to his man in London."

"Why would the French want to see Lord Bossley prime minister?"

"So they can have him in their pocket. The earl has grand ambitions. He's made friends in high places. He confided in me one night when he was in his cups."

"Lord Bossley doesn't drink that deeply," Will said with certainty.

"He has started to. Haven't you noticed?"

There had been lines of dissipation on Bossley's face, but Will had thought that a matter of age. The man was over sixty and had spent a good number of years under the Barbados sun.

Will's guard was up. Would Bossley have said something, even while drinking, to a man like Rhys-Morton? "This is a serious charge, Squire. Are you certain your confession shouldn't be for spreading a falsehood about a good man?"

"There are French ties to Scotland. Not all of Bossley's money comes from his crofters and tenants. Everyone thinks it does, but they are wrong.

Take this knowledge from me. I can't bear it any longer," the squire said. "Now you know. If you think it should be reported, then you do it."

"Me? All I have is your hearsay. Speak to Major Ashcroft. He is the Crown's Authority in the area. Tell him what you've told me."

"I'm not certain he isn't in on it. You do know that once Sherwin marries that duke's daughter, Bossley will have more power than any man in England. The duke is very well connected. No one will question Bossley's actions until it might be too late. There is a reason he's paying Banfield a pretty penny to marry Sherwin to that girl."

Will wondered if Lady Corinne knew about the money.

The squire let go of Will's hand and clumsily climbed to his feet. His features sagged as if he'd been broken. Will rose with him.

"It's on your head now," the squire told him. "I've relieved my conscience. I've been a self-ish man and followed the master, but I will endeavor to do better in the future. Isn't that right, Reverend?"

"No, it isn't enough. Take care of your tenants, Squire. Show them the compassion you want from our God."

Rhys-Morton nodded. "I will. I will. But I

can't protect them for having to pay Bossley. He's the law here. You ken? This is best between us? Yes?"

"Of course." The words were bitter in Will's mouth.

"Good. I mean no disrespect to your foster father. Thought it better I talk to you than anyone else."

"That was a wise decision," Will murmured, uncertain if that was how he felt. This information was valuable. It added pieces to the puzzle that was Bossley.

"Thank you, Reverend. Thank you. Like a confessional, right?"

Will wanted to sigh. "As you say."

The squire didn't look at Will as he let himself out.

Will stood alone in the kitchen. Bossley was being paid by the French?

His foster father's ambition was unsettling. He liked to scheme.

This wasn't the first time Will had confronted it. Bossley had played him against Freddie all his life. But how could he imagine to escape with treason?

Or was this the way things were done in halls of power? A man "bought" his way in.

Last night, Will had taken a small chest from the coach and tucked it into the sack where he'd been carrying his fire torches. What with Lady Corinne being shot, he'd not stopped to break the lock to see its contents. It was currently hidden in the rock wall of the reiver's hut.

But what if there wasn't money in it? The chest had a lock and had been quite heavy—like the others Will had stolen. Except Bossley had taken great pains to see that the chest reached London. To whom was he sending it?

A knock on the door and "Reverend Norwich?" told him the elders had arrived and were tired of waiting. Will opened the door on John McBride, Lem Carlson, and Joshua Gowan.

"Here you are now, Reverend. We were waiting at the church, but you are right late," McBride said. He had a burr to his voice, proof of his adventurous years spent in Glasgow.

"I'm sorry. I seem to be chasing myself this morning," Will apologized.

"We don't mind the wait," Gowan said. He was the blacksmith and his wife cleaned the parsonage, along with cooking Will's meals. "But I must say, you look the worse for wear."

"I was called out for a sick child," Will lied.

"Whose child?" McBride wanted to know.

"On the other side of the parish. You wouldn't know them," Will answered. He had to be careful. His lies were stacking up. He needed to keep track of them.

Before the Thorn, he'd prided himself on his honesty. What did they say—pride goes before the fall?

"You are always running somewhere in the middle of the night," McBride observed. "I'm glad I don't have your job. I like my bed too much."

"You like your warm wife too much," Carlson responded. He was the oldest of the three, and he had iron-gray hair, a long beard, and a liking for whiskey.

McBride gave him a playful cuff to the ear but laughed. "You are right, you jealous dog."

"Come, gentlemen, let us have a look at the tower's bell," Will said, wanting them out the door and their minds on other things.

Gowan spent a good hour weighing the damage and wondering if he could or could not do the repair. There was concern about funds. Money was tight.

Will found it interesting that no one in the parish mentioned the small packs of money he put on doorsteps, money he'd stolen as the

Thorn. Well, he really didn't consider it stealing. He thought of it as a redistribution. The money had belonged to the crofters in the beginning.

Or the French.

In the end, Gowan decided he couldn't do the repair. The bell would have to be taken to a foundry in Manchester. Another expense.

The men climbed down from the tower. Will was the last to descend. It had been a busy morning, yet thoughts of Lady Corinne hadn't been far from his mind. He wondered if they had discovered her missing or if Ashcroft had said anything—

"Hello, Will."

Bossley's voice gave Will a start. The earl never visited the church; then again, they should have been looking everywhere for Lady Corinne.

A calmness settled over Will, the same calmness he felt before he pulled the mask over his head and became the Thorn. God help him, but he enjoyed the challenge. He savored righting the wrong. He craved the danger—and Rhys-Morton's confession had raised the stakes.

Will turned from the ladder. The elders stood to the side, silent. They did not make eye contact with the earl.

He did.

"Hello, my lord," Will said with the ease of one greeting a family member.

His lordship was decked out in a light coat trimmed in velvet with piping. His boots shone like mirrors, and the gold buttons on his jacket had the dull gleam of true metal.

"Problems with the bell tower?" Bossley asked, addressing the question to the elders. None would answer. The tenants and crofters kept their silence around the earl. Will sensed that the earl enjoyed toying with them, of encouraging their fear.

There had been a time when the earl had attempted to make Will fear him. He'd failed.

"The bell has a crack," Will replied.

"Someone rang it too hard?" Bossley said with a mild smile, as if he'd made a joke. The elders gave the weak chuckles expected of them.

This teasing, this pretense of a casual visit, was not what it seemed. Will turned to the elders. "Gentlemen, I shall send to Manchester for information."

"Very good, Reverend," Gowan said, but the others only nodded their heads, gratefully accepting his words as a dismissal.

Bossley waited until they'd left the building to say, "Good men. Hard workers. The church looks in fine form, Will."

His foster father rarely involved himself in the goings-on of Holy Name. Either his visit was about Lady Corinne . . . or, possibly, the squire's visit.

"Is there something I can do for you, my lord?"

Bossley waved the question away, moving past the stone baptismal font and walking into the sanctuary.

The interior was a fine example of Tudor craftsmanship. The first earl of Bossley had been most generous in his day but he'd also been extremely vain. He'd given the church the carved pews, the grand pulpit, and an ornate rood screen decorated with imaginative scenes, including one representing himself spearing a lion.

The story was told that the lion represented Scotland and the reivers the earl had greatly despised. Will had no doubt the story was true. Many would have liked to have seen that portion of the screen removed. Centuries of intermarriage should have blurred the lines between Scot and English in this small borderland, but such had not been the case. Most of the parishioners were proud of their Scottish ancestors and had a tendency to see the earl of Bossley as some medieval English warlord—something this earl certainly played upon with his demands.

Bossley scowled at Will. "You should find your razor. No proper parson would go around looking like an outlaw."

Will forced an easy smile and rubbed his chin, wondering if Bossley knew how close to the truth his criticism was. "You are right, my lord. Unfortunately I had a sick call last night and returned just in time for my meeting with the elders."

"And your neck cloth? And your shirt? You aren't wearing a shirt."

"I gave the shirt to the crofter and must have tossed aside the bands at the same time. I have more."

Bossley studied him for a moment. Will had to admit, the man had presence. With little more than a lift of his brow, Bossley had always been able to make Will squirm. It took all Will's resolve to stand calm and assured in front of his foster father.

"I do admire you," Bossley said at last. "You take such care of your flock. Giving them the shirt off your back, as it were."

"They are your flock as well, my lord," Will couldn't resist reminding him. They'd had this discussion. Several times, back in the early days, when Will had protested against what

Bossley had been doing to the crofters and had thought his arguments could overcome the earl's greed.

"Yes, yes," his lordship answered. "But I'm not here for an argument. This is a social call, Will." He smiled, the expression not reaching his eyes. "What did you think of Lady Corinne last night?"

"Why do you ask?" Will's voice betrayed nothing but casual interest. Oh, he was becoming an adept liar—although his nerves were stretched thin.

"Curiosity," Lord Bossley said. "It struck me over dinner last night that it is time you married."

That was not the direction Will had expected the conversation to take. *"Marry?"*

Bossley laughed. "Yes, man, marry, or are you like some papist and thinking to remain celibate? I won't have it, you hear." He'd changed his tone. Lightened it. Filled it with goodwill. Will's guard went up. "You need a woman, Will."

"I won't argue the fact," Will agreed with complete honesty. "But I've yet to meet the right one." Or one who wouldn't have minded his outlaw activities or seeing him hanged. Still, there had been a time he'd dreamed of marriage, of a wife to grace his life. She'd always looked like Lady Corinne. . . .

Will shut the thought from his mind. He was a dreamer, a fool. And now that he was learning how difficult, headstrong, and willful she was, Lady Corinne was the last woman he would wish for a wife.

Come to think of it, he was doing Freddie a service by helping her run away.

"I shall find one for you," Lord Bossley promised. "A bishop's daughter who can help further your ambitions . . . and mine. I told you I wanted to see you archbishop of Canterbury someday. Don't believe it couldn't happen."

"Canterbury?" Will's gesture took in the confines of the country church. "I might as well aim for the moon."

"I am the moon, Will." There was not a trace of doubt in the earl's voice. "Do you believe me?"

Slowly, Will nodded his head. It was what Bossley expected, what he felt was his due.

"Good," Bossley said. "I don't want you to forget what you owe me; what I owe you."

"You've given me enough, my lord," Will answered.

"So modest," he observed. "You make a good clergyman. I chose well for you. The woman I choose will be good for you also. Two of the bishops have marriageable daughters. I shall pay a call to them once we have Frederick married."

No mention of the missing bride.

"How is the duke of Banfield and his family today?" Will prodded, wanting information. Bossley's whole manner puzzled him. He acted as if nothing had been amiss. Could he not know that Lady Corinne had run away?

"They left this morning," was the reply. "Sad to see them off. Banfield and I think alike on many important matters. But I shall see him in a few weeks at the wedding."

"Did you have the chance to say your farewells?" Will had to ask, fishing to see if Lady Corinne's absence had been discovered.

"Oh, yes. We breakfasted together."

"How nice."

Either Bossley didn't know Lady Corinne was gone, or he was pretending.

"Lady Corinne will be a good breeder," Bossley predicted, "as well as a lovely bit on a man's arm. Freddie is a lucky man. But don't you worry, Will," he said, coming down the aisle toward him and giving him a clap on the arm. "I won't saddle you with an ugly wife either. Trust me.

Here now. Good seeing you last night. Don't be a stranger. Come by the house any time you are about. You know you are welcome."

"Yes, my lord," Will said, following his foster father out of the church.

A young boy named Jamie Broxter held the earl's horse, a huge grey that always looked as if he would snort fire. The earl swung himself up into the saddle.

"Enjoyed our chat, Will," Bossley said. With a wave, he put his heels to his horse and took off, not bothering to toss the lad a coin.

Pondering his lordship's true purpose for the call, Will watched him ride away . . . and wondered whether he was capable of treason.

"He promised me a shilling," Jamie complained. "Said he would give it to me."

"Here," Will answered, pulling a coin from his own pocket. "Spend it wisely."

"Thank you, Mr. Norwich. Thank you."

Will watched the lad, his mind whirling with a dozen possibilities, none of them boding well for him. He needed to remove Lady Corinne as far from him as possible.

Bossley never did anything on a whim.

Chapter Six

The day's shadows had almost turned into evening by the time Will could make his way back to the reiver's hut. He was not pleased to see Lady Corinne pacing impatiently in front of it.

She stopped at the sound of his approach and waited for him, her eyes alive with indignation, her arms crossed. "I'm hungry, bored, and ill-tempered," she warned as he dismounted.

His response was to shove the basket he carried into her arms. "What are you doing outside the cottage?" he countered. "I thought you had better sense than to parade yourself around the country-side in hardly anything more than your petticoats."

"And whose fault is that?" she snapped back, having to put both hands on the basket's handle to lift its weight. She was using her wounded shoulder. Will was pleased. It was a sign she would recover quickly.

"I couldn't sit inside all day," she answered in her defense. "There is only so much sleeping or braiding my hair I can do." She flipped the single long plait over her shoulder for emphasis.

Will had seen her dressed in her finest, her hair carefully styled—and he found he liked her better this way. She appeared younger, less jaded, well, except for the scowl on her face.

"You'd best be careful with that frown, my lady," he murmured as he tied Roman's rein to the rough-hewn station holding up the lean-to. "Your face might freeze that way." He'd overheard Mrs. Gowan say this to her daughter Amanda, and apparently it wasn't new advice to Lady Corinne.

"A wife's tale," she shot back. "My face is fine."

And it was. The color had returned to her cheeks.

"How's the shoulder?" he asked, keeping his voice brusque, keeping the distance between them.

"It's sore," she replied, rooting through the

basket, so it couldn't have been bothering her that much. "I slept most of the day. What is in this kettle?" She lifted it up, inhaled the perfume of meat, potatoes, carrots, and peas. "*Supper*," she said with pleasure. "What is it?"

"Mrs. Gowan's stew."

"Mrs. Gowan?"

"She's the village lady who tends the parsonage and makes the meals."

"It smells delicious," she replied, picking up the basket with her free hand. "Or else I am very hungry. My head was starting to ache, but I am happy now." She went inside the hut and sank down on the wobbly chair, her petticoats spreading out in a perfect fan, as if she'd been in court. His shirt was so big that she'd had to roll up the sleeves, and the hem almost reached her knees.

"Is there a spoon?" She frowned down into the basket even as Will made a sound of annoyance.

"I forgot eating utensils," he confessed.

He had not followed her into the hut but hung back by the doorway. He needed to keep distance between them.

Of course, his presence appeared not to have any impact on her. She worried about food and a spoon while he worried that she'd notice he was hard as an iron rod.

"I'm so famished I could eat with my fingers," she said without bothering to look at him. "Or lap it up like a dog. Oh, here, there is bread." She pulled out the half loaf of Mrs. Gowan's bread, tore off a hunk, and attacked the stew. She *mm*'ed her opinion. "What meat is this?" she asked after several bites.

"Mutton."

She pulled a face. "I'm not fond of mutton. I prefer lamb. But hungry people eat what they must, and this is tasty. And," she continued after another big bite, "I think when one is having an adventure, one should eat things that are not the usual."

"An adventure?" The woman was eating his supper, had disrupted his life and his peace of mind, and she called it an adventure?

"Yes, that's what I've decided," she said. "I'm going to make the best of this and enjoy myself immensely. By the way, have you heard about my missing? I suppose everyone is up in arms."

"No, no one is," he answered, almost enjoying the saying of it.

She stopped eating. "What do you mean? There is no search for me?"

"You have stew on your cheek," he said.

Lady Corinne searched it out with fingers and

wiped it away. "Thank you," she said before confessing self-consciously, "I've been gobbling." She took a deep breath, as if resolving to have better manners. "Well?" she prodded. "What is the story? What have you learned?"

Will barely heard her questions. He was lost in his own quandary. He didn't want to like her. He didn't want her personable and relaxed. This was too intimate between them. It almost bordered on friendship, and, he realized, he couldn't be friends with her.

Or he didn't want to be. She was too potent, like a craving, a desire, a threat.

He shifted his weight in the doorway. She noticed then that he hadn't entered the room. "Oh, please, come in," she said as if just remembering her manners and they were in some drawing room.

"I'm not here to stay," he said, standing his ground. "I saw Bossley today. He said your parents have left and made it sound as if you went with them."

"They left?" She lowered the hand that had been about to deliver a hunk of stew-dipped bread to her mouth.

"I can only think that they believe you went to London," Will said. "They must not know you were shot last night, so that means Ashcroft is keeping quiet. What had you anticipated them to do? How did you believe they would react?"

She reached for the jug containing cider that he had put in the basket and took a drink before saying, "I didn't think they'd leave. I hadn't really thought about it. I assumed there would be a search."

"Bossley said he breakfasted with you this morning and that he plans to be in London in a few weeks for your wedding."

"He is obviously lying." A frown line formed between her brows. She set both the cider jug and the kettle on the hard dirt floor beside her chair and came to her feet. "Do you believe he suspects you know where I am or what happened?"

"That *is* the important question," Will said grimly. "Although he didn't give the impression he suspects me. If anything, during our short conversation, he sounds as if he still sees me as some benign and befuddled country parson."

"What shall we do?"

"We shall do what we are doing," he answered.

"What if someone comes by here? Or notices smoke coming from the chimney?"

"Or sees you marching back and forth in your petticoats?"

She ignored the jab. "What if this is all a ruse and they suspect you?"

"Then my wisest course is to act completely normal," he said.

Lady Corinne took a moment to digest this. "I've created problems for you, haven't I?"

"Just a few," he remarked dryly.

A frown came to her brow. "You don't like me overmuch, do you?"

I like you too much. "I have no personal feelings toward you," he answered. "That being said, yes, you are a burden. What am I going to do with you now?"

"I'm safe here," she suggested.

"Provided no one discovers you. People pass this way all the time. I'm certain if you stay here, in this one place for a long period of time—such as four weeks—your presence will be discovered. See? I wasn't being difficult this morning. Is there someplace you can go?"

She collapsed onto the chair. "No. Relatives would contact my parents. My friends, what few I have that are true, would not appreciate my involving them in such a scandal. But this—" She indicated the hut with a wave of her hand. "Works perfectly. I believe I must stay here."

"No."

He doubted if anyone told her no very often. He seemed to find himself saying it to her all the time.

But instead of showing a flash of temper, she considered him a moment and then smiled, an expression that was welcoming, confiding, intoxicating—

"I could come and stay in the parsonage," she suggested. "We could tell people I'm a maiden aunt or, perhaps better yet, a cousin."

Will forgot about her smile. "That is the most harebrained idea you've put forth yet," he said.

"I don't believe you have thought this through," she said without taking offense at his charge.

"*You* are talking to me about thinking things through?" Will forgot all of his lust and yearnings and vows to stay away from her. He walked into the hut, marching from one side of the room to the other while he tried to take control of his temper. He turned to her. "No. No, no, *no*."

"Well, you don't want me to stay here because you are afraid I'll be discovered, so where could I go? Why don't I stay in the one place that it would make sense? Our parson in Suffolk has a cousin living with him. No one thinks anything about it."

"The people of Ferris will," Will assured her.

"I'm an orphan. Have you forgotten that? You don't think people will wonder about cousins or maiden aunts who crop up out of nowhere?"

Besides, she was suggesting staying with him. Under his roof.

Here he was yearning, lusting, wanting—and she saw him as a eunuch.

That was the greatest insult of all.

"I'll keep out of sight," she promised, coming to her feet. "No one will know I'm at the parsonage. I'll be a shadow, a mere sliver of a presence."

"You can stay out of sight here."

"You didn't want me here."

"I've changed my mind."

"There are no doors or windows. And there are holes in the thatch. What if it rains? I'll be even more of a burden if I take sick."

"A moment ago, you were perfectly happy to be here," he pointed out.

"But I've thought things through," she said ingenuously. "This is what you wanted, isn't it? For me to think things through?"

All Will's life he'd heard the expression "seeing red." He had assumed it was some idiom, rather meaningless.

Now he discovered a person really could see red. A haze came over him, a mixture of anger, exasperation, and frustration. This woman knew exactly how to boil his blood. "I should have left you on the road."

"You wouldn't do that," she said with conviction, and apparently not taking any offense. "It's not your nature."

"You've *changed* my nature. You are willful, headstrong, and *rude*."

That last word brought her chin up. For a long moment they squared off, two fighters, each bent on having his or her own way.

Then to his surprise, she backed down. "I thought it was a good idea," she murmured, breaking eye contact and picking up the basket. "I haven't meant to be rude. I don't like rude people or pushy ones. It's just that sometimes one must be a bit forward when he is in a dire situation—" She pulled out the dress he had brought for her. "Oh, look at this." She held the serviceable green wool up to her person. "Not the first stare of fashion, but I'll be able to return your shirt. Did you ask one of the ladies in the village for this?"

"I'm a bachelor, Lady Corinne," he said, sounding a bit priggish, even to his own ears. But she had to understand the great lengths he was being forced to take on her behalf. And for his. What if his parishioners or, worse, his bishop discovered he was hiding a peer of the realm's daughter? The consequences could be brutal. "I can't knock on doors asking for women's dresses."

"No, I suppose you can't," she said lightly, and there was a smile on her lips, as if she found what he said humorous.

And Will felt stiff, unyielding, and churlish. To compound the impression, he added, "I found it in the poor box."

"It will do," she responded graciously. "Thank you. And I see you have socks and shoes." She retrieved the leather walking shoes. "How stiff. I imagine I could walk the hills in these and have blisters to show for them."

"That's why the socks are so heavy. Good woolen socks. Better for you than silk and cotton."

"I thank you for them as well," she said, and Will felt the knot of his anger unravel. She held the dress against her body, lifting the skirt and swaying as if dancing, her movements feminine.

His was a solitary world. A masculine one.

And she had the power to upend it.

Especially when she said, "Here, let me change, and you may have your shirt back."

"It's not necessary—"

But she'd flitted into the next room.

Will stood, ill at ease. He didn't like himself when he was rigid. His eye fell on the cold hearth. He had never restarted his fire that morning, and the kindling was still there.

And she was right, the hut was very exposed and far from suitable for any gentlewoman to inhabit. Rain would flood the place. He knew that, since he'd been here after a bad storm.

The corner of his eye caught movement in the other room. He should have looked away. Since there was no door, she couldn't close it. She relied on his honor to know his place while she changed.

Except from where he'd moved before the heath, he could see clearly. She stood with her back to him, struggling to take off his shirt with one hand. She lifted the hem. The sight of that curving indentation where her waist met her hips threatened to bring him to his knees.

He remembered too clearly applying that bandage the night before. The vision had haunted him throughout the day.

Will knew he should have looked away, but he lacked the ability to do so. The blood had left his brain. Again.

She pushed one arm through the sleeve, then winced as the upward movement shot pain through the injured shoulder. She stood for a moment, her head down.

His feet moved forward. He told himself he was being kind.

Maybe he was.

"Let me help," he said.

She stiffened, dropped the shirt hem. "I can do it."

"At what cost?" he asked, pretending his impatience was for her sake. He gathered the material of the dress. "Leave the shirt on. I don't need it, and it will be added warmth."

For once, she did as instructed, her manner as obedient as a child's.

Gently he eased the dress down over her wounded shoulder. "I will have to change the bandage," he told her. "I thought I would do it tomorrow. There's a salve in the basket that I plan to apply, but if there is pain or itching, don't hesitate to rub it on the skin around the wound."

"What is in the salve?" she asked.

"It's a recipe that Alma McBride cooks up. I've seen it do good things for cuts."

"Thank you," she replied.

The dress was too big and too short. The hem

barely reached her ankles. He began tightening the laces.

She pulled her braid over one shoulder so it wouldn't be in his way. The top of her head actually reached his chin. Her hair smelled of clear air and the sweetness he identified as her.

He'd rarely noticed the scent of a woman before, unless she'd been wearing a strong perfume, but this was different. He was keenly aware of every facet of her. And it had been such from the moment he'd laid eyes on her all those many years ago.

"I brought candles," he said, feeling the need to be practical. "And I'll start a fire."

"You aren't afraid someone will see the light burning in the window?" she wondered. There was an edge to her tone, a mocking.

"I want you safe," he said. He'd tied her laces in a bow. He should have moved his hand, let go of the strings . . . but he held on.

She turned, looked up at him.

For a moment they stood so close that they breathed each other's air.

She knew she could conquer him. She had to have known. Men threw themselves at her at every party, every rout, every opportunity.

He was a country parson, an orphan, a thief.

A besotted idiot. A fool.

Life experience had taught Will not to long for what he could not have. It was how he'd learned to make peace with childhood jealousies over being an outsider.

But that didn't mean he couldn't want.

"Thank you," she said softly.

He watched her lips move, mesmerized by them. Her bottom lip was fuller than her top. How easy it would have been to lean forward and press his lips against hers—

"You are welcome," he said briskly, releasing the laces. Of course his thumb was caught in the loop of one. He fumbled a bit as he freed himself.

He stepped back, and then stepped back again. "I need to start the fire." He turned and all but ran to the chore, thankful to have something to do.

Unlike this morning, he didn't have difficulty setting the kindling on fire, but it didn't make the hut any more hospitable. It also didn't alleviate his concerns for her safety.

But she had to stay here. She had to—until he could find a place to send her. She was not good for his peace of mind. "I'll see if I can't think of a safe hiding place for you. Preferably one in Scotland. It might afford some protection against being forced to marry, although, truly, Lady Corinne, perhaps you *should* marry Freddie?"

"Would *you* marry him?" She had come to the doorway between the two rooms. The deep green of the dress seemed to emphasize her pale blonde hair and bring out the blue in her eyes.

She had a point. At one time he and Freddie had been close, but the school years and their many differences had driven them apart. Freddie was a man in the shadow of an ambitious father, one with high expectations. Will could understand what motivated his foster brother while still not admiring the man he'd become.

Will rose to his feet. "Keep wood on the fire," he said. "I'll bring in enough for tonight, but in case it isn't enough, there is a stack in the lean-to."

Outside, birds called the end of the day. Will carried two loads of wood into the hut for her. He did worry about her safety, but what could be done?

"Until morning," he said. He started toward the door, feeling like a miserable excuse for a man, but he couldn't have taken her with him. He mustn't have.

She followed him outside. "Would you mind leaving your horse?"

He looked at her, surprised by the suggestion.

"I know I sound petted and silly to you," she said. "I realize I have made a nuisance of myself . . . but I've never been alone before. I thought I would go mad today without anything to do. I swept out the cottage the best that I could. Did you notice? It's lonely here, and I have many thoughts weighing on my mind. If you won't take me with you, then please, may I have the animal for company?" She scratched Roman's ear, right where he liked it.

Her words and his own guilt and worries for her finally influenced him. He looked in the distance beyond the knoll leading to this part of the stream and outcropping of rocks. "Do you know about horses?" he asked.

"More than I do about housekeeping," she assured him. "I rode before I could walk, and the head groomsman always made us take care of our own animals. This old boy will be safe with me."

He released his breath in a heavy sigh. "Very well. Roman will be your guard tonight."

"Thank you," she said with such enthusiasm that Will was pleased with himself. "Do you have far to walk?"

"Far enough," he said. "I'll have to take him from you in the morning."

"Of course."

"He'll keep you safe," Will continued, warming up to the idea. "Roman is better than the most trusted dog."

The look in the horse's eye said that he understood he was being discussed. He turned his head and nuzzled her hand. She'd made another conquest.

"I'll take very good care of him," she promised, reaching for the reins. "Now you go on. I'll unsaddle him. I can manage with one arm. You look tired, and I don't want to keep you from your rest."

"My lady, if you felt that way, you wouldn't have run away in the first place." He didn't give her a chance to respond but started marching up the knoll.

One remedy for lust was exercise. Will was reminded of this on the long walk home.

Did Lady Corinne know how those defenseless looks and longing sighs affected a man? Of course she also infuriated him as well.

One moment she was asking his opinion, and in the next she would countermand it. Nothing was more irritating to him, and the sooner he rid himself of her, the better. He was determined to see her as far from his parish as possible within the next forty-eight hours.

She was young and strong, and with Alma McBride's salve, she'd heal with only a small scar to remind her of her foolishness.

"Are you out for a bit of a walk, Reverend?" Tommy Meecham asked, coming upon Will as he returned to Ferris.

"I lent Roman to Sean Hayward," Will answered.

"Oh, you are a good man, Reverend."

Lies, lies, lies. Will was heartily sick of lies.

The fire in his kitchen grate was dying down by the time he returned home. He liked a chill in the air when he slept.

Besides the kitchen and sitting room, the parsonage had an upstairs with two bedrooms. It was a snug little home, a peaceful one.

Sometimes, too peaceful. Too lonely.

Perhaps that was why he'd responded to Lady Corinne's plea for company. Many a night he'd sat before his hearth and wished for another voice, another presence besides his own.

Bed felt good this night.

Will had no trouble falling asleep, but his dreams were not what he wished. He dreamed he was caught in a maze, and everywhere he turned

Lady Corinne would appear. Sometimes her image would be that of the fifteen-year-old he'd met years ago. Or she would be as she'd been the other night at dinner—cool, regal, sulky.

Or as he'd left her this evening, eager to please, needing his help.

And she was the first thought on his mind when he woke. It was already past dawn. He threw back the covers and pushed his hand through his hair. He'd overslept. Even now he felt groggy, leaden.

Pulling on his breeches, and wearing little else, he went downstairs. He needed to wake up. A good draught of cider would have him going. Then he'd best dress and hurry out to the hut before Mrs. Gowan came to do the cooking and cleaning. He didn't want to answer questions with more lies if she noticed Roman missing.

He walked into the kitchen, picked the cider jug off the dry sink beneath the window, and, forgoing a glass, lifted it to his lips—

Roman was out in his stall, his head hanging over the door.

Will turned, suddenly realizing he wasn't alone.

Lady Corinne sat at his kitchen table, her braided hair tidy, her face scrubbed clean.

Her expression was both hopeful *and* defiant.

Will choked on the cider in his surprise. He wiped his mouth with the back of his hand. "What? How?" he sputtered, stunned by the thought that she had found her way to Ferris.

"A horse always knows his way home," she said, obviously pleased with her cleverness.

And Will let his temper explode.

Chapter Seven

Corinne was rather proud of the way she'd managed to reach Ferris.

Roman had been a willing compatriot. Horses always knew the way home, and the dark hadn't bothered him. After all, he was the Thorn's gallant charger. Saddling him and climbing on his back had been a challenge, but Corinne had managed. Roman had then carried her all the way to his stall, where he was now peacefully munching on his hay.

While riding through the night, Corinne had started to picture herself an adventuress—like Lady Hester Stanhope, who'd set all of London buzzing last year when she'd sailed off with her maid, her doctor, and a guard for Greece and parts beyond. Corinne's parents had thought Lady Hester foolish in the extreme. Her father had claimed the woman unnatural. A woman's place was under a man's protection and by home and hearth—but Corinne had been envious.

Lady Hester was the first woman who'd made Corinne start to think that perhaps there might be more to life than the cycle of marriage, having children, and dying.

And now *she* was a bold woman. She had taken her destiny into her own hands. The world was spread out before her—*or* she had thought it was until she'd caught sight of Reverend Norwich's naked chest.

It wasn't as if she was clueless about the male anatomy. She'd viewed the Elgin Marbles. She'd perused paintings of men wearing little more than fig leaves. She was sophisticated, a Londoner.

But no piece of cold stone or painted canvas could emulate the real thing. His chest was hard planes, the muscles lean. His skin was darker than Freddie's pasty whiteness, almost a golden tan. Furthermore, attractive nakedness aside, Reverend Norwich was also the most intriguing man of her acquaintance. That alone set him apart.

He was also furious with her.

Anger boiled in his eyes. In one abrupt movement, he threw the pottery jug in the corner of the room, where it shattered into heavy pieces and splattered liquid. The sweet smell of cider filled the air.

"Why, my lady, *why*?" He didn't wait for an answer but demanded, "This is some sort of game to you, isn't it? My life means nothing."

"That is not true," Corinne said, coming to her feet. "I have the deepest respect for you. I don't want to endanger you. I think the 'cousin' plan will work, especially if I stay out of sight—" She stopped. "Don't you think it wise for you to put on a shirt?"

He spread his arms, his straight brows deepening into a frown. "Does this offend you? What did you expect when you sneaked into a man's house uninvited? That I would be waiting for you in evening dress?"

"I didn't 'sneak.' The door was unlocked," she corrected him.

"That's because it is Ferris. We don't go stealing into each other's homes. However, be assured, I shall put a lock on it within the hour—but first I am telling you to leave. Go back to the hut."

"Please, Mr. Norwich, this will work—"

"*No*. This is not a discussion. First, I'm not a servant or one of your love-smitten swains. I don't jump to the snap of your fingers, my lady. And second, we have already discussed how I'm an orphan? No relatives? Can't you grasp that?"

Corinne didn't appreciate his tone. He spoke as if she'd been simple. "Well, you don't order me around either," she shot back. His feet were bare. She'd never thought of how intimate it would be to see a man's bare feet, especially such well-formed feet. Indeed, there was little of him that was not well formed—

She had to keep her mind on her argument.

"And let me tell you," she said, pointing a finger at him, "I don't have love-smitten swains. And I am increasingly vexed by your accusing me of being some . . . some heartless Delilah or selfish princess. I know Freddie is considered a catch in London, but *we*"—she pointed her finger back and forth between herself and Reverend Norwich—"know his true nature. The more I know his character, the more I detest him. He's selfish and vain . . ." She broke off, frustrated by his stony-eyed face. "I am *not* marrying Lord Sherwin. I will not. And you *could* put a lock on your door, but I would just sit on your step. *Then* what would happen?"

"You wouldn't be a problem for me. Freddie would see you and scoop you right up and away to the parson. In fact, he wouldn't even have to go anywhere. I'd happily perform the marriage, anything to have you out of my life."

Those words hurt. "That was unkind," Corinne said.

"Unkind is mistreating a puppy or pushing an old person or berating a child. Unkind is *not* explaining to an overindulged, cosseted aristocrat that she can't go every place or do everything she wishes. You, my lady, are no different than anyone else on God's earth. I didn't invite you to run away, and I'm quickly tiring of having to take care of you—*especially*," he emphasized, seeing she'd opened her mouth to protest another unflattering portrait of her character, "when you don't appear to have the common sense God gave a sheep."

How could she ever have thought him handsome?

"You are a disagreeable toad." There, she'd thrown an insult of her own, and it felt good. "My intelligence is not to be questioned, sir."

"Prove me wrong," he challenged. "Take the intelligent action. Return to the hut."

"And what? Stay out of sight for *four* weeks?"

"Lady Corinne, we've had this discussion. You are not going to be around Ferris that long. As soon as I think of a place to ship you, off you go. You are the one who wants to hide. I see no reason to endanger my neck."

Corinne shifted her weight from one foot to the other. "All right, so perhaps I am selfish for wishing to hide in your home rather than an abandoned reiver's hut without a proper door or any physical comforts. But it is lonely out in the moors. There were night sounds that are quite discomforting. Please, I will stay out of sight. No one will see me."

"*I'll* see you." He took a step away, pushing his fingers through his dark, straight hair. "You upset *me*, my *peace*, my *life*. The parishioners use the parsonage. They walk in at all times. Your presence *will* be discovered."

"Then we are at a deadlock." She used her duke's daughter voice, the icy one. He'd accused her of being an aristocrat. Well, she was. "I know your secret and you know mine. You can complain, foam at the mouth, and howl at the moon, but it won't change the fact that you can't make me do something I refuse to do. Not without consequences."

"Would you really turn me in?" he challenged. "Do you want my death on your conscience? Is not marrying Freddie worth that to you?"

He was testing her. He thought her weak.

Well, Corinne wasn't ready to cry quarter. "To keep from marrying Freddie? Yes. You are a common outlaw, Reverend Norwich. A villain of the worst order. A man of God who steals. A hypocrite. There are some names for you. How do you like that plainspokenness?"

His jaw tightened with her every word. She had no doubt he would like to take her by the scruff of the neck and toss her out the door.

But he wouldn't. She saw that now. His bark was worse than his bite—she hoped.

"Now, please go dress," she instructed him. "Your standing there half naked is not proper, even amongst cousins." And as for herself, she resolved to no longer romanticize him. She had to remember her own words, but it was hard to keep from staring at his bare chest.

"You think you have me cowed, don't you?" he said, his quiet tone dangerously low. He took a step toward her.

Corinne held her ground, although she leaned away from him. "Do not come closer, sir."

"I will come closer," he assured her. "You are going back to the hut if I must hog-tie you and stuff you in a bag."

"You lay a hand on me and I shall scream so loud, all of Ferris will hear me."

"And then what if you do?" he asked. "Who are they going to believe? Their parson who tends to their needs, or the willful woman who is to become the next Lady Sherwin? Don't think Freddie won't take you back. Your marriage is what his father wants, and he always does as Bossley says. Scandal or no."

Pride vanished. Corinne hurried around to the other side of the table. "You do *not* want to do this."

"*Yes, I do.*" He kept coming toward her.

She edged around the table from him. Of all the scenarios she'd pictured in her mind of what would happen when she presented herself to him, *this* had not been one of them. She'd assumed he'd be angry at having his hand forced, but she'd thought she could manage him. Most men usually did what she wished of them. "Reverend Norwich, we must work together. Remember what is at stake."

"I've decided it might be worth the hanging to have you off my hands."

And Corinne decided she might be wise to run—but she'd only taken three steps toward the front sitting room when he caught up with her. He picked her up, throwing her over his shoulder like a sack of grain. "My lady, you have met your match."

"Stop this," she ordered, trying to squirm loose of his ironclad hold on her legs. She doubled a fist and pounded his back. Her fist bounced off it without seeming to break his stride toward the back door. "You are being foolish."

"*You* have the amazing ability to make me feel that way," he countered, speaking as if through clenched teeth. "Now stop wiggling—"

"Oh, that's an order I'll obey," Corinne shot back, trying to twist her hips free. Her fists didn't work, but a sharp elbow did. His hold loosened. She started to fall, which was not her intent. His arms juggled her, then held her safe—just as the kitchen door opened.

A woman entered and came to a startled halt. She was of middling years, petite, and ready for work. An apron covered a gray wool skirt, and she had a mobcap over her black hair. She carried a basket on one arm, which she almost dropped when she saw them.

Reverend Norwich froze.

Corinne felt his body tense. He was holding her with both arms, her breasts were against his chest, her hands on his shoulder for balance. She sensed they were in trouble, and she stopped moving, even breathing.

The head of a young woman of some sixteen or eighteen years of age with the same dark hair attempted to peer around the woman in the door. "What is going on?" the girl asked, her shocked mother continuing to block her way.

Mr. Norwich took a step away from Corinne. "Mrs. Gowan—is it that late already?"

"Yes, sir," Mrs. Gowan answered, still not recovered from her surprise. "I knocked. You must not have heard us?" Abruptly, she turned to the girl. "Mandy, see if Roman has been fed."

"Is something the matter?" Mandy wondered. Her voice dropped a notch. "Who is that woman?"

"My cousin," Reverend Norwich said without missing a beat. "Go on, Amanda, do as your mother said. You know how Roman is about receiving his oats."

"Yes, Mr. Norwich," Amanda said, although she lingered a moment, craning her neck for a better look. A spot of color appeared on each of her cheeks, and Corinne surmised that Amanda had been as duly affected by the sight of her pastor *en dishabille* as she had been. She withdrew reluctantly.

Corinne knew this was her opportunity to seal her new position in his life. She stepped forward. "There is nothing to be alarmed over. William—*Will*—and I were remembering a step to a country jig we used to dance as children." She forced a hearty laugh and even attempted a jig step. Dancing seemed a plausible enough excuse for her to be in his arms. "I'm a relative on the maternal side," Corinne senselessly added. A duke's daughter didn't have to explain herself, but a "cousin" found in a half-naked parson's kitchen had better do some talking.

"How very nice," Mrs. Gowan murmured. She shifted her weight and her shoe crunched on one of the broken pottery pieces. She frowned down at it.

"Would you give us a moment?" Will said. "My cousin"—he spoke as if the label left a bad taste in his mouth—"arrived late last night and I overslept this morning. I am embarrassed to not be dressed for you, but that is as it is."

Mrs. Gowan leaped at the chance to escape. "I forgot the cheese, the one you like? I meant to bring it but left it on my table. Let me run home and I'll return shortly."

"Thank you," Will said.

However, the moment the door shut behind her, he whirled on Corinne. "On the maternal side?" he repeated with disbelief at her gall.

"Lady Bossley's people. That was a bit of truth I added," Corinne said, taking a side step away from him. He was not happy. Not happy at all. "Everyone knows Lord Bossley doesn't have much family. All of Freddie's relatives are from your mother's side. I think it made it sound like the possibility exists."

"And why are you here and not at Glenhoward?"

"Because you and I are close. Just as I said to Mrs. Gowan. We were childhood playmates. And I don't like Freddie. She will believe that as well if she's met him."

"The woman is not a fool."

"But she accepted the story," Corinne pressed.

"Because she is in shock."

"However she feels, I'm here. You've agreed to it. I'm your cousin."

Mr. Norwich's face lit with fury.

Before he jumped down her throat, she defended herself by saying, "What is done is done. I can't think about the gossip. I started this venture on nothing but nerve. It's all I have . . . but I've been reasonably successful."

"And at what cost?" he ground out.

"Whatever it takes, sir," she responded fearlessly, "including abusing and fraying your goodwill."

His response was to march out of the kitchen. A beat later, he stomped up the stairs.

Corinne crossed to the door and began picking up shards of the pottery jug. "He needs time," she murmured to herself. "He'll come round."

And she sincerely prayed he would.

Will couldn't remember a time when he'd lost his temper so completely. Yes, he could. Yesterday afternoon when he'd talked to Lady Corinne.

She did that to him. Made him mad with rage.

He paced the perimeter of his small bedroom, going from one side to the other in four steps.

His anger had been a living, breathing thing that had taken over his mind and his common sense. *Why had he picked her up? Why had he touched her?* That's when everything had gone wrong. If he'd stayed on his side of the kitchen, he could have . . . what? Had her do exactly what she'd done downstairs anyway?

Of course, the scene would have been more discreet when Mrs. Gowan entered. And there would be no stories of him chasing women around his kitchen.

He prided himself on his reputation. It was all

he had that was truly his. That, and his own personal code of honor.

And what of Lady Corinne?

Only a ninny would believe Mrs. Gowan had swallowed that silly story about cousins. It was as lame as he'd warned her it would be—*especially* after Mrs. Gowan had caught Lady Corinne in his arms. "God, it looked terrible."

He'd spoken aloud. That was one of the drawbacks—or benefits—of living alone, except he wasn't alone any longer.

A fact borne home by the sound of a footstep on the stair tread.

She was coming upstairs.

Uninvited. Unwanted.

Was there no end to her presumption?

He turned his back to the doorway. If there had been a door, he would have slammed it, but the rooms up here didn't have doors. At one time, the upstairs had all been one room, and the walls had been built shortly before Will had taken up residency. There was no call to put in doors for a bachelor.

His bed was still unmade, the mattress indented where he'd spent the night. He needed to dress. He had a busy schedule. He didn't have time for nonsense—

"I'm sorry."

Will stiffened. He knew she stood in his doorway. "I'll remember you are sorry when I'm standing on the gallows with the hangman's noose around my neck."

"It won't happen—at least not because of me," she promised. "The people in this village don't know me. My family and I had just arrived at Lord Bossley's house. I travel with my own maid. No one should identify me."

He didn't know how to answer that piece of fantasy. Of course someone would know who she was—sooner or later.

At his continued silence, she said, "I'll stay out of view. I promise. I know you don't have a reason to trust me, but I beg you to give me the opportunity to meet your standards. You will not be disappointed."

"I need to dress." He turned then, giving her a pointed look that it was time for her to leave.

Her cheeks turned pink, as if she'd just realized how little he was wearing. "Of course, I beg your pardon." She withdrew, but she didn't go down the stairs. She moved into the bedroom across the hall from his.

The room his "cousin" would have used if he'd had a cousin.

In one angry stride, Will crossed to his wardrobe and threw open the doors so hard that they slammed the sides of the chest.

"Damn it all," he muttered. He shouldn't swear. It was his vice. He tried to keep it mild. Sometimes, it was difficult. He pushed a hand through his hair. It needed to be cut. He needed a shave. He needed, he needed, he needed . . . *Dear Lord, she was beautiful.*

The worst part of their tussle downstairs was that he'd enjoyed it. She'd felt good in his arms. And that scent of hers. . .

A perfumer should capture it in a bottle. The man would make a fortune.

Will tried to put her out of his mind as he unfolded a clean shirt and put himself in order. He focused on the task at hand, the sharpening of his razor, the scrape of metal against skin, the tying of his preaching bands around his neck.

In the mirror he appeared a man who knew his place in the world. A man who was correct and upright. A man who wasn't lying to everyone he knew.

Lady Corinne had called him a hypocrite. She'd been right.

Mrs. Gowan had returned. He could hear her and Amanda busy in the kitchen, the sound rising through a vent in the floorboards that let the heat from the kitchen rise to warm the upper rooms. He was going to have to talk to Mrs. Gowan, to beg her to pretend about his cousin.

Properly dressed, Will went out into the hall. The bedrooms were so close that his doorway was only feet from hers.

Lady Corinne sat on her bed, her hands folded in her lap. She looked up at the sound of his step.

Their eyes met, held.

She pressed her lips together, her distress clear in her clear blue eyes. Sad eyes. She wasn't one to hide her emotions. Her brow wrinkled in concern. "I know you don't like me," she admitted quietly. "I'm sorry."

Those last two words lingered in the air between them. They pierced his anger. Made him a fool.

Oh, he hurt . . . but not in the way she imagined. And this was the second time she'd accused him of disliking her.

"It's not that I *don't* like you, my lady," he conceded and went downstairs, chased by his own folly.

Amanda lay in wait for him in the sitting room. She was a bit lovesick for him. It amused her parents, and yes, he was flattered. He'd long ago

discovered women were fascinated by the clergy.
He assumed it was because of their leadership
role. He was too old for Amanda but wished to
be gentle with her feelings, especially since he
could understand yearning for the Unattainable.

"There is going to be a dance after Luddy and
Jillian MacKay's wedding next Saturday," she
said to him.

"That what I understand," he answered. He
pulled his prayer book down from the shelf. His
sitting room doubled as his library and study. "I
shall be seeing Miss Jillian this morning."

"You'll be going to the dance, won't you?"
Amanda wondered. She'd clasped her hands
behind her back, a movement that brought her
pert breasts to his attention. He'd noticed her use
this same movement on many of the parish lads
with devastating effect. He would not be conquered. He kept his gaze on his prayer book.

"I shall make an appearance," he said, opening
the book and riffling a few pages. "But I won't
be there long." He closed the book and started
for the kitchen.

But Amanda was feeling bold today. She
stepped in his path. "Your cousin just said you
could dance, and you should," she told him.
"You should come out in the village more often."

She was close. Too close. He forced a smile and sidestepped away from her. "Thank you, Amanda, but people want their parson in the church and not dancing away on the green."

"I believe you are wrong about that, Mr. Norwich. Some of us would like to see you dance."

"So they can laugh," he assured her. He started once again around her. She wouldn't let him go.

She placed a hand on his arm. "I wouldn't laugh," she said, raising earnest eyes to his face.

Emotions were strong at her age and very real. He knew. "I know you wouldn't, Amanda, but I'm too old for you."

"You aren't that old."

"I'm ancient. You need a brawny lad."

"I prefer brains," she said.

"We men grow into good sense . . . sometimes," he had to add with a smile. Then, with quiet seriousness, he added, "I am not for you, Amanda. You wouldn't be happy with my life."

Tears welled in her eyes. "You're wrong," she said. "*Wrong.*" Before he could respond, she turned and ran through the kitchen and out the door.

Her mother had overheard. She'd been in the corner by the door scrubbing the floor. She now sat back on her heels.

Will felt terrible at causing Amanda dismay. "I'm sorry. I didn't mean to upset her."

"When a lass is that age, looking cross-eyed will upset her." Mrs. Gowan came to her feet. She pressed a hand against her back. She'd had six children, Amanda being the youngest, and she often told Will that each one of them had marked her body. "You were fine, Reverend. Very kind," she said. "In fact, I appreciate your honesty to her. Mandy has been yearning for you since she was this high." She held her hand up to a point close to the height of her waist.

"Now I do feel old."

Mrs. Gowan laughed. She had the habit many short women did of looking up to talk to a person, so she always appeared to have her nose in the air. "You should be her parents," she told him. "She's a lovely lass, but she is a handful. Joshua thinks we should be arranging a marriage for her. She has her sights set on you, and that is not good."

"It's not that I don't believe she is lovely," he wanted to stress.

"Go on now, I know what you mean. I understand." She walked over to the dry sink. Will followed.

"So," she said, changing the subject, "is your cousin here for a long stay?"

He should say something noncommittal. Mrs. Gowan really didn't care about the details of his life. Oh, she'd warmed up to him over the past few months, but Will remembered how it had been when he'd first arrived in Ferris. The parishioners had not been happy to see the foster son of Lord Bossley appointed to living at Ferris. They'd not trusted him. Mrs. Gowan had carried out her duties as housekeeper, but there had been no easy discussions, no confidences.

Will had been lonely in those days. A pastor's role was never easy, especially for a single man, but his relationship to Lord Bossley made it all the more difficult.

Over time, especially recently, the distrust seemed to have lifted. His parishioners now came to him with their concerns, and he was glad for it.

And he wanted that goodwill. His was a true calling. In a life when he'd often felt confused, out of place, and alone, the Church and the good Lord's mercy had sustained him.

He was also certain Mrs. Gowan's feelings toward him played a strong part in what the villagers thought of him. She saw that he was fed well, fussed over the long hours he worked, and provided friendship.

Today, she'd brought him a loaf of bread from her daily baking. It rested on the windowsill. Before she left, she'd have a chicken roasted on the hearth's spit or one of her tasty stews for his dinner.

He realized that if ever there was a person whom he could not lie to, it must be Mrs. Gowan. He couldn't abuse her friendship in that manner.

"She's not my cousin," he heard himself confess. The words just came right out of their own volition. "Although what was happening when you first arrived is not what it might have seemed."

Mrs. Gowan turned from the dry sink, her brows raised. She gave him a considering look and then said quietly, "I know she isn't your cousin, and I have enough understanding of your character, sir, to not let my mind assume the worst."

"Do you know who she is?"

"No."

"It's best that way, Mrs. Gowan. Please don't ask questions, and let's not discuss her being here. She may be living in the parish for a few months," he continued, humbled by her confidence. "I don't know how long, but I would appreciate it if I could count upon your discretion."

"Aye, Reverend, you may. But I also want you to know, you can trust us in Ferris. We consider you one of our own. After all, we've known you were the Thorn these past five months and more, and nary a word has passed our lips."

Chapter Eight

Mrs. Gowan's words, offered in that practical, borderland tone, stunned Will.

A smile lit her eyes. "See? You didn't even know we knew. If you wish to have a 'cousin,' then we trust you. Believe me when I say we have tight lips and you are one of us."

One of them. Will had thought himself completely alone . . . but now, thinking on it, he realized he couldn't have managed to escape notice or to accomplish half of what he'd done without help.

His housekeeper nodded, as if she understood what he was thinking. "When the soldiers come asking questions, we make it sound as if you are right here amongst us all the time. They don't suspect you, but we want to be certain they don't."

"I'm humbled."

She laughed. "No, tis us that are humbled. We'd given up. We'd been swallowed whole. Lost our pride. But you gave it back to us."

"I wanted justice."

"And you helped us to discover faith. There isn't anything we wouldn't do for you."

"Does everyone know?" he wondered, alarmed.

"Not everyone. Just those whom we can trust. None of the gentry, of course," she answered, picking up the water bucket she'd used to clean the floor. "But my husband, the elders, most in the village and a few others, they know."

Her husband knew as well?

Will leaned against the dry sink. "I saw him yesterday. We discussed repairing the bell. He's never said a word."

"And he won't." She opened the door, poured the water out on the step, and picked up a broom to sweep it clean. "We understand what that money is for. You've given it out evenly. Wisely. Honestly."

"I took great care to keep it quiet." He heard her praise, but if anyone leaked a word . . . "How did you reason it out?"

"You were a bit awkward at first. Not half as clever as you'd thought. And I'm in and out of this house, and there have been signs. Once I noticed the church coffers always had money to help those who were in danger of losing their livelihoods, then I started to suspect."

Will thought of the chest he'd stolen, of the warning from Squire Rhys-Morton—or had the squire's confession been part of a plot?

He'd go mad thinking about all the possibilities. He wasn't one for intrigue, and there were many times, especially of late, when he wished he'd never started the Thorn.

"I know what you are thinking, sir," she said. "You are into this deep, but I've been wanting to tell you not to busy your conscience over the death of one like Simon Porledge. What he did to Seth was beyond cruelty. I say you handed out justice, a justice no one would have had without your courage."

And they thought he'd murdered Porledge as well.

The only one who naturally thought him innocent was annoying Lady Corinne. Will wanted to explain, but he dared not. "Mrs. Gowan, you must never breathe a word of our conversation to anyone. You must erase from your mind what you know. I beg you to do this for your own safety and that of your family."

She shut the back door and propped the broom on the floor, her hand on the handle, posing as if she'd been a courageous adventurer. "Pshaw, Mr. Norwich. I'm descended from reiver's stock. My family has lived on this land for as many generations and more than Bossley's own ancestors. I'll not hide in fear. There was a time I was afraid, but you gave me courage. We are proud that you are the pastor of Holy Name."

"Is that why the pews at Holy Name have grown crowded?" he queried, a touch of irony in his voice. "When I first arrived, it was often myself and old Andrew at service."

"You support us. We support you . . . and your sermons are growing on me." She put the broom away by the side of the dry sink. "You still talk over my head. You are too intelligent for your own good, Mr. Norwich, but we like you. And if you say that young woman is your cousin, well, then, so she is. Anyone who dares think different had best keep her tongue in her head. You know I'm thinking about Maude Clemson. A busybody always thinking the worst. But I'll see that she is kept in her place."

"Thank you," he said, meaning the words. The

truth was until he'd created the Thorn, he'd felt ill at ease in his profession. It had been hard to stand aside and do nothing while a great wrong was being lowered on the people of this parish.

"You know," Mrs. Gowan continued, wiping her hands on her apron, "our current Lord Bossley may be a mighty man in London, but there are few of us here who would offer a hand to help him if he was drowning in the Liddell, begging your pardon, Reverend," she added as a way of penance. "It's a shame now. You should have known his father, the old Lord Bossley. He was a grand man. Good to all of us, the way a lord should be."

"Times are changing, Mrs. Gowan," Will offered, feeling that out of loyalty alone he should say something in the defense of his foster father. "We can't keep all the old customs."

"Some things *should* change," she agreed. "Here, I've brewed myself a cup of tea. Would you like one?"

She'd never made that offer before. A threshold had been crossed between them, one that he'd hoped to cross months before when he'd first arrived as their clergyman.

"Yes, I would."

"Sit down then," she ordered while she

poured two cups and carried them over to the table. "I know you feel you must be respectful to Lord Bossley," she said in motherly tones as she took the chair across from his. "I want you to know that when he came back from that island he'd been living on, we all wished to serve him well. He was our peer. It's him that betrayed us."

Will turned the handle of his teacup without taking a sip. "What was he like then?"

"When he first came? Different than what we expected. No one knew him well. After all, he'd been away to school from the day he came out of skirts. The old lord and his lady didn't live together well."

"What do you mean?"

"They didn't like each other. He stayed on the estate and she spent all her time in London. Her son stayed with her, although from what I've heard, she never was a doting parent."

"Bossley's father didn't protest?" He couldn't imagine a man letting his child grow up without him.

She made a disparaging sound. "Some men are good with children. My Joshua is one of the best fathers. But the old lord seemed to care more for his hunting dogs than his wife and son. My mother used to say that most of us had forgotten the old lord even had an heir until the current lord showed up one day almost a year to the day after his father's death. We'd started to believe he'd never return to Ferris. I mean, we'd received word he was on his way, but he took his time in coming."

Her expression softened. "I remember you when you were no higher than a chair leg. I was one of the girls Lady Bossley interviewed to care for you and Lord Sherwin. I wasn't hired. She thought me too young. Two years later I was married and had a child of my own."

"Well, we've come full circle, haven't we?" he observed dryly. "You *are* taking care of me now."

She laughed and stood up from the table, finished with her tea. "I wouldn't have been happy in London. But I understand why our Lord Bossley enjoys himself there. It is all he has known. That must be his mother's mark on him. I wonder what happened to her?"

"The dowager Lady Bossley? She is still in London." Will had only met her once or twice. She was a strange woman, who gave him an unsettled feeling. "From my understanding, she is extremely frail. Only Bossley calls on her."

"It's too bad. Perhaps if he'd had more of a father's influence, he wouldn't be so greedy, if you will pardon my speaking my mind."

Will laughed. "Speak your mind whenever you wish, Mrs. Gowan. I appreciate it *and*," he added pointedly, "I appreciate and value your discretion."

"You've earned my loyalty, Mr. Norwich. If you are asking me to keep my lips sealed, that's already done. Porledge deserved his death." She picked up the basket she usually carried, a sign she was ready to leave for the day. "You see the bread here." She placed her hand on the loaf on the sill. "I have a chicken and potatoes in that pot on the hook." She nodded toward the fire, where a covered pot had been set off from the heat. "Mandy will be at the churn this afternoon. I'll send her over later with some fresh butter . . . ?" Her voice broke off. Her manner changed as she stared at a point beyond his shoulder.

Will turned in the chair and then came to his feet at the sight of Lady Corinne in the doorway. She'd replaited her hair and held the pitcher from the washbasin.

She looked very young, very innocent, and very lovely—although the dress threatened to swallow her up. Of course, not even sackcloth could disguise her curves or take away from her natural grace.

Lady Corinne's chin came up, as if she expected him to censure her for coming down the stairs. "I'm Corinne Rosemont," she said to Mrs. Gowan. "Mr. Norwich's cousin." Abruptly, she held her hand out as if wishing for the other woman to shake it.

A surmising glint came to Mrs. Gowan's eyes. Her glance slid from Corinne to Will. She was an earthy woman, and Will feared what conclusion she had jumped to. She stuck her hand out and took Lady Corinne's. "It's my pleasure to meet you, Miss Rosemont," she said, bobbing a small curtsey anyway. "I'm Rachel Gowan. My husband's the blacksmith, and I have been Reverend Norwich's housekeeper this past year. I hope you enjoy your stay here in Ferris. If there is anything you need, ask. I'll be happy to help."

"Thank you, Mrs. Gowan. I appreciate your kindness," Lady Corinne answered, her initial defiance giving way to genuine warmth. Mrs. Gowan melted.

It did Will no good to watch that Lady Corinne conquered everyone around him. Was he the only one who knew to keep his guard up?

"Well, now, I'll be off," the housekeeper said. "Don't forget tomorrow is washing day."

"I won't," Will said.

Corinne took a step after her. "Do you have needle and thread?"

"Aye."

"Could you bring it on the morrow?"

Mrs. Gowan's gaze dropped to Lady Corinne's overlarge dress. "I'll have my Mandy bring it when she runs the butter over later today. I have a seam ripper as well. You may need to take down the hem."

"Yes, I do need to do that," Lady Corinne said.

"I also have another dress I can send. And a bonnet. You'll need a bonnet to go to church. It's a shabby thing, but a clever girl can fancy it up."

"I will appreciate both," Lady Corinne murmured.

"Good day, Reverend. Miss Rosemont." Mrs. Gowan was out the door.

There was a moment of silence after she'd left. They could hear her calling to see if Mandy had finished her chores, then ordering the girl to follow her home for the churning that needed to be done.

Will wished he could have left with her. Instead, he hid awkwardness behind silence.

Lady Corinne spoke first. "I heard what she said about the Thorn." She waited a beat, as if expecting him to respond. When he didn't, she asked, "Why did she say Simon Porledge deserved to die?"

There was something he could attach his temper to and use to put distance between them. He didn't want to like her. He mustn't. "Sometimes, my lady, you are too curious. Stay out of what doesn't concern you."

With those curt words he left the rectory and kept walking. He needed to release anxiousness, and it took him a good five minutes before he realized he'd tramped into the woods surrounding Ferris.

This wasn't the first time he'd blindly walked out doubts, fears . . . shame.

Simon Porledge. The man haunted him.

Will considered himself a practical man, but he carried guilt for Porledge's death. Guilt for what had happened to the people of Ferris.

And now, in the middle of everything, God had delivered *her*.

She was willful, arrogant, disturbingly beautiful, and honest. More honest than he was with himself. Ironic how an infatuation he'd suffered as a youth was carried with him still.

He played the offended party well . . . even as he was secretly glad she didn't want to marry Freddie. He knew his foster brother's true nature better than any. She'd been wise to run.

However, although she was an innocent in this cat's game he played with Lord Bossley, she could very well be the cause of him losing his head.

"Keep your distance, Will," he reminded himself. "Keep your distance."

The sooner he shipped her away, the better.

The small rectory seemed to shrink even more with Will's exit.

Funny how she had no difficulty thinking of him as Will—her cousin Will. She liked the name. It fit him. The title "Reverend" was old and stuffy. Will was a strong name and worthy of this complex man. A man who was also handsome, dashing, angry, alone . . .

He wasn't like any man she'd ever met before. She'd be wise to keep her distance. Will had secrets. She sensed it. Not everything was what it seemed, but she couldn't decide if that was just a fanciful notion of her own or a threat.

She filled her pitcher with water heating in a kettle beside the fire, then walked through the sitting room, acquainting herself with her new home. The whole rectory was the size of the reception room in her father's London house.

The books on the shelves in the sitting room were religious tomes, many in Latin or Greek. No wonder he was so serious all the time. She'd have been cross-eyed if she'd had to spend her reading time translating. She could do it, but she'd never understood the purpose of reading Greek.

She climbed the stairs. Her night of wandering was catching up to her, and her shoulder ached from overuse.

Her room had a single bed covered with a patchwork counterpane, a washstand, a chair and table by the window. The window overlooked the shed that stabled Roman, who stood munching his grass. She'd discovered last night that the horse was down to his last four good teeth. It took him a great deal of chewing to finish a meal, but Corinne was learning to respect the beast as Will did. Roman was surprisingly strong and forward-moving for his age. He'd not shirked in carrying her through the dark.

On the other side of the shed, not far from the back kitchen door, a garden had been tilled for spring planting.

If she leaned against the windowpane, she

could see the stone edifice of Will's church. A graveyard filled most of the surrounding space around the church with carefully manicured walkways to keep visitors off the graves. A huge cherry tree, just now coming into bloom, glorified and sheltered this hallowed ground.

And beyond the church was Ferris.

Corinne wished she dared open the window and stick her head out for a better view. The risk that she could have been seen and recognized was too great, and even if she did do so, the church blocked most of what she could see.

But she had a hint of what it was like in the two buildings in her line of sight. Thatched roofs, well-tended gardens, children chasing a hoop down the dirt road. Peaceful. Pleasant. And yet there was a darkness here as well.

She pulled back. This sense of foreboding was not like her.

They said her great-grandmother had the "sight." She'd often predicted events well before they'd happened.

Corinne had not thought she shared her ancestress's gift, but she couldn't shake this sense that she was where she was meant to be.

And that something was afoot. Something she couldn't define but "felt."

Curiosity made her bold enough to enter his room.

The wooden-post bed was larger than hers, but not by much. Considering his height, he must have had to sleep doubled up.

There was a woven rag rug on the floor, and the counterpane on his bed was a deep blue. The sunlight coming through the window struck the color and reflected it around the room. The sandalwood scent of his shaving soap lingered in the air.

In contrast to the two pegs in the wall of her room, he had a wardrobe. It was a rough-hewn thing, obviously locally made out of oak. His riding boots had been placed side by side in front of it. They'd been polished so that there would be no reminder of the Thorn's escapade the other night.

Corinne opened the wardrobe door. She was not surprised to see two black jackets, two black vests, and one cleaned and pressed white shirt. A parson's life didn't allow for much color. She wondered where he kept his vestments. Probably over at the church.

She closed the door and noticed one place where Will was not neat and orderly. There was a stack of books on the floor beside the bed. Some were left open, as if he'd found an item of particular interest and had wanted to refer back to it later.

She couldn't resist seeing what he read and was pleasantly surprised by the miscellaneous assortment. These were not the decorative books of a gentleman's library, books placed on shelves for show.

No, these were well-loved books. Judging by their spines, they'd been read repeatedly. There was Daniel Defoe's *Robinson Crusoe,* as well as *Letters of a Turkish Spy* and other tales of adventure and foreign places. She'd read two of the books on his stack—*One Thousand and One Nights,* although she'd read it in English under the title *The Arabian Nights* and not this French translation, and *Castle Rackrent,* one of female author Maria Edgeworth's entertaining novels.

Corinne held these books in her hand as she glanced over at the boots, polished and waiting for their master's next adventure.

Infatuation was a dangerous thing. It clouded judgment. In spite of his calling, Will Norwich was a dangerous man.

She'd be wise to remember it.

But he was also one who craved adventure.

This, Corinne could understand.

* * *

Will did not return home until late. At some point, he'd fetched Roman and ridden off, but Corinne had fallen asleep across her bed and so had missed the chance to speak a few words to him.

Mrs. Gowan's personable daughter Amanda had come by with fresh butter, needle and thread, and the promised clothing. Corinne set to work on the green wool, attempting to give it, if not a more stylish line, then a better-fitting one.

She was definitely ready to eat by the time Will returned. She'd set the table in anticipation of his arrival. Amanda had reminded Corinne about cooking the chicken. Corinne had never cooked anything before except biscuits with the cook when she was a child, so she was pleased that her efforts of hanging the chicken pot over the fire had resulted in a hot, tasty dish.

Furthermore, her natural enthusiasm for life wanted conversation. She'd longed for it all day, and now that he'd returned, she was ready to talk.

He wasn't.

Will went about chores. He pumped a fresh bucket of water, which he set on the floor beside the dry sink. Then he took the stewed chicken off the fire and set the pot on the table. He took his chair without waiting for Corinne to have her seat first.

She didn't complain. She folded her hands and waited dutifully as he said a few ministerial words over the chicken. Her family was not particularly religious. They went to church for show, but she wasn't going to tell him that. He seemed truly devoted.

He then ate his dinner in silence, focusing on his food, which he ate with an economy of movement.

When at last she couldn't take being ignored any longer, Corinne said, "Perhaps we should discuss our story about my being your cousin?"

He didn't answer immediately. She kept a pleasant smile on her face, but her grip on her fork tightened at his rudeness. Just when she was ready to reach over and pop him on the head with the fork, he said, "It's not necessary. You won't be out and about. Mrs. Gowan will keep your presence to herself." He buttered his bread and started eating it. He had not looked at her as he'd spoken.

Corinne pushed her chicken around her plate. "I think we should play a game this evening. It will while away the time."

"I don't like games," he answered, shifting his attention from his bread to the last of his chicken.

"Not even cards? I'm very lucky."

"I don't play cards."

"Do you have an instrument? Music is a good way to entertain both mind and soul—"

"No."

Corinne took a deep breath. He was being deliberately difficult. She wondered what imaginary crime he was placing beside her name now. "We could converse? Play a game of ten questions? I ask you questions and then you ask me—"

"*I* shall read this evening."

A solitary endeavor. She set down her fork and frowned at him, although he didn't notice, since he refused to look at her. She decided to take the direct route. "Why are you being this way? What have I done to upset you?"

He lifted his head, looking at her with mild surprise—and she was struck anew by how handsome he was, even when she was vexed with him. "Let me see . . . you've forced yourself on me, compromised my position, jilted my foster brother—"

"Oh, please," she interrupted. "We've already hashed this out. You are unhappy with me. I understand. It's clear. You may stop acting out in such a bad fashion."

Her reward was to have his gaze finally hone

in on her. She was surprised to realize his eyes weren't brown, as she'd supposed, but green. A woody, dark green.

"I am not acting out. I am eating my dinner."

But she had engaged him. Triumph made her smile. He saw that smile and deepened his own frown. He pushed away from the table. "You are the most frivolous woman I've ever met."

"Yes? Well, with your present grumpiness, I can't imagine you've met many women. Or interested one of them."

His head snapped around in her direction.

"You must be careful, Will," she chided, deliberately using his given name. "You are in danger of being dudly."

His brows crossed. "Dudly? That's not even a word."

"It is. I just used it in conversation. That makes it a word. It's worse than being dull. Dudly is *more* boring than being dull, a state to be avoided at all costs."

"Your using it doesn't make it a word. A word has to be one everyone knows." He rose from the table, carried his plate to the dry sink, and put it in a bucket of water on the floor. "You may think you have control of the world, Lady Corinne, but you don't have control of the English language."

"Corinne," she said softly, pleased that she'd breached his wall of silence. "You must call me Corinne." In fact, she wanted to hear him say her name.

"No," he said, a considering look in his eye. "I'm too dudly to do that." He walked out of the room.

Corinne was on her feet in a flash. She picked up her own plate, went to the back door and tossed the scraps outside, not knowing what else to do with them, then dropped her silver and plate in the bucket and hurried to join him in the next room.

Will was lighting a lamp. He sat in the chair beside it and reached for the book on his reading table. It was a heavy one about theology.

"I believe I shall read as well," Corinne announced, wondering if she could pull him out of his shell once again.

"I don't have any books that would interest you," he muttered, settling his heels on a footstool and crossing his booted feet at the ankles.

Corinne couldn't remember ever having to work so hard to attract the attention of a man.

She came over to his chair and, pushing his feet off the footstool, took their place on its needle-pointed cushion. "What sort of books do you mean?" she challenged. "Poetry? Romance?" He had both those books by his bed upstairs.

"One with made-up words in it," he replied, not bothering to look at her—but that was all right. She was charmed.

No one ever teased her. She was always treated as different and set apart because of her father's rank.

"You don't dislike me," she said.

He turned the page of his book, raising it a touch higher as if to shut her out. "Lady Corinne, I'm not an admirer."

"You were once. And you didn't even know me."

"Now I'm starting to know you." He kept his voice flat, too flat. He was trying too hard.

"How do you do it?" she asked softly. "How can you be two men? One is staid and disciplined. The other has an adventurer's heart. Are you both one and the same, or is one trying to overcome the other?"

A tension vibrated from him. She'd found a chink in his armor—

Will slammed his book shut. His hand came down on her wrist, his eyes alive with anger. "Lady Corinne, I am not your lady's companion, your confidant, your *cousin,* or a toothless dog for you to badger at will. I'm a man, Corinne.

And you'd be wise to remember that and stop being so naive."

"Naive?"

"Yes," he said drawing out the word. "Grow up, my lady."

Infatuation evaporated. Corinne twisted her wrist, and he let her free.

He sat back and reopened his book. His attention returned to his reading; supposedly, she had been dismissed.

Corinne rose to her feet. "You can growl at me all you wish, sir, but I like being mistress of my own fate. You have always been free to decide what you wish to do, where you want to go. I never have been. So, if my satisfaction with the turn of events isn't to your liking, *Cousin* Will, then so be it."

She walked over to the stairs and started up the first step, but then she turned. He sat in the lamp's pool of light surrounded by darkness, a man alone.

"And I don't need to grow up. I'm not the one throwing tantrums. I'm a woman full grown. You'd best remember that, Will."

Corinne went upstairs, not looking back. She undressed and climbed into her bed . . . but it took her a long time to fall asleep.

She listened for him.

* * *

Will waited a decent amount of time before stealing out of the rectory. Riding Roman, he headed back to the reiver's hut. Using the lamp he'd brought with him, he removed the chest from its hiding place.

When he'd stolen it, he'd been surprised at the size. So small, and yet Bossley had gone to great pains to keep it safe—even to the point of hosting a dinner party in honor of his son's future marriage. He'd wanted to be in Ferris—because it was so close to Scotland and those who sympathized with the French?

Will opened the chest and was so stunned by its contents that he almost dropped it. Gold coins, the size of halfpennies, tumbled out into his hand. One side was engraved with Napoleon the Emperor's head. On the other were the words *"Empire Française,"* along with the amount of each coin— *40 francs*—surrounded by a laurel wreath.

There were close to a hundred coins. Four thousand francs in gold. Such an amount could buy much goodwill.

Ashcroft obviously hadn't known what he'd been carrying, because he'd left the chest sitting in the coach seat, where Will hadn't had to strain to look for it.

Will closed the chest, his hands shaking. Of all the things he'd thought of Bossley, traitor had not been one of them. And it truly had been by chance that Will had come by this bounty. He'd thought Bossley had been making the usual shipment of British coin unfairly taken from the crofters. This was something quite different. Deadly different.

What would Bossley do to have this returned? Or to keep his secret dealings with the French quiet?

Will feared the answer.

Chapter Nine

Shortly before noon the next day, Will burst through the kitchen door to announce, "The whole village knows my *cousin* has come to visit." He was hatless, as if he'd left the church in a hurry. "*Everyone*. I've had three people ask after you."

Corinne sat reading at the table. She looked up in a show of mild surprise. "Oh, are you *speaking* to me now?" This morning, when she'd come downstairs, he'd kept his nose buried in a book and had refused to look at her, let alone say a good morning.

He stabbed his fingers through his hair in frustration. "This is what I feared. Gossip will

spread through the village faster than a fire.
Before supper this evening, everyone will know
my cousin is here. Mrs. Gowan promised to
keep your presence secret. I can't imagine she'd
break such a promise—" His eyes narrowed on
the bucket by the dry sink. "What is this? Fresh
water?" He picked up the bucket and gave it a
sniff. "Did you pump this?" He didn't wait for
her response but launched into the diatribe she
knew he wanted to deliver. "I *told* you to stay
inside. You assured me no one would see you if
I let you stay here. And you were wrong. If you
had stayed at the reiver's hut, no one would have
known you were *here* because you wouldn't be
here. Now everyone is speculating and asking
questions. It's the questions they *don't* ask to my
face I need to worry over."

"Mrs. Gowan told me this morning no one
will say anything to Lord Bossley or Major Ashcroft."

"Oh, yes? The two of you are cozying it up,
aren't you? Well, let me inform the two of you
that gossip doesn't work that way. And Bossley aside, what if the bishop hears word of this?
That I'm keeping a woman who pretends to be
my cousin in the rectory. Then he will say something to Bossley. Or to Freddie."

That last sobered Corinne immediately. "I didn't go out. Mrs. Gowan pumped the water for me. And she said she told her husband but no one else."

"Then how does anyone know you are here?" he said to himself, pacing from one end of the small kitchen to the other.

Corinne immediately knew the answer. "Her daughter. Mandy is a chatterbox."

"Yes, but who would listen to her?"

Men never understood the workings of society.

"Anyone. Everyone," Corinne replied. "You are an important person in the village."

"I'm just the rector."

"You *are* the rector, the *only* one in the whole parish with that title," Corinne said, then began ticking off other important points on her fingers. "You are also single, handsome, related to Bossley." She shrugged. "It's a wonder the gossips aren't camped out in your garden."

He pulled a frown, shook his head, half-turning from her . . . but then he said, "Would they really pay that close attention?"

"Is there something else to take their minds off of their own lives? Father always said gossip is for the bored, but I've noticed that in London it runs rampant even with people whom I think should know better."

Will stood very still, and Corinne realized he was actually upset.

"What is it?" she asked. When he didn't respond, she said, "They won't betray you, Will. I can tell that just in my morning's conversation with Mrs. Gowan. They consider you as close as family."

His eyes brightened with a fury that caught her off guard. "So now you are telling me you know my own parishioners better than I do myself?"

Corinne sat back in her chair. His anger was out of proportion. She didn't sense fear from him, but a fierce protectiveness. "Is something wrong?" she asked.

Her simple question only made him retreat further. "I have to prepare my sermon," he said and went into the sitting room. She heard him pull books from his shelf. A moment later, he went out the front door.

For a long moment, Corinne sat, going over the scene in her mind. She understood his concern. Keeping her presence quiet was important and, yes, he did live a double life. But there was more at work here.

Will Norwich had demons.

He was also the most complicated, fascinating man she'd ever met.

Only four days ago, she'd been confused about life, about her purpose, about what she wanted. Running away had made perfect sense. It had felt right.

Being here, with him, made sense as well. She didn't understand why, but for whatever reason, life's twisting course had brought her here. And this, too, for whatever unfathomable reason, also felt right.

She returned to her reading.

She was not what he had expected.

Will knew he was hiding in the church. True, he always practiced his sermon from the pulpit . . . but today he took longer than usual.

He had to avoid her. It wasn't just that she attracted him, that his infatuation for her had never died—oh, no, it seemed stronger than ever the more he was around her—but she had a way of seeing right to the heart of a matter. He sensed it.

Their earlier conversation had seemed innocuous, and yet she seemed to have divined his troubled spirit.

Perhaps he felt this way because he was not accustomed to having anyone around. His was a solitary life. He'd discovered it was easier that way.

He'd grown up with the knowledge that he was "different." He didn't know his parentage, he was a charity case, he had no family.

The Church was the perfect calling for one such as himself. It gave him purpose—and an excuse for being "apart" from the rest of humanity. The preaching bands around his neck were his identity. God was his family.

When he'd arrived in Ferris, his ties to Bossley had kept him separate from the community. He'd understood their distrust. He'd accepted it, even had anticipated it. Wasn't distrust the motive behind Freddie's and his companions' teasing? Behind those hostesses over the years who had felt they'd had to invite him but hadn't been able to welcome him?

Then he'd created the Thorn. With the Thorn, he'd set himself apart even more. This secret of his was dangerous to know.

He hadn't yet come to terms with Mrs. Gowan's claim that there were those in the parish who knew. It was not wise to trust.

And why should he have trusted? He'd never been able to trust anyone in his life.

Lady Corinne knew that. He didn't know how—but she knew. In the kitchen, there had been a moment when he'd felt as if she'd been able to see all the way to his soul, that she'd understood he was weak. Alone.

God help him.

He tried to concentrate on the words he'd written on the sheet of paper in front of him, but his mind kept returning to her.

A footfall in the back of the church warned Will he wasn't alone. He looked up. *She* was standing there, her pale blonde hair a beacon in the church's gloom.

For a second, Will couldn't think. He reached out to the pulpit's sides, gripping them tight. It took a moment and the out-of-place sound of a yowling cat before he realized she wasn't alone.

Sarah Pearson, the miller's wife, stood by Lady Corinne. In one arm she held the baby she'd given birth to two months ago. Her son Little Seth held onto her skirts. Her other arm rested on her oldest child's shoulder. Maggie Pearson had always been a somber child. What had happened to her father, the violence against him and his withdrawal from the village society, could not have been easy for a child to understand, but they told Will that Maggie had never shed a tear or spoken a word after that horrible night. She now held a yellow tabby in her arm that, from his panting and plaintive yowls, appeared to be in distress.

"Will," Lady Corinne said, her tone urgent as she came forward, bringing the family with her. "Mrs. Pearson and her children came knocking at the rectory's door. They have a request that's very important." In her eyes, he could read the rest of her message. She was anxious that he would be angry with her for disobeying his order to stay out of sight. Her gaze pleaded for him to listen to what she had to say.

"What is it?" he asked, not moving from his place in the pulpit.

Mrs. Pearson took a step toward him. "Begging your pardon, Mr. Norwich. I need help. My daughter's little cat is ill. Something is wrong."

A cat? What did he know about cats?

"All she does is cry." Maggie took a step forward as she spoke. The words had burst out of her, and now huge tears welled in her eyes. She blinked them back, her face pinched, as if she struggled to keep herself together.

He understood that feeling. How brave she felt she had to be.

Will's worries about Lady Corinne being discovered vanished. He came down from the pulpit, his focus on Maggie. "I don't know much about cats. What do you wish me to do?"

"Just look at her," Maggie urged. "You can make her right. I know you can."

Her mother spoke up. "Actually, I brought the children here thinking it might be good to have a blessing," she suggested. "I know there isn't much you can do, Mr. Norwich. I know that. But I couldn't let the cat . . ." Her voice trailed off into a heavy sigh. "Not at the house," she finished.

He understood. Too many bad things had happened to these children already.

"Well now, let me see," he said. He sat down next to Maggie in the pew and offered his hands. The child placed the cat there with great and somber trust. She moved around so that she sat in the pew beside him, her manner one of complete confidence in him.

Had he really wasted prayers earlier on his lust for Lady Corinne? Had he been so selfish?

God forgive him.

He now placed his prayers where they should have been. *Please don't let me disappoint this child.*

"I told them you would know what to do," he heard Lady Corinne say.

Not her too.

Gently Will probed the cat's sides, trying to identify the problem. The animal was not fat, and it didn't take a heavy touch for him to realize a rib was broken. He could feel it laid across the cat's belly. The animal shifted in his hands, meowed in great distress, and growled a warning.

The loose rib caused discomfort, but if it was not removed, it could puncture the cat's lung or another organ.

A calmness fell over Will. He did know what to do.

He pulled a small penknife from his pocket and opened the side of the cat where he felt the loose bone. The cut was only half an inch long. He pulled out the broken rib.

Though there was hardly any blood, Kitty did not thank him for his work. She hissed and lashed out with her claws before jumping to the ground. She dashed a few feet from them, then stopped, as if finally realizing the pain was gone. She shot a regal look in his direction, the blessing of cat, before she sat back on her haunches and began cleaning her wound. While they all watched in wonder, she moved on to cleaning her face, as natural as could be.

Will looked down at the tiny rib in his hand with disbelief.

"You did it," Maggie said, hopping up from the pew. "I told Mother we must go see Mr. Norwich. I said we must." She hurried to her pet, who let herself be gathered up into Maggie's arms.

"Be careful, Maggie. Watch that wound," Will said.

"Thank you, Mr. Norwich," Sarah Pearson said. Tears were streaming down her face. "Thank you."

"It wasn't much, I assure you," Will said.

"It was a miracle," she answered.

"No, miracles are far stronger than realizing the cat had broken a rib," he assured her, standing.

"Well, *I* didn't know what to do," Mrs. Pearson said. "But you did." Little Seth had even come out from behind his mother's skirts to join his sister in petting the cat.

"It really wasn't anything of my doing," Will repeated.

"I know, I know, God and all that," Mrs. Pearson said. "But when God is not there, *you* have been the one to do His work. When I see a pouch of money left on the doorstep, I know who it is from—and I'm thankful for it, Mr. Norwich. Seth is angry and more than difficult. I needed a bit of blessing from God. Come along, children. Let Mr. Norwich finish preparing for his sermon."

Her children dutifully obeyed. Maggie cradled the cat on her shoulder as if she carried a baby. The cat looked back at Will, staring at him with sphinx-eyed wisdom all the way out of the church.

Will stood where he was until the door in the vestibule shut behind them.

"That was amazing," Lady Corinne said.

He could feel heat rise up his neck at the compliment. He turned away, embarrassed, and started for the pulpit. "I didn't do very much."

"Will, you cut the cat open and saved its life," she countered.

Keeping his attention on his notes, all too aware of her watching him with admiration in her eyes, he said, "I guessed. It was a cat. I felt I couldn't cause any harm."

He expected her to leave. She didn't. He could feel her studying him. "What?" he said at last, impatient with himself as much as with her. He was too aware of her. She was almost overwhelming.

"You don't want to feel as if you are a part of them," she said. "But you are. And you did know exactly what to do. Have you studied medicine?"

"I read a book on anatomy," he muttered.

"This is more than that. You *knew*," she insisted. "Just as you knew how to care for my wound. You were born with a gift, Will, something passed on to you . . . perhaps by your father?"

Immediately, Will rejected the idea. His mind closed against it. He could feel the wall come down. "My father? Chances are my mother never knew who my father was. He probably was any number of sailors who docked in Barbados port. As for my mother, I prefer not to think how much my father paid to bed her. I've heard the whores there can be had for a penny and the streets run rampant with their by-blows."

"You've heard? But you don't know?" she challenged. "I'm surprised you haven't gone on a quest for the story."

"Lady Corinne, this is not an argument. I understand a woman's desire to romanticize my parentage, but a man can't afford such nonsense. I live in the here and now. By the way, speaking of wounds," he continued briskly, "does your wound bother you?" He realized he'd been so focused on keeping a distance between them that he hadn't thought about it.

"It's healing," she said, sounding almost cheery in spite of his set down. "I use the salve all the time. Please don't be late for supper." She gifted him with her dazzling smile and left, her step so light that she was practically skipping.

Did the woman understand the power of that smile? How it made him want to follow her?

Or what hearing her praise did to him? It was as if she chipped away at the armor he'd built around himself as protection.

And what would be left after she was gone? He feared the answer.

Maybe she didn't understand that she could hurt him. He wasn't like her usual swain. Freddie wasn't the sort to be heartbroken. He had few feelings for anyone other than himself.

But Will wasn't made of the same stuff as Freddie. He had something to lose. Even her criticism of his not knowing the facts of his birth rankled a bit.

He waited until it was past dark and he knew she would already be in bed before he returned to the rectory. There were errands to keep him busy. He checked on Maggie and her cat. The story of his operation had spread through Ferris.

There were many nods of approval as he walked by. The lads still didn't invite him in for a drink at the pub, but those sitting out front nodded and tipped their hats to him.

Most of these men couldn't have known he was the Thorn. He had no idea what they thought of him, because he kept his distance and they didn't attend services. He could have entered the pub without an invite, but he chose not to.

Upstairs, Will couldn't resist a glance past her open doorway to be certain she was all right.

She slept and looked like an angel, her face relaxed in repose and her silky hair spread out over the pillow. He backed away, moving to the safety of his own room.

The next morning, a Sunday, Will made certain he was up and gone to the church before Lady Corinne rose. There, he busied himself preparing for the service.

He was pleased that the pews started filling a good half hour early. Will walked up and down the aisle, greeting parishioners.

The time was almost ready to start. Will went over to his chair beside the pulpit. His deacon would start the service.

However, before the man could offer the opening prayer, Lady Corinne arrived in the back of the church. She was wearing a bonnet and a dress of blue wool.

Her bonnet couldn't have been the one Mrs. Gowan had given her. Will had seen it, and the hat had been very shabby. This one was white, with a sprig of cherry blossoms tucked in a red ribbon. Her dress was the one he'd brought to her from the poor box, only it now fit far better than when she'd first taken a needle to it.

She came down the aisle and took a seat next to Rachel Gowan. She kept her head bowed as if in deep prayer.

He scoffed at her prayerful demeanor. What she was really doing was worrying about his re-action once this service was over. And she was right to be worried. He'd ordered her to stay out of sight and now here she was, parading around Ferris. She placed far too much trust in Mrs. Gowan's assurances.

If Will could have picked her up and carried her out of the church without making a scene, he would have done so.

As it was, he was forced to quietly fume while she flouted his authority—and then another pa-rishioner arrived, one Will had never expected to see in his church.

Seth Pearson had to be carried in a makeshift sedan chair. Four of the local lads, none of them churchgoers, held the poles bearing him up. His family—Maggie carrying a doll this time, not a cat—followed him in.

The lads carried Seth to the front left side of the church. Sarah and the children sat beside Seth. The lads took the pew behind theirs.

For a moment, all Will could do was stare in amazed silence, much as the rest of the congregation was doing.

Since the attack, Seth rarely went out. He'd lost the use of his legs and could no longer grind the parish's grain into flour. He didn't even try but left the work to others, who lacked his touch and would have appreciated his advice. They said the days were miserable for him. He'd refused all visitors and spent his time drinking.

And now he was here, looking cleaned up and sober. Because of a cat. God did work in mysterious ways.

Will turned to the deacon and gave him a nod. The service started.

Corinne knew Will wasn't happy with her. She almost wanted to thank Mr. Pearson for claiming Will's attention and taking it off of her. One didn't have to be a resident of Ferris to realize all were surprised by this man's appearance.

Maggie saw her looking in their direction and waved, a smile transforming her face. Corinne had to wave back. A small one, suitable for church. She turned her attention back to Will and saw him frowning.

She frowned back. She didn't have to fake her frown. She wasn't happy with Will's avoiding her. He was being rude. He was being judgmental.

She was thankful Mrs. Gowan was there next to her.

The service started. It was the traditional, the standard. He took to his pulpit and surprised her at how ill at ease he was. She would not have thought that. She had expected a thought-provoking sermon, and there was one, somewhere in his ramblings. It was his delivery that was difficult. He was stiff, tight, self-conscious. Certainly his awkwardness was not because of her. She couldn't have made him that poor a homilist in a week.

Thank the Lord he was a better highwayman than he was a minister.

After the service, Corinne quickly joined the tide of people leaving the church. She skillfully managed to bypass Will at the door, as Mr. Pearson had been carried to him and most people were interested in speaking to both of them.

Out in the yard, Maggie came over to see her. The child was smiling and assured Corinne that kitty was doing well before hurrying off to run circles around the gravestones with the other children.

"This is a wonderful day," Mrs. Gowan confided. "I didn't think we'd ever see Seth Pearson back in church."

"What happened to him?" Corinne had to ask.

"An accident," Mrs. Gowan said, starting to sound distracted, as if she didn't want to discuss the topic. She began to turn away.

Corinne placed a hand on her arm. "Please, I believe I know it includes Lord Bossley. What is happening? What is going on? And who is that Simon Porledge?" At the sharp, questioning look Mrs. Gowan sent her, Corinne pressed on, "Yes, I've heard of him but I don't know the story. Tell me about it. Please."

"It doesn't involve you and I'm certain Mr. Norwich would not approve."

"Mr. Norwich doesn't approve of anything I do, including attending church," Corinne said, nodding over to where Will stood visiting with parishioners. He saw her and, although he kept smiling, his eyes promised there would be a reckoning.

Good. He'd have to *talk* to her for a reckoning.

"I mustn't involve you in this," Mrs. Gowan protested. She smiled her regret and moved off.

"I can tell you," Mandy said.

She'd been standing to the side, obviously mooning over Will. He definitely had made a conquest in her.

It stood to reason she would know the story. A young girl with an infatuation would know everything she could about the object of her desire.

If Corinne had pangs of conscience about asking Mandy, curiosity squelched them.

Mandy motioned for her to move closer to the cherry tree, away from the others. "Everyone thinks I don't know what is going on, but I do," Mandy said and proudly told Corinne the story of Lord Bossley's man breaking the miller's legs so badly that he'd not been able to walk again.

"They thought he was going to heal," Mandy confided. "But his legs are crooked and give him great pain. He can't ply his trade or anything." She lowered her voice to add, "It's the Thorn that keeps them fed. He brings money to the family and to others in need in the parish. We've all been safe since the Thorn started guarding us.

Some would have lost their homes where their families have lived since the beginning of England if it wasn't for him."

Guarding them. What an interesting way to look at the highwayman's actions. He was providing more than justice. He offered protection.

And now Corinne understood Will's motives. He robbed to feed his flock, to take care of those who needed help. No wonder the villagers wanted him to trust in their silence.

Corinne gazed across the churchyard to where he stood, tall, handsome, forthright—and that is when she fell in love.

He was St. George and Sir Galahad combined. He was noble beyond any man she had ever met. And he was also very handsome.

"Isn't he the most wonderful man?" Mandy asked, summing up Corinne's thoughts completely. "You are so lucky to be his cousin," she continued, reminding Corinne of her role.

"Yes, I am," Corinne agreed. She gave Mandy's hand a little squeeze. "Thank you for sharing that information with me."

"Don't tell anyone," Mandy warned.

"I'd never betray him," Corinne said.

"Neither would I," Mandy agreed. Her mother called her name. She shot a cross look in the direction of her parents. "They treat me as if I'm a child," she said, "but I must go. I'll see you tomorrow, Miss Rosemont."

"Yes, thank you, Mandy."

The girl smiled a look of farewell and hurried off.

As for Corinne, she was wanted as well. Will was frowning at her again. He nodded toward the rectory and started walking, expecting her to follow.

"I'm a man, Corinne." That's what he'd said to her the other evening, and that one line had haunted her dreams for the last two nights.

The time of the promised reckoning had indeed arrived.

Chapter Ten

Will was ready to set Lady Corinne in her place. He wanted her to stay at the rectory and out of sight. She might have believed she was safe in Ferris, but she risked recognition, and someone from the garrison—or a member of the gentry—could ride through at any time.

He had a list of people who could endanger both of them.

Still wearing his vestments, he waited for her inside the rectory sitting room, his hands clasped behind his back, his face set in a serious mien.

The kitchen door opened. He heard it close and her footsteps across the kitchen floor. She entered the sitting room, smiling at him.

Please, God, her smile. He had to frown so that he wouldn't smile back.

Before he could say anything, she said, "The service was lovely, Will, and I know you don't want me going out and about, and I won't. I also know that you really have just my best interests in mind. I'm very fortunate to have your care and concern. You are the most noble, handsome, generous man of my acquaintance. I admire you greatly in a way I've never felt toward any other." And then, before he could gather his stunned wits, she crossed over to him and kissed him.

She pressed her lips to his and held them there for the barest minimum of a moment.

But what a moment it was.

Will couldn't think. His mind ceased to function. *She was kissing him*. She had risen up on her toes and kissed *him*. It felt completely right and natural—and he wanted more.

But before he dared to reach out, to take hold of her and kiss her the way he wanted to kiss her, the way he'd dreamed of kissing her, she released her hold. Lowering her heels to the ground, she stepped back, turned, and walked up the stairs.

For a moment, Will stood, stupefied. He heard her humming.

Twice now that she had called him handsome. *Him*. Lanky him.

She might have meant it.

Upon hearing her come down the stairs, he panicked. Women weren't attracted to him. Well, some were . . . but never the ones he wanted. Lady Corinne was on a pedestal. She couldn't have admired the likes of him.

More important—he had nothing to offer if she did.

Knowing he couldn't talk to her right now, he walked into the kitchen before she reached the sitting room.

And so he opened the kitchen door and escaped. He walked back to the church. He needed to change from his vestments as it was, but here was sanctuary.

Here he could sit searching for the remnants of peace her presence disrupted.

Lady Corinne admired him. But she shouldn't have. She was a duke's daughter, a fixture in the highest rankings of society.

A footstep sounded behind him. *She was here*. She walked to where he was sitting, stood close to him. The light scent of her swirled around him.

"Another woman would be angry that her gesture had been rejected," she said.

Will didn't speak. He didn't trust his voice.

"My grandmother had a sense of things. A knowing. I have a touch of it. If it wasn't for that, Will, I'd be hurt. You think I don't know how challenging this is for you? You have no sense of your own worth and you can't see me as anything other than the duke of Banfield's daughter."

"I see you as the woman my foster brother planned to marry."

"That won't happen."

He turned to her then. "Only bad can come from this, Corinne. You believe you can weather the scandal of jilting my foster brother. You've *seduced* yourself into believing all will be right and therefore you take frightening risks. I can't compound the scandal of you jilting Freddie by taking you for myself. If not for Lord Bossley's saving me from the streets, I don't know where I'd be. And here I am—stealing from him, Corinne. My own foster father. But I don't do it for myself. That's my one saving grace. I don't take from him for my own sake. But if I take you, it *will* be for myself."

"And I'm telling you, Will, this is where *I* was meant to be."

"You couldn't have noticed the fact years ago

when I fell at your feet?" he wondered, half jesting. "Then we could have avoided all of this messiness."

Her shoulders rose in a small, graceful shrug. "I don't understand the ways of the world any better than you do, Reverend. I know only what I feel. And I'll be honest, Will, this is a new emotion for me. I'm not certain all that it is . . . but I believe it might be love."

"Might?" He stood, latching onto the word. "*Might* be love? It *can't* be. We are not free to love." There, he'd made the decision. "Go back to the rectory now, my lady."

"Will, I don't think you are listening to me—"

"I am. I have enough complications in my life without this one. And you've created enough problems in yours that you don't need a parson who is also, what did you call me, a thief and a hypocrite. It's the hypocrite that bothers me the most because you are right. I owe loyalty to Lord Bossley, and yet I'm torn over what he is doing to these people. To love you would mean I must choose to walk away from both. I can't do it, Corinne. For whatever reason, my roots are here."

"I know," she said. "And it makes me love you more."

"A love like that is only successful in one of those tragic novels where love withers and dies. Don't be like that, Corinne. Love whomever you wish, but escape Freddie and me. Give your love to someone who can return it freely, clearly."

"I can't do that, Will. It is already gone. It's yours."

God in Heaven.

How easy it would have been to take her in his arms. She stood as proud as a duchess and yet unafraid to be vulnerable to him. She was everything he'd dreamed of, and the real woman was more intelligent, more imaginative, more honest than he could ever have predicted.

"We can't," he whispered. "We are of two worlds, and they are very different."

She didn't fight him then. She nodded. "You will return for supper?" she asked. "Don't worry. I won't toss myself at you."

"Corinne—"

Warding him off with an upraised hand, she said, "Let's leave it be, Will. For right now, let's attempt to be kind to each other."

He nodded, accepting her suggestion, realizing it was far more mature than denying what existed between them. "I'll be home for dinner."

"Good," she replied. "And we will play a game

of some sort this evening. You don't need to be traipsing around all the time. You are in want of a good night's rest."

How true that was. But as he watched her leave the church, he doubted that he'd ever have one as long as she was under his roof.

For the next two days, Will and Corinne provided each other good company. Will didn't linger around the rectory, but he didn't run from her either. He pretended that all was fine—or, at least, as it should have been. They spoke of the weather, of hobbies, or of books they'd read.

She did not make any more declarations and he reminded himself he was being honorable, and completely miserable.

Shortly after four on Wednesday, the Broxters' son, Jamie, a lad of twelve or so, came running to fetch Will. His mother had gone into labor and had birthed her baby, but the pains had not stopped. Mrs. Grady, the midwife, had said the family needed to send for their confessor.

The Broxter home was on the outskirts of Ferris and easily reached by foot.

When Will arrived at the Broxters' cottage, a good number of village women had already gathered around the door. They stood in the front garden, their brows knitted in worry as they huddled together and spoke in whispers. He nodded as they solemnly parted ranks to let him pass.

Inside the three-room cottage, Emily Broxter still labored even though her baby had been born. Her breathing was heavy, anguished. The smell of sweat and blood mingled with the homey scents of cooked food and clean laundry. Her newborn squalled for sustenance.

Mrs. Broxter had always come to Sunday service and was the sort of woman every parish needed. Everyone liked her. She was always willing to lend a hand or offer a smile. She had made no secret that she'd been praying for another baby. Jamie was her and her husband's only child, and she had desperately wanted another.

Shortly after Will had first arrived at Ferris, she'd asked him why her prayers for another baby hadn't been answered. He'd been so green, so naive, that he'd been embarrassed by their earthy discussion. He'd counseled her to accept her barrenness as God's will.

The woman had not done that. Rumor had it around the village she'd traveled to Carlisle to a crone who boasted she had a secret to end barrenness. Will had thought it a superstitious waste of time and good money, but four months later, Emily had been with child.

Will had feared quite rightly that it would have been a challenge to the Church, and it had been in some quarters. There had been whispers and questions, especially as Emily had blossomed during her time. Her cheeks had turned rosier, her hair shinier, her spirits sunnier. She'd still come to church, but she had teased Will that if God didn't provide an answer, there was always another way a determined border woman could contrive one. She'd hoped for another son.

Will had not appreciated her jibes. But he had never wished her harm.

The birthing bed had been set up in the main room, close to a roaring fire.

"She's cold," Mrs. Grady, the midwife, told him, knowing he understood what that meant.

Emily's husband sat on a stool in a corner, his gaze watching his wife, his hands resting on his knees, as if he felt useless and drained of all energy. "I'm here, Mark," Will said, not certain the man had registered his presence.

Mark Broxter didn't react, not even to give a nod. Jamie, having accomplished his mission to fetch the reverend, took guard by his father's side, placing a small arm around his sire's massive shoulders. Mark's mother, old Mrs. Broxter, stood off to one side, trying to stave off the newborn's hungry cries by letting the babe suck her knuckle.

"Is there a nurse for the baby?" Will asked.

"Aye," Mrs. Grady answered. "Muriel McKinnion has milk. Her babe is about to come off the teat."

"Have you sent for her?"

Mrs. Grady shot a look in Broxter's direction. "He won't let her come. Says his Emily wants to nurse the baby herself." She moved closer to Will. "There's another one in there, probably unformed. Her body can't rid itself of it."

Jamie spoke. "You saved Maggie's cat, Mr. Norwich. Do something now. Can you?"

The weight of fear fell on Will's shoulders. Everyone watched him. Waited.

He gave his attention to Emily on the bed. Her eyes were closed. Her red hair and brow dripped with sweat, yet her hands were like ice.

Someone offered him a stool and he sat. "Emily?" he asked, his voice a whisper. She gave his fingers a weak squeeze but did not open her eyes.

He looked over to Mrs. Grady. He wanted to know if there was a chance Emily would recover. She understood his silent question and bowed her head.

In the corner, Emily's husband still hadn't moved.

Will turned to ritual. He was going to disappoint Jamie. In times like this, he wondered about his calling. He knew this woman was going to die. This giving, vibrant woman. Emily had a wonderful laugh, the sort that encouraged others to join in her delight of life.

The cottage was silent now.

He began with the scriptures and those verses offering comfort and the balm of mercy . . . and all the time he was wondering, Why? Why, when she'd just had her child, the one thing she'd begged God for, why was her life being taken from her? What sort of perverse wisdom was this?

Emily responded. Every once in a while she squeezed his fingers to let him know she listened. But her strength grew weaker.

He was going to fail Jamie. This was beyond his understanding, his power.

Will couldn't leave her. He couldn't come in, say words, and then be off to parish duties. She deserved his support by her bedside. He lost track of time. He spoke of God's redeeming love, of the promise of angels and a life everlasting. He spoke with belief, conviction, even as his voice grew hoarse and as his words repeated themselves. This is what Emily needed from him now. She needed his faith. His tutors had taught him that this was so. He *must* believe, even in the face of his own doubts—

Her eyes opened.

She looked around, lucid.

There was a murmur behind Will, a reminder that they were not alone in this room.

Mark Broxter tumbled forward to stand on bended knees by his wife's side. "Emily?" He reached for her hand, clasping it in his large, callused one.

She smiled at him. Her skin was translucent in the firelight. "My husband," she whispered. She looked beyond him to where her son Jamie had come forward. "You are such a good lad."

The boy's face was pinched tight with emotion. "Are you going to be all right, Ma?"

Emily turned toward Will. He didn't sense that she saw him. "Where's my baby? I want to see my child."

Old Mrs. Broxter came to the side of the bed

near Will and held the now exhausted newborn for Emily to see.

"A boy?" Emily asked. "Did they tell me he was a boy?"

"He is," her husband confirmed. The tension had left the lines of his face. He was eager, loving, devoted.

"He was worth it," Emily whispered, her gaze never wavering from the sleeping child, her eyes full of maternal love. "So worth all of it . . ."

And in that moment, she slipped away.

It happened so quietly, so quickly, that Will was not prepared. One second she had been with them, and in the next she was gone.

"Emily?" her husband asked. "Em?"

There was no response. There wouldn't be.

"Mark—," Will started.

"She's gone?" Mark interrupted in disbelief. "She's not coming back?"

"Sometimes they have a last moment," Will tried to explain. "It's as if they give us a gift of their presence, a time to say good-bye—"

"*My wife is dead?*" Mark reached for his Emily, took her by the shoulders and gave her a shake.

The women in the room came out of their initial shock. His mother doubled over as if in pain. The cries of the others sent the message quicker than words that a tragedy had happened.

"She's not here," Will said. "She left."

"*I want her back,*" Mark demanded. He let go of her body and she dropped to the bed, all life, all vitality vanished away.

Mark sat back on his heels. His son stood sobbing silently beside him, but the father was in such shock that he could do nothing to comfort the child.

Will came around to their side of the bed. Mrs. Grady had buried her face in her hands. She now took his place and closed Emily's eyes before giving in to her own grief.

"*Why?*" Mark demanded of Will. "Why did God take her?"

"I-It's not our place to reason why," Will said, falling back on the platitudes that had barely sustained him over the last hour. "We can't understand the mind of God."

"It wasn't *God* that took her," Mark said, coming to his feet. He turned toward his mother, pointing his finger at the baby she held, the baby who had been startled awake and screamed for his mother. "*He* took her," Mark declared. "He *murdered* my wife."

"Mark, he is a baby," Will started. "He's your son—"

"He's no son of mine. *No son of mine*," Mark repeated at a shout, aiming his words at that innocent child.

Jamie broke down uncontrollably. He reached for his father, wanting him to take him up in his arms as if he'd been a babe.

But Mark could not do that. His soul was on fire. "Remove that child from my house," he demanded. "Take it from here or I shall grab him and bash his brains on the floor in front of my dead wife."

Will was horrified at the man's grief. Mark's mother was shaking, denying her son could say such a thing.

It was Mrs. Grady who grabbed the now screaming infant from old Mrs. Broxter's arms. Mrs. Grady who took Will's elbow and pushed him toward the door.

Fresh air slapped Will in the face. He blinked, as if not realizing how late the hour was. The moon was high in the sky.

"I need to go back in there," he said, turning. "I must talk to him—"

Mrs. Grady's hand blocked his passage. "You'll do no such thing, Reverend." She held the squalling newborn with one arm. "That man is in grief. He doesn't need you. He needs time to face what's happened to him."

"But I might offer him comfort," Will said, realizing even as he spoke the words that there was nothing he could say that would alleviate the horror of what had just happened. "And his baby. He can't turn his back on his own child."

"He can right now." Mrs. Grady moved him along to the road, away from the women gathered to offer help and support. "I've seen this before. Aye, I agree with you that his wee life has done nothing wrong, and Mark Broxter will come to that same mind. But right now, his grief is all he can feel."

"What will happen to the baby?" Will asked and found himself reaching to hold the child.

Mrs. Grady let him have the child. "It's so puny," Will observed. He'd not been around newborns, never held one. The bones were so fine; his body lacked muscle. He chewed on his fists, whimpering in his hunger, his strength spent.

"He'll grow," Mrs. Grady said, "and be a strong one. That's what happens to them that is cast off."

Cast off. The description struck Will in a way he'd not anticipated. He'd been cast off. "But I thought you said his father would come for him when he is of clearer mind?"

The heavy sigh she gave didn't bode well for that premise. "Men are funny," she admitted, taking the baby back and cradling him in her arms. "A mother can't walk away from her child, but a man can. *Some* men can," she corrected herself. "Not all. It is as if they go half mad in grief. Don't plague yourself over it, Mr. Norwich. You've done your job and I know you'll be seeing Mark Broxter again. Once the hurt isn't so intense, then the reason will set in. In the meantime, I need to see this wee one to Mrs. McKinnion. She's a godsend, she is. I had a babe three months ago that died because her mother didn't have her milk and there was no nurse close at hand."

"I don't remember a baby dying."

Her face took on a sympathetic look in the moonlight, part pity, part practical. "We didn't bring her to you. We returned her to the earth from whence she'd come. 'Twas the mother's wishes." She took a step closer to him. "I can see you are rattled a bit by all this, but trust me, it's all a part of God's plan. The good and the bad, we must take it all." She started walking up the road.

Will watched her until she was out of sight. People were leaving the Broxter cottage. Will offered a prayer that God would grant this family peace, but he found no sense of peace in the offering. Words were inadequate, and what was a prayer? Words of hope, wants, wishes . . . selfish words. Ineffective ones.

He began walking back to the rectory. As he moved, images hovered on the edge of his mind. Faces he could barely see. Voices he couldn't understand. The parents of his dreams.

The midwife had been right. Broxter's actions had shaken Will to his core.

The headache started. His head felt gripped in a vise. Those images grew fuzzy, distant. Will stumbled back and then pushed himself to move forward. He had to reach the rectory. He couldn't be found here on the street, stumbling blindly around.

Will reached the rectory kitchen door. He slammed into it, turning the handle at the same time, and fell to the kitchen floor.

For a long moment, he lay there. He was dizzy, his head pounded. He waited, praying for this to pass—

"You are home," he heard Corinne say before giving a soft cry. "Will, what has happened?"

She knelt beside him. Her face, her worried expression came into view.

He frowned up at her. This was not how he wanted her to see him. He rolled over, attempted to push himself to his feet.

Her hands slid under his arms and she helped him up into a kitchen chair.

"I feel like a fool," he muttered, his throat dry, sore. The pounding in his head wouldn't stop.

She pushed a mug of cider into his hands. The drink helped. It cleared his mind. She was kneeling on the floor at his feet, both of her hands holding his free one. Her brow wrinkled with concern . . . concern for him.

"What was it?" she asked. "Did you fall?"

He was grateful for the drink. Grateful for the company. The headache started to recede. She'd banished it. "I'm fine. Sad case this evening."

"Do you wish to talk about it?"

Will had learned to keep his own counsel. There had never been anyone to discuss his experiences with. He'd been alone. Singular and alone—until now.

She waited patiently.

He should have told her it was nothing, a momentary lapse, silly, really—

"A friend died tonight." And then the rest of the story came pouring forth: Emily's desire for child, how the baby had killed her, how now her family was bereft with grief.

How the father had rejected his newborn son. . . .

She listened. The wick in the lamp she had carried in burned low, but she didn't move.

"How you saw me come in the door," Will said, "was just my being—" How was he being? How could he describe it? He'd never said anything to anyone about the images, the headaches.

He sat a moment, silent, uncomprehending.

"I understand your being upset," she said. "That poor child, blamed for his mother's death." She shifted her weight. The brick floor had to have been uncomfortable, but she'd not moved. "Do you ever think about your own past?"

The question caught him off guard. "What do you mean?"

"What do you know about the time before Lord Bossley took you in?"

"I remember nothing," he said.

"Perhaps you remember more than you know? That could create pain in your head, couldn't it? The struggle to remember?" She rose and pulled the other chair at the table closer to his.

He fought the urge to move away. Her suggestions nettled him.

"Will, Lord Bossley found you wandering in the streets at . . . . what did he claim? No more than the age of three?"

"That is what he says."

"Well, there was a time before him," she replied. "And who knows what your life was like, what horrors you had seen?"

He didn't want to discuss this. He realized he even feared it. "What matter does it make? The present is all that counts." He hated appearing weak in front of her. It was unmanly of him.

She sat back. "You confuse me. You serve at the will of Lord Bossley in this parish. He pays your living . . . and yet you rob from him. It's your way of righting the wrong he does, no? You are too loyal to go to a magistrate or take your case to your bishop."

"I've talked to Bossley. He knows how I feel."

"But you wouldn't testify against him?"

"He saved my life," Will pointed out.

"You have a problem," she said. "You see a wrong but can't ignore it like other men would. You feel powerless to go to the magistrate, so you create this highwayman to right the wrong."

"I had to do something."

"And that attitude, sir, is completely at odds with your upbringing. I could not imagine Freddie making such an insistence. Will, have you ever thought that what you feel, some of the man you are—your compassion, your sense of honor and responsibility—could have come from perhaps your parents? No, don't protest," she ordered when he opened his mouth to deny her suggestion. "You witness a father abandoning his own child and it unsettles you. It unsettles me to hear of it! But, Will, don't you think your reaction this evening might be connected with the part of you that you don't know? Just think on it. You need not agree, but be open to the possibility."

"Are you saying I could be recalling my father?"

"Yes."

The thought challenged him. He shook his head, would have pushed away, but he covered his hand with hers.

"What if Lord Bossley isn't telling the truth about finding you?" she asked.

Will immediately rejected the idea. "To what gain? Who am I to him? If anything, I've cost him a pretty penny. He's educated me, clothed me, fed me—"

"I don't know his motives," she said. "But thinking on it, he doesn't strike me as a charitable person."

"He boasts about taking me in," Will said.

"And people think well of him for it. But I don't sense being kind is a part of his nature. And you may laugh at me if you like, but I put great faith in my initial impressions of people. When I met Freddie, even when he was supposedly interested in my cousin, I didn't trust him. I was not wrong, was I?"

He didn't answer.

"Lord Bossley keeps you close at hand," she observed.

"The bishop suggested I take the living here."

"And you weren't tempted to strike out just a little?"

"I like it here," he felt forced to admit. "Yes, I know it's unambitious of me, but I feel a need to be here."

"There must be a reason for that," she concluded. "If I continue on, you will think I've been touched by that full moon outside. But don't discount these things that bother you," she urged in a low tone. "There is a mystery here, Will, and this sounds outlandish, but I sense you may be a key. Think on it." She rose to her feet. "I'm tired. I'm for my bed. Are you staying up?"

That was their habit. He always waited until she was asleep and often slept in the sitting room. "A bit. Here, take the lamp." He lit the stub of a candle off of it.

At the door, she hesitated. "Please don't worry about the baby. The villagers will take care of him."

Will nodded.

"Good night," she said and then she was gone.

He listened to the sound of her bare feet climbing the stairs. She'd stunned him, and not with her beauty but her insight.

The images that had been swirling in his mind since Broxter's outburst seemed to slow. A face came into focus. A man's nose, his smile—

Will walked through the dark to the sitting room. Moonlight streamed through his front window. He found paper and pen and began sketching the face. He set it aside. His exhausted mind could take no more. He fell asleep.

However, the next morning, he rose with the dawn and was anxious to see in the daylight whose face he'd drawn.

He was disappointed to realize he'd drawn his own.

Chapter Eleven

T he early-morning fog clung to the ground
longer than usual.

Looking out her window, Corinne felt restless,
uncertain.

She didn't know if her sense of foreboding
had anything to do with the death of the young
mother or if she was uneasy with last night's conversation.

Her worries escalated when she caught a
glimpse of red military coats walking down
the street. Even though they couldn't possibly
have seen her, Corinne stepped away from the
window. Will had warned her that men from the
garrison patrolled Ferris, but she hadn't seen any

of them until now. Their presence reminded her of what was at stake if she was not careful.

The rectory was becoming her prison. Will was gone every morning before she came down, no matter how early she rose. She had tried to catch him. Had wanted to breach the gap of distrust.

Perhaps her instincts were wrong. Maybe she *wasn't* meant to be here. That extra sense of purpose that she'd always trusted to point her in the right direction might have failed her.

As she stood there watching the soldiers move out of her range of vision, she realized Will might not be able to give her what she wanted, what it was that she longed for. She wanted love, but not love like the poets promised. She didn't want itchy yearning and proud neediness that could never be fulfilled.

No, she wanted the sort of love that her aunt Catherine had for her husband. She had eloped with a banker. Granted, Banker Montross was highly respected now, but back then her ducal grandfather had been furious. He'd cut Catherine off, not that her aunt had cared. She'd always seemed content. Once Corinne had even caught her aunt and uncle stealing a kiss by the back stairs in spite of their age.

Corinne couldn't imagine her parents doing such a thing. Her father kept a mistress and rarely came home when they were in London. Except for the rare occasions that they traveled together, such as coming to Glenhoward, or entertained, her parents didn't spend time in each other's company. They were a couple for social purposes and producing an heir or two.

But Corinne wanted more. She wanted to be her husband's helpmate. She wanted the connection she'd felt with Will last night. Her insight, her advice had had meaning to him.

Of course, she was completely prepared to go downstairs and find him gone . . .

She heard a sound from downstairs. Someone was there, moving around. It was probably Mrs. Gowan come early. Still, Corinne grabbed a last look at herself in the glass over her washbasin. She'd pulled her hair back in a neat chignon at the nape of her neck and secured it with a few pins. She was wearing the green dress today.

As she left her room, she could see through the doorway of his bedroom that his bed, once again, looked as if he hadn't slept in it. She suspected he didn't sleep in his room but in the chair in the sitting room. His purpose was to stay away from her, and he was the sort of man who was very good at what he set out to do. Corinne knew he was attracted to her. She couldn't have felt this pull toward Will without his feeling something in return.

She hurried downstairs, entered the kitchen, and came to a halt, surprised by the sight of Will pouring a mug of tea.

"Good morning," he said, smiling at her. There was something changed about him, something she wasn't quite able to place.

"Good morning?" She moved into the kitchen, cautious.

"I trust you slept well?" he said as he set the tea at her place at the table. He pulled out her chair. "For you."

"Me?" She sounded dumbstruck. She was.

He smiled and she realized the difference she'd noticed was that he appeared relaxed. "Yes, you." He turned toward the dry sink. "I'm having cider." He carried a mug with his cider and a plate of cheese and bread over for their breakfast.

Corinne sat in her chair, but she watched him, uncertain.

Taking his place at the table, he took a piece of bread and cheese, smiled at her, took a bite.

She didn't move.

He swallowed and said, "Your tea will grow cold."

"You are usually gone when I wake." It was an accusation.

"I was gone," he said breezily, adding a slice of cheese on his bread. "But now I'm back."

"What has happened?" she demanded. "Last night you were not happy, and this morning you appear as if you haven't a care."

"I don't," he said. "I went to see Broxter this morning." He took a sip of his cider.

"How is he?"

"Not good. He loved her."

He loved her. Such a simple statement, yet it held a wealth of emotion.

Will said, "I told him he must love his sons as well as he'd loved her. They are a product of that love and that baby could not have harmed his mother. I don't know why Emily died, except that childbirth is hard for any woman. But I know she thought the baby was worth the cost of her life. If Mark tosses him aside, what does that say about his love for his wife?"

"You told him this?" she asked, impressed.

"Yes. I also reminded him that God doesn't think of death the way we do. I know about how it is the beginning of eternal life and all of that, but what do we really know? I said to him that I couldn't believe that something as vibrant and real as the love Emily Broxter had for him and for those children could ever die. She was a strong woman. A strong soul. She wouldn't leave him. I truly believe she is close."

"And what was his answer?"

"I didn't wait for an answer. I left him then."

"You left him?" Corinne repeated in disbelief. "Did you not want to know if anything you said bore fruit and made a difference to him?"

"It's out of my hands," he said, then brought his whole attention upon her.

Corinne went still, suddenly self-conscious. He wasn't just looking at her hair, her eyes, the surface. No, it was as if he looked into the very depths of her, and then he said, "Thank you."

"For what?"

"For challenging me. For not being afraid to speak your mind." He turned his attention to his breakfast.

"That is the first time anyone has said that to me," she said, still confused, and he laughed. The sound filled the kitchen and she was riveted by this new side of him, the one that wasn't worried or angry.

"Cory, you can't help yourself . . ."

Cory? He'd called her Cory. No one had ever called her such before, and she adored it.

". . . you are the most clear-eyed, honest person of my acquaintance," he was saying. "Emily would not want her child to be cast aside; for the good of the child I had to speak, because I understand what could happen to him. My life would have been so different if Bossley hadn't stepped in. I always felt guilty for it, but now—" He shook his head. "Perhaps asking Broxter to take his son to his heart is my atonement. My purpose for being here."

He looked to her for agreement, and Corinne felt a bit dizzy. No wonder she was falling in love with him. She couldn't help herself.

Will waved his hand at her, forcing her to blink. "Are you all right?" he asked.

"Yes, yes, I am," she replied, wondering if he realized how utterly charming he was when he was like this. He came across as stronger, more confident, more attractive, handsome, appealing . . . the list went on and on. She thought him perfect.

"You will attend the funeral today?" he asked.

Considering the direction of her thoughts, it took a second to make the change of subject with him. "The funeral?"

"Yes, as my cousin, you will be expected to pay your respects."

"I saw soldiers today," she answered.

"I saw them as well," he said. "They were passing through. They should be gone by now, but I doubt if anyone would consider looking for the Unattainable at a country funeral."

Corinne didn't like his use of that detested nickname. "I'm not unattainable," she muttered, rising from her chair and picking up her untouched tea, then setting it back down.

"My lady . . . ?" he started, as if realizing she was upset, though he felt a bit clueless as to how he'd offended her. It was the nickname. It made Corinne even more frustrated and sad. She'd been wrong. He didn't "see" her. He had no clue what she felt for him.

And she wasn't going to tell him again. She had pride.

"What time is the funeral?" she said, cutting him off.

"At eleven."

"I assume you have duties before the service?" He usually did, or at least that was his excuse.

"I do—"

"I shall see you at the church then," she said

and left the room before he could say anything else to upset her.

And *why* was she so upset?

She didn't even understand herself. But as she tromped up the stairs, she knew she was angry.

In her room, she sat on the end of the bed. Her arms crossed tightly against her chest, she suddenly knew the answer.

He'd spoken to her as if he'd valued her opinion. He didn't treat her the way her parents and her family did. *He listened. He heard.*

But he didn't understand.

She admired him so much . . . . but in spite of his admiration of her, he did not return the same level of feeling. He did not love her.

Corinne felt her heart break. It hurt, physically hurt, and she didn't think she would recover. Never in her life had she thought that she might find the man she could love but he would not love her in return.

Her poor heart didn't know what to do.

She'd taken offense. Will knew that. He went over to the door of the kitchen and leaned against it, listening to her march up the stairs.

Cory. She was beautiful. Vibrant, warm, caring . . . and he'd hurt her because she wanted more than he could, or should, give her. For her own good, one of them had to keep his wits about him. She might survive the scandal of jilting Freddie—she was lovely enough and well connected enough to do so—but *not* if she ran off with Freddie's foster brother.

She'd given Will so much.

In the week and a half she'd been with him, she'd graced his world with her humor, common sense, and refreshing candor. His youthful worship of her had been well placed.

But now was the time to think of her best interests. Rusticating as the wife of a parish parson or being the widow of a highwayman was not for the likes of her. She deserved silk gowns, a fleet of servants, and so much more.

For a moment, Will allowed himself to dream of her being his, longing with a passion that threatened to bring him to his knees. His Cory. His beautiful, beautiful Cory.

"But it must not be," he reminded himself. "It must not be."

The church was crowded by the time Corinne made her way over for the funeral. Everyone in the parish attended, all dressed in their best. The sanctuary was a sea of bonnets.

Mrs. Gowan saw her and motioned for her to come join her family in their pew. Corinne gratefully sank down next to her, taking a moment to adjust the angle of her own bonnet.

"You've changed the style again," Mrs. Gowan said with admiration. "You have a good way with a needle."

"Thank you," Corinne replied. She gave Mandy a wave of her gloved fingers before the funeral started.

Will and the deacon walked in behind an altar boy carrying a cross.

Corinne couldn't look at him very long. Her disappointment still lay heavy upon her. She'd almost convinced herself it was all for the best, but she knew she could not continue this way. He was the man she wanted, the one she could never have.

She was going to have to leave. She'd made up her mind to do so.

The pallbearers entered carrying a closed coffin. They were followed by a barrel-chested young man with flaming red hair. His son, the lad that fetched Will yesterday, held his hand. This was the widower, and he looked, and moved, like a man destroyed.

In his free arm, he cradled a newborn—and

Corinne wanted to stand and cheer. Will had convinced him. He'd done it.

Her battered heart filled with pride.

And, she realized, *that* was love. Even in her misery, she could be happy for Will. He'd persuaded a father to claim his son. How heroic was that?

The service was a sad affair but Corinne felt hope. She hadn't known Emily Broxter, but she did know that every mother would want her family to stay together.

The baby started crying during the burial. Several of the women offered hands to help, but Mr. Broxter warned them off with a shake of his head. "He's right to mourn," he said, his own voice laden with his pent-up tears.

After the burial, Corinne and Will somberly walked back to the rectory. They'd gone to the wake for a minute and left at the proper time. Will broke the silence first. "He claimed his son," he said.

Corinne nodded. Her mind wasn't on the deceased woman. She waited until they'd reached the house to speak. "I'm ready to leave."

He stopped. She took a few steps, then faced him. His moss green eyes had darkened with concern.

Concern. She'd wanted an emotion stronger than that. She wanted something more. . . .

"It's time," she said. "I've had a lovely sojourn in the country, but I'd best return to my life."

"You'd go back?"

"Not to London. I've been thinking of where I could go. Making a plan, what you'd wished I'd done in the beginning." There was bitterness in her voice. She couldn't help herself. The disappointment of being unloved combined with pride made her curt. "I have a great-aunt in Edinburgh. She's a very distant relation and we are strangers, but I need to hide for only a week or so more." She found it hard to look at him. "Just out of human kindness, let alone family loyalty, she should take me in for what little time I have left to miss the wedding. You will help me make arrangements?"

"Of course."

"I won't mention your name. No one will know your involvement with my running away." Her throat tightened. The finality of her decision hurt. She started to turn away—

"Cory," he said.

Hope leapt inside her, whirled her around to him.

"What?" she asked, hating how anxious, how eager she sounded.

He stood a moment, his jaw uncompromising, his brows together. A shadow seemed to cross his eyes, a regret. And then he said quietly, "I'll make the arrangements in the morning."

She stood, suddenly loving him so much that she couldn't believe he didn't love her in return. She wanted a declaration, a sign of passion, or good regard . . . a sign of anything other than this stiff civility. What she wanted to do was rail at him. To demand why he couldn't love her. Why couldn't he open himself to at least the possibility of returning her affections? Of caring as deeply for her as she did for him?

"Thank you," she murmured and went into the house.

Will didn't follow.

That was probably just as well. Really. It must have been.

She'd marched through the kitchen, but in the sitting room she was overwhelmed by a forceful thought: it wasn't right that she left without telling him how she felt. Yes, she might look like a fool—no, she quickly amended, being married to Freddie, a man she could never love, would have been foolish.

Loving Will was not.

She couldn't just let him go.

Corinne performed an about-face and walked back through the kitchen, ready to open the door and make her declaration—until she heard a male voice outside that was not Will's. She rocked back, stepped to the window over the dry sink, and peered outside. She immediately drew back when she caught sight of a messenger wearing the colors of Lord Bossley's livery.

A moment later, the messenger left and Will entered the rectory, the set of his mouth grave.

"What is it?" she asked.

"Lord Bossley has requested my presence for dinner," Will said. "He sent the coach for me."

"Why would he do that?" she asked.

"He doesn't do it often, but occasionally he likes to have me as a guest. Part of family unity and all that," he answered, distracted.

A warning sense of dread fell upon Corinne. Something was not right. "I don't believe you should go," she said stoutly. "In fact, I *know* you shouldn't."

He shot her a sharp look. "Why is that?" he said.

Corinne shifted her weight. "I sense things, Will. Some would say premonitions. I don't feel good about this invitation."

"I don't feel good about it either," Will answered, "and I have no special gifts. It is unlike Bossley to have me over more than once in a month. He says he has some local matters to discuss, and that could be true. But just to be careful, I want you to stay out of sight, Cory. Don't answer the door for anyone. Roman will be here. If anything happens, I want you to ride to the reiver's hut. Do you understand? You leave. Promise you will do so."

"Of course. But what of you?"

"I shall be fine if I needn't worry about you. Bossley's man is waiting for me outside," he threw over his shoulder as he took the stairs to his room two at a time. "Follow me. We haven't much time."

She found him beside his wardrobe. There was a false drawer in it. He pulled out pound notes and pushed them into her hands.

"What do you want me to do with this?" she asked.

"You might need it," he said. "If I come home tonight, we'll use it for your passage to Scotland. It's mine. I didn't steal it, if that is what you are wondering."

"I didn't think you had," she said and then realized that even the little time she had left to be with him was being taken from her. "Will," she started, before she lost courage. "I want you to know . . ." She let her voice drop off as her courage failed.

I love you.

Hard words to speak aloud.

They stood so close. He reached up and tucked a stray curl back under her bonnet. "I know, Cory," he said as if she'd spoken. "I know." He let his hand drop. "It's better this way. You deserve more than I can offer."

"What if I don't want more?" she answered, daring to step forward.

He gripped her shoulders. "No, Corinne. I—"

His voice broke off. She leaned forward. "What, Will?"

He raised a finger, ran it along the bottom of her lip. She couldn't breathe. For one sweet moment, she thought he would kiss her. She knew he wanted to—

"No," he said, his voice shaky, as if holding back came at great cost. "I can't let you throw aside everything for me."

Her temper flared. "Stop protecting me. I know what I want."

"And that is why I must think clearly for both of us." He took a step back. "If only we *could* see the future," he said. "I'll return later, Cory. We'll talk then—"

"Or will you put me off once more?" she demanded.

"We'll talk," he answered, moving around her toward the door. "Put the bars across the doors. Let us be cautious." He was gone.

She started to follow, then changed her mind, letting her steps end at the top of the stairs.

The money felt heavy in her hands.

Evening's shadows were deepening when a frantic knock sounded at the door.

Sitting in Will's chair reading, Corinne hesitated.

"Mr. Norwich," she heard Mandy's worried voice call out and then another pounding on the kitchen door. "*Please,* you must help us." She tried the door handle but could not open the door because Corinne had obeyed Will's order to slide the bar in place.

Corinne rose and crossed into the kitchen. "What is it, Mandy?" she asked.

"It's my father. The soldiers came for him. They believe he is the Thorn."

Shoving the bar out of the way, Corinne opened the door. Mandy's face was streaked with tears. "Where is Mr. Norwich?" she begged. "He'll know what to do."

"What is this about your father?"

"The soldiers came," Mandy said, pushing past Corinne to look wildly around the kitchen, as if she thought Will was hiding there. "They broke down the door. They've torn up everything we own. They accused Father of being the Thorn and kept hitting him when he wouldn't tell him where some chest was hidden."

Alarmed, Corinne asked, "Where is your mother?"

"She went with some of the women after the wake to help Mr. Broxter settle into his mother's house. She lives a mile away. I came here first. Where is Mr. Norwich?"

"He's not here," Corinne admitted.

Mandy gave a sharp cry. "But I need him. My father needs him."

"Please, Mandy, be brave," Corinne said. "Go to your mother. I shall do what I must to send word to Mr. Norwich. Which way did they take your father?"

With huge, hiccuping sobs, Mandy pointed in a direction. "Toward the garrison."

There was only one road in and out of Ferris. Corinne stood a moment, struggling to think of the best thing to do. She couldn't ride to Glenhoward, not without giving herself away—and how would that save Mr. Gowan?

And what could she expect Will to do? If he rode to rescue Mr. Gowan, he could be captured himself.

No, she had to make the soldiers see that they had the wrong man, while still protecting Will.

An idea came to her, a daring one—but she no longer feared the daring. From that fateful moment that Corinne had hidden herself in Bossley's coach, her life had become more exciting, more meaningful than she could ever have hoped.

Why should she not have taken another risk now?

Upstairs in his room, she pulled on his breeches. They were way too large for her, but she tied rope around her waist. She couldn't wear his boots, but his black stockings and her kid slippers would suffice. With one of his black jackets, his wide brimmed hat, and a flour sack, her costume was complete. She didn't bind her breasts. His clothes swallowed her whole, making her look like a scarecrow—but she had transformed herself into the Thorn.

Well, not the real Thorn, but if she rode Roman fast enough past the soldiers, they wouldn't know the difference and give chase. She was about to test Will's boast that Roman could outrun any horse half his age. She picked up the boot blacking for Roman's blaze and set off for the stable.

Chapter Twelve

Corinne rode along the outskirts of Ferris, just inside the line of trees bordering the forest. She kept her hat low on her head and prayed the evening's long shadows would give her protection. She saw no movement from the village and believed chances were good she could escape without notice. Most people were still involved with the wake and supporting the young family.

Roman's head picked up once he realized they were going out of town. Of course, Corinne had only a vague idea of what she wanted to do. Her goal was to ride up on the soldiers, surprise them, and keep riding. They might give chase, but she knew Roman could outrun them.

In truth, this horse was fabulous, ancient, wise, and wily.

She gave him a pat. He snorted his response and his pace picked up. Unaccustomed to riding astride like a man, Corinne had to grab his mane and hold on. She'd adjusted the stirrups, but they were still too long for her legs. She'd had this problem the last time she'd ridden Roman, but speed had not been an issue.

Finally, she tired of fighting the stirrups and threw them over the saddle. She hadn't been misleading Will when she'd said she could ride. She could jump hedgerows all day without stirrups, but having to fuss with them could lead to a problem when she had to ride fast.

They traveled parallel to the road. It wasn't hard. Roman understood what was expected, so she let him dictate how they would go about things. In fact, he appeared to be enjoying himself.

His ears picked up. Corinne reined in, listening. There were the sounds of grumbling men.

The hour was dusk. She wished she had some of Will's flaming gourds to throw at the soldiers and distract them.

Instead, she gathered her courage and pulled the mask down over her face. The bag smelled of grain and she couldn't see out of the sides of the holes at her eyes, but her biggest concern was that she had no weapon. She couldn't believe she hadn't thought of that before this moment. She had nothing. Not a pistol, a sword, not even a stick—although she'd know how to use a stick. She hadn't a clue how to fight with pistol or sword.

Why, oh, why had her mother insisted on embroidery instruction and not a lesson in good weaponry? She might ask her that someday.

For right now, her only recourse was to ride straight through the soldiers, swooping in with her cape flying.

"*Allez,* Roman," she shouted, thinking the command sounded smarter in French. Then, quickly realizing she sounded like a girl, she lowered her voice and repeated the command, "*Allez*—"

Roman rocked back and took off with such energy, such force, that he reminded Corinne of nothing less than one of those Chinese rockets.

All she had to do was hold on, which she did for dear life.

Roman rounded a bend and they came upon the small group of three or four soldiers marching Mr. Gowan. His hands were tied behind his back and there was a hood over his head. The soldiers turned at the sound of Roman's pounding hooves.

"Hurry, Roman, hurry," she pleaded, knowing she needed the element of surprise, and he heard her. His pace picked up.

A shout of warning went out from the soldiers. Corinne kept her head low, ready to race right past them—

From the trees, a score of soldiers came out into the road. Their presence threw Roman off. The horse tried to swerve to avoid hitting the men running at him, but his age caught up with him.

Corinne could feel the muscles tighten beneath her. The horse lacked the agility to change direction. He stumbled, tripped, almost fell.

By the time both she and the horse recovered, the soldiers had surrounded her, their rifles aimed for her heart.

Roman reared like a mighty warhorse, but Corinne was not ready for it. She slid off his back and fell to the earth.

For a second, she lay there, the breath knocked out of her.

A soldier stepped up to her. Major Ashcroft. He smiled, very pleased with himself.

Corinne was afraid to move, knowing he'd recognize her immediately once he pulled off her mask.

"Well, well," he said. "We knew if Gowan wasn't our man, then we'd flesh out the real Thorn. All it took was patience."

It had been a trap all along. Corinne thought herself a fool.

"You are much smaller than I had thought," Major Ashcroft said, almost to himself. "But now, sir, let us take off your mask, see who you are—"

A sharp whistle rent the air. Roman snorted a response.

Major Ashcroft looked up just as a dark shadow dropped upon the horse's back. In triumph, Roman reared, rising straight up, and the shadow took the form of a man—*the Thorn*—who whirled the horse around to charge the soldiers.

Caught by surprise and their own fear, the soldiers scattered, leaving Major Ashcroft standing over Corinne. The Thorn knocked him down as Roman galloped past. Corinne belly crawled out of the way.

The Thorn leapt from Roman's back and pulled the sword from another officer's scabbard. Major Ashcroft tried to rise, but the Thorn placed a booted foot on his backside and pushed him down again. "I didn't tell you to move, Major," he said, pointing the sword at him.

Corinne could hear Will in his voice, but, like all good actors, he took on a role when he was the Thorn. She doubted if anyone, even his foster father, would know it was him.

"Free the blacksmith," the Thorn instructed her, and she hurried to obey. The soldiers didn't move. They could have overpowered them, but such was the Thorn's presence that they were either frightened or in awe.

"Return home," the Thorn ordered Mr. Gowan, who immediately began walking.

"You'll hang," Major Ashcroft dared to boast. "I shall see to it."

"Then I shall await your future plans," the Thorn said with a small bow. He whistled and Roman came trotting to him. "Mount up," he ordered Corinne.

She placed a foot in the stirrup and pulled herself up, glancing over at the Thorn as she hit the saddle. She gave a shout of warning.

Major Ashcroft had come to his feet, pulling out his own sword and attacking the Thorn.

Her cry alerted Will just in time. He turned, avoiding being run through.

The major regained his footing and attacked again. Steel met steel—but the Thorn was the better swordsman.

Corinne was amazed at how quickly Will's sword could feint and parry. He made the officer appear ridiculously clumsy and slow in front of his men. The tip of Will's sword was here, there, removing a button, brushing Major Ashcroft's hat off his head, flicking off his wig, and all the time he was forcing him back toward the woods, until the major ran into a tree and could go no farther.

The Thorn's sword tip was aimed at the major's throat. The officer swallowed, his Adam's apple moving against the sharp, deadly point.

"You've been bested this time, Major. Perhaps you will be more fortunate the next."

"Go ahead. Finish me off," Major Ashcroft said. "What is one more murder after Porledge's?"

Corinne saw the tension in Will's body, knew that Ashcroft's taunt had found its mark. He changed from the confident, daring Thorn to preacher with a conscience.

Major Ashcroft noticed as well. He smiled grimly, a smile the Thorn wiped from his face by thrusting forward and driving the sword into the tree by the major's head.

Will gave a low whistle and Roman obeyed. Corinne would have been dumped if she hadn't grabbed hold of the saddle. Will mounted behind her in a blink. "Good-bye, Major," he called out, then put heels to horse and they were off, racing past the startled soldiers.

She heard Major Ashcroft shout for his men to follow them, but it was too late. Roman was the wind.

Corinne had no fears riding with Will. His body protected her. She was cradled between his strong legs, sheltered by his back, and balanced by his arms. He rode this horse as if they'd been one and she was all a part of it.

Will took them through the forest and across the moors, heading in this direction and that. They seemed to ride for hours. He sent Roman into a stream. They followed its curve before climbing up the bank and arriving at the reiver's hut. Will jumped off the horse, pulling her with him. He set her aside and quickly saw to Roman's needs.

Even in the moonlight, Corinne could see that the magnificent beast was tired. He gratefully went into the stable, rooting and finding the hay left there for him.

Corinne pulled off her mask. The air felt good

on her flushed cheeks. She walked into the cottage, hoping the stool was still there for her to sit on.

She was exhausted. Spent. And at the same time exhilarated. This had been the most amazing night of her life.

Will's tall body filled the doorway, blocking out the moonlight. He'd taken off his own mask.

"I understand why you do it," she confided happily. "That was beyond anything I've ever experienced. You were brilliant. Brilliant, brilliant, brilliant! We saved Mr. Gowan's life. We took on a whole garrison—"

Her praise came to an abrupt halt as his hands grabbed her arms and he lifted her to give her a small shake. "That was the most foolhardy, dangerous, ridiculous thing you've ever done," he lashed out.

Corinne's elation died. "Ridiculous? We saved Mr. Gowan's life. And you took on Major Ashcroft in a sword fight. He couldn't keep up with you—"

He gave her another shake. "You could have died."

The heat and the anger of his voice penetrated her giddiness. His grip was hard. "But I didn't," she said.

"You came damn close." His eyes were angry slits in the moonlit darkness. "What do you think would have happened if Ashcroft had used his sword on you? Or if they had strung you up without bothering with a magistrate?"

She'd not thought of any of that at all.

"Whatever possessed you to do it?" he demanded.

"Fear for Mr. Gowan's life." She twisted her shoulders, trying to release herself from his hold.

His grip did not relax. "By risking your own? Do you know what would have happened if they had discovered who you were?"

"But they didn't learn who I was," Corinne answered, resentful of his questioning. "Will, we did it. We did what we set out to do."

"We did nothing. You made the escapade twice as hard by involving yourself in it."

"Well, I beg your pardon," she said, her own temper rising. "If you had been home to receive Mandy's message, you could have gone yourself. I would have sat by the fire waiting for your return as patient as Penelope."

He snorted his opinion of that image.

"As it is," she continued, "you were busy toadying up to Lord Bossley and you weren't anyplace close enough for us to reach you. Oh, wait! I know. I could have sent one of the village boys over to Lord Bossley's table with a note addressed to the Thorn. 'Excuse me, Lord Bossley, but the man who has been robbing you blind is sitting at your dinner table. Would you like me to fetch the noose now? Or should we do it later?' "

"Stop your sarcasm," he said, his face contorting in anger. "This is not a jest. The danger of the soldiers aside, you could have broken your neck riding Roman."

"We did right well this evening," she returned stoutly. "And I'm sorry if you want me to wait upon your bidding, but a decision had to be made and I made it. Perhaps you think I thought wrong, but an innocent man's life was at stake."

"And you were the only one who could rescue him? Lady Corinne, darling of the *ton*. From the moment I set eyes on you, you've been nothing but a problem. Always prying into what doesn't concern you—"

"I care about people," she shot back, but his words hurt.

"If you cared about them, *you'd stay out of the way.*"

Corinne doubled her hands into fists. She'd have loved to box him around the ears. What hurt was the fact that there was some truth to what he was saying. If he hadn't arrived, she would have been in trouble. She'd imagined a daring rescue, not a trap.

"*You make me so angry,*" she said. "I don't even know how you knew where we were."

"John McBride ran into Mandy, who told him the story," Will said. "He came riding for me. No note at the table, so very sorry. And I'm not angry at you, Cory—no, yes, *maybe I am*. You foolishly risked your life."

"And what would it matter to you?" she charged. There were tears in her eyes now. She blinked them back. "I've been a nuisance, a pest—"

He shut her up with a kiss.

And not just a normal kiss, either.

She'd been kissed before. Pecks, slobbers, fish swallows—but she'd not been kissed like this.

The moment his lips met hers, it was as if she'd been born to kiss him. Their mouths melded together as if this was the most natural state for the two of them.

Corinne couldn't think, couldn't reason, all she could do was close her eyes and savor.

He smelled of the night.

He smelled of man.

He smelled *good*. He *felt* good.

Will broke the kiss. He released his hold on her and, fortunately, kept a hand on her arm or she would have just fallen face forward.

"I shouldn't have done that," he said. "It wasn't right."

"Wasn't right?" she repeated, still befuddled by the kiss. His words confused her. "Will, you've never done anything more right."

And to show him what she meant, she came up on her toes, threw her arms around his neck, and gave him a kiss of her own right back.

There was a momentary hesitation from him. A last pang of his good conscience, she supposed—but she would not be denied. Not any longer.

Kiss me, she silently ordered and pressed her lips to his harder. *Kiss me, kiss me, kiss me . . .*

And, at sweet, wonderful last, he did.

Chapter Thirteen

Will had never been as frightened in his life as when he'd been confronted with the scene of Cory dressed as the Thorn and surrounded by soldiers. Fear had made him powerful.

And fear had made him angry with her.

Fear had also been what had kept him away from her. He'd feared what would happen when she left, whether or not he could recover, whether he could ever love anyone the way he'd come to love her.

Yes, love.

His being pulsed with it—and in her kiss, he realized she loved him in return. No hesitation, no doubt, just love.

Of all God's glorious gifts, love humbled, amazed, and stirred him in a way he'd never anticipated.

Suddenly, the journey of his life made sense. Every experience, every challenge, every passage had been moving him to her. She now kissed him as if she could connect their souls—and she did.

He was hers. Forever.

Will touched her tongue with his, experimenting, wanting more.

Her lips curved into a ticklish smile, then, tentatively, she returned that intimate touch.

Will thought he'd lose it right there. Lust was a heady thing and he'd held his in check for far too long. It was a wonder he had an ounce of brains left.

He didn't know who started undressing whom. Their hands seemed to be everywhere. He wanted to feel her bare skin against his, to be inside her. And she was equally anxious.

Theologians who argued for a chaste life obviously didn't know what it was like to have Cory in one's arms. She was his siren. He'd wanted her from the very second he'd laid eyes on her all those years ago, but over the past weeks he'd come to know and respect her. She was everything he admired. Resilient, honest, independent . . . and the greatest blessing of all, she was *his*.

His senses were full of her. He untied the rope at her waist, swept aside her jacket, pulled the shirt over her head, discovered her breasts.

She was perfectly formed. Her skin was warm, hot even. Strong muscles flexed and played beneath his hands. Her nipples were shell pink and hard.

Her hand slipped inside his breeches. She found him, stroked him as boldly as she did everything in her life, and it was his undoing.

How could he hold back when she wouldn't?

His lips found her ears, her neck, her eyes, her nose. His hands grew bolder, slid beneath her clothing to cup her buttocks, pulling her closer to him.

She bit his ear, whispered an urgent, "Please, please . . ."

He was mindless with arousal. With need. He lifted her up. Her breeches fell to the ground. He wrapped her stockinged legs around his waist. If he didn't have a release fairly soon, he would combust into thin air like a flame that escaped its fire—

He entered her in one fluid, deep, smooth movement.

Startled, Cory broke the kiss. Her eyes widened, her body tensed.

Will felt the tear.

Reason asserted itself. He feared he'd hurt her. He held very still. His breathing was tight, labored. "Cory?"

She didn't answer.

"I've hurt you," he said and started to back away.

Her hands grabbed his shoulders. "*Don't you dare move,*" she ordered. "It was just unexpected. But it's . . . nice?" She released the breath she was holding. He felt her expand, accept him. Her clear eyes met his. She frowned.

"Is this all there is? After all that, this is it?"

Will gave a shaky laugh and her brows raised in surprise. "I felt that," she whispered. "I felt your laugh all the way through me."

"And how does it feel?" he wondered, uncertain how much longer he could keep himself at bay. Love had turned him greedy. He had to have all of her.

"Laugh again," she ordered softly. "I think I like this."

Music to his ears. "Cory, I'm going to do more than laugh," he promised and began moving.

She gasped, sighed, and then moved with him.

Her arms tightened their hold around his neck. Her lips kissed a line along his jaw. Her tongue found his ear, and when she whispered, "This makes running around the countryside so worthwhile," Will thought he came undone.

He thrust now, deep and hard, his arm around her waist, holding her for him. That they were both partially dressed added to the moment. The scent of her, the scent of them drove him to madness. He moved faster, his straining muscles begging for release while his soul begged for them to go on forever.

If Ashcroft, Freddie, Bossley, her parents, and the whole of London had stormed the reiver's hut, they could not have taken him off of her. He adored her vitality, her perfect feminine beauty, her ability to fit exactly right with him.

"My beautiful man," she murmured. "My beautiful, perfect man."

He didn't talk. He couldn't. He was using all his energy to pleasure her.

This was the meaning of life. This moment, this woman, this—dare he say it? *Holy,* yes, holy connection. She'd been meant to be in his arms. And he never wanted to let her go.

Her breathing came out in small, shaky gasps. There was a tightening in her, a quickening. He held her tighter, finding his voice to whisper her name.

Deep muscles claimed him. He experienced her satisfaction just as he found his own release. He was deep, deep within her, and for a second, they were suspended in time.

Dear God, how he loved her.

The life force of this man flowed through her. The world as Corinne had known it ceased to exist. It was replaced by stars, thousands and thousands of blinding stars. No one could have brought her here. Only him. Wonderful him.

He came down to his knees, bringing her with him. He held her with gentle concern.

She knew he'd experienced exactly what she had. She could see it in his face.

Oh, yes, life made perfect sense.

Of course she'd had to run away from Freddie, from expectations, from duty—otherwise, she wouldn't have been *here*.

For a long moment, she rested in his arms. Her bones had turned to jelly. She had no wish to move. But eventually, the cool night air tickled her backside.

He pressed a fervent kiss against the top of her head. When she looked up, he kissed her mouth.

She practically purred with enjoyment. He was kneeling and balancing her on one knee. She combed his hair with her fingers, liking the silky feel of it.

"I hurt you?" he asked, concerned eyes pleading with hers.

"I'll be sore on the morrow," she predicted. "But," she added as his concern started to turn to alarm, "that was the most incredible experience in my life. Is it always like that?"

"Only when one is in love," he said, leaning down for another kiss.

She stayed him by placing her fingers against his mouth. "*Are* you in love?"

His eyes were still dark with spent desire. They must have mirrored hers.

Her mother had warned that men needn't feel passion or even attraction to claim a woman. She'd heard her brothers sniggering over conquests. She'd been so caught up in Will's kisses that she'd not questioned her actions . . . but *wait*. This was Will. He wasn't like any other person in the whole world, let alone the rest of his sex. This man had honor, integrity.

"I'm in love," he said.

If she hadn't been in his arms, she would have jumped and danced. As it was, she threw her arms around his neck and happily declared, "I'm in love, too."

The force of her movement cost him his balance. They fell to the floor in each others' arms, kissing, smiling, kissing again.

Love. He *loved* her.

She would glue herself to his body and make him take her everywhere with him.

He sat up first, came to his feet, and helped her up.

Their kisses grew tender, loving.

They were both still half dressed. It was comical, and they had to laugh, until he started helping her undress completely. She helped him and in short order they both stood naked in the moonlight.

Will took her hand and led her to the cot in the other room. This time, their lovemaking wasn't desperate. They'd crossed a barrier. They discovered trust.

When he entered her this time, there was bit of pinch of soreness, but passion eased it. She cradled him between her legs, reveling in his weight on her body.

This time was even better than the last. The cot was as rickety as she remembered, and the threat of it collapsing caused much laughter.

Laughter and love. Corinne felt she had the best of all worlds.

They didn't leave the hut until the wee hours of the morning. Riding Roman home, they were decidedly an odd couple, what with both of them wearing breeches. Corinne sat sideways, safe in Will's arms. She'd stretched muscles she hadn't known she had, but he held her as if she was the most precious thing to him.

Will had proven to be a good lover. A strong one. She ran a hand over the shadow of his beard. It scratched the back of her fingers.

His lips curved into a smile and he caught one of her fingers with a kiss.

"I don't want to return," she said.

"I know," he answered, but he kept riding.

"How did you ride to find me with the soldiers?" she wondered.

"I took McBride's horse."

"How did you explain leaving to Lord Bossley?"

"Any of the many excuses I've used for parish duties. He never questions them."

"Excuses?" A thought came to Corinne. She frowned. "You were late to the dinner party for Freddie and me. Was that an excuse?"

His smile widened into a grin. "I hadn't

planned on attending that night. After all, Freddie was marrying the woman I'd loved from afar."

"Did you really love me back then?" she wondered softly, touched by the thought.

Will turned serious. "Yes. Not only do I think I did, I now know I did."

"And you couldn't stay away from me, and so that is why you arrived late to the dinner party?" she guessed, delighted with his admission.

"Yes," he admitted with a laughing sigh. "It is true. I couldn't stand being away wondering if you were still as beautiful as you were years ago."

"What did you think?" she had to ask.

"I thought you were beautiful, but I was certain I could walk away from you. In fact, as I remember, you were the one following me—"

"I was not—"

"In the library?" he reminded her. "In the coach?"

Corinne laughed. "It all did work to my advantage, didn't it?"

"And to mine," he agreed, pressing a kiss to her forehead.

She sobered. "I'm not leaving, Will. I'm staying with you, wherever you go, whatever you do."

"I don't know, Cory—"

"You said you love me."

"I do."

"Then wherever you are, I will be," she promised. "Don't you understand, Will, by running away I've defied my parents, my family, society, and I couldn't be happier. At last, I'm living my life. And I've found you. The life the two of us will have together is worth giving up all that I've known. I don't care if we leave England. I won't lose you."

"And I won't let anything happen to you. Cory, for my own well-being, I must know that you will protect yourself."

"*You* will protect me," she insisted.

"With my life," he vowed. He was silent a moment, then said, "I have something Bossley wants."

"What is it?"

"No, I won't tell you. But that is why he's hunting for the Thorn. If he catches me, take care of yourself, Cory. I'd be driven to madness if I thought any action of mine would hurt you. Promise me you will do this."

"Nothing will harm us," she answered. "We were meant to be with each other. I know this."

He shook his head. "I'm not superstitious. I

pray, but in the end, I know we make our own choices. Be wise, Cory. Please don't hesitate to deny me if it means your safety."

She could never do that, but she understood he would not accept her claim. She also knew that if he kept playing the Thorn, they would capture him.

"How much simpler life would be if you were just a parson and I some village maid. Or perhaps you'd be what you are in your heart, a healer? Mr. Norwich, physician." She liked the sound of it.

"That's not our world," he told her.

"I can wish."

"If wishes were horses—"

"—then beggars would ride," she finished.

They'd reached the rectory. All was quiet. Will let her off at the back door before he took Roman to his stall and settled him in.

Corinne waited for him in the kitchen. He took her hand, led her upstairs to his bed, and made love to her again.

Later, as he slept in her arms, she reflected on how she really wasn't going to walk well in the morning, but being in his arms, coupling with him, was worth the price of a few sore muscles.

Her one regret was a sense of foreboding that had settled upon her and wouldn't leave.

Will called her superstitious. He was wrong. Something was coming their way. She could feel it, and the only thing she could do was hold him tight and pray they could see it through.

The next morning, Will did not want to leave the bed. However, he also knew that the wisest course, after having seen the soldiers last night, was to be seen out and about. His goal now was to protect Corinne. At all costs.

He tried to be very quiet as he dressed. He knew she was tired and needed rest. Yesterday had been a long one for the two of them, but he'd woken this morning feeling more content and at peace than he ever had before in his life. His Cory not only fascinated him but she also said things he needed to hear.

The time *had* arrived to make the Thorn disappear. Perhaps there was another way to help Bossley's crofters and tenants. Will had gone to an extreme.

He also knew that no matter how desperate circumstances became around Ferris, he couldn't touch the French gold. Bossley was looking for it.

Will wasn't about to turn Bossley in. He owed

his foster father some loyalty. As long as the gold stayed hidden, then Bossley couldn't betray England and Will couldn't betray Bossley.

It seemed too simple.

And what of Freddie? Will dismissed him. Cory was his and he'd let no man take her away from him. Scandal or not. If they had to leave Ferris, he would go. They could travel to the Netherlands or Italy. Perhaps even cross the ocean to the American continent.

He could even think about going to Barbados. The idea had been forming in the back of his mind. Corinne had nurtured it with her questions about his parentage. What if his father had been as caring as Mark Broxter? What if he'd made a decision in haste and regretted it?

What if his father was looking for him? That had been a boyhood fantasy—that his real father searched for him. Will had set it aside years ago, but there was always a "what if?"

Setting the kettle on the fire to boil, Will planned to make tea for Corinne and carry it upstairs to her. Of course, what he wanted to do was climb back into bed with her. He could spend his life making love to her. He amended the thought—he *would* spend the rest of his life making love to her.

He sensed someone behind him and turned. Cory stood in the doorway wearing nothing more than the sheet from his bed. Her eyes were lazy with sleepiness. Her smile stretched across her face. Her glorious hair fell past her shoulders in a tangled messiness that begged a man to touch it. He hardened immediately.

"Good morning," she said.

"Will you marry me?" he answered.

The words came right out of his mouth without preamble or thought—and they were exactly right. He did want to marry her.

Her smile widened. "You still love me then?" she asked.

"More today than I did yesterday. But you are the one who needs to consider. Cory, I have so little, but everything I have is yours. Heart and soul."

"*You* are my fortune," she answered. "I woke up this morning, Will, and life is absolutely wonderful. You are my destiny."

"We will have to leave Ferris."

She smiled, understanding. "I know. This is hard. You belong here, don't you? You care for the people here."

He shook his head. "I spent most of my life in school and rarely came to Glenhoward. But from the moment I took over this living, it has been a good home. However, my life has now changed. Wherever you are is home to me."

"Yes, I will marry you," she answered. "Yes, yes, *yes*. Now come here so I can seal my pledge with a kiss." She stretched her arms, opening the sheet and spreading it out like giant butterfly wings, displaying the angry scar on her shoulder from where she'd been shot and all the beauty God had given her.

Will was in front of her in a beat. He gathered her up with the intention of kissing her senseless before carrying her back up to bed. It was his one thought, his only thought—

But then he realized that his initial feeling that he wasn't alone didn't stem from Cory's appearance.

They weren't alone.

He froze, looked up—and there, staring at them through the window over the dry sink, was Amanda Gowan, her face pale with shock.

Chapter Fourteen

Corinne saw Amanda at the same time Will did. They broke apart like two magnets with the same pull. Corinne hurriedly covered her nakedness while Will went to the window.

The girl took off running. Will knew he had to stop her. He didn't know what he would say, but he couldn't let her share what she'd just seen.

He headed to the door. "Dress, Cory, and pack my things. We must leave. This can't stay a secret."

"What are you going to say to Mandy?" Corinne asked.

"I don't know. But we need her silence, just for a few hours longer."

Corinne placed a hand on his arm. "Be careful, Will. She's in love with you."

"She is infatuated," he corrected.

"Sometimes that is worse," she said.

"I've done nothing to encourage her feelings," he said in his defense. "I've been courteous to her, but no more, Cory."

"I know that. However, we women are strange creatures. We form attachments in our dreams. If a man is nice to us, just in passing, that is sometimes enough for us to nurse hopes. Will, every day she comes here hoping you'll speak to her and then she probably cherishes those words. Her heart *is* involved."

"It can't be. She's too young."

"And you are being very male. You aren't noticing what is right in front of you."

"Perhaps you should talk to her?" he suggested.

"No, it must come from you," Corinne said with regret. "I am now her rival."

"I just hope I can catch up with her," he muttered. "I'll return as soon as I am able." He pressed a kiss on her lips and forced himself to push away. She was too tempting. Too warm, too loving.

He picked up his hat and let himself out the kitchen door. Amanda was nowhere to be seen around the rectory or the churchyard. He started walking into Ferris and a few moments later was knocking on Gowan's door.

Mrs. Gowan answered. "Good to see you, Reverend. Amanda delivered my message?"

Now he understood why Amanda had been at the rectory. "No, I mean, she came by, but I couldn't talk to her," he said. "In fact, I'm looking for her. I need to know what she wanted."

Her mother gave a world-weary sigh. "She didn't deliver the message? I don't know what to do with that girl. I would have brought it to you myself but I was with Mrs. Broxter caring for the boys last night and was hoping for a bit of a lie down. Poor Mark is still not himself, although he's in a better frame of mind, thanks to you."

"What is it you wanted me to know?" Will asked.

"David Bishop's mother has taken a turn for the worst."

"Not another death." Bishop was a farmer to the south. He was a good-natured man with twelve children.

"Bad news comes in threes," said Mrs. Gowan with her customary practicality. "He came by the Broxters' last night to pay his respects and was wondering if you would come sit by his mother's side. You know she's in her eighties, and David says she is doing poorly. She was fond of you, although we didn't see much of her these past few months."

"Understandably," he answered. Guilt was an uncomfortable feeling. He was about ready to run out on these people who had come to mean a great deal to him over the year. He'd done nothing but think of Corinne these past few days and barely knew what was going on in the parish.

"I know it is a hike for you and poor old Roman, but David asked me to ask."

He could pay a visit. It would take half a day, but he could travel to Mother Bishop's side, then he and Corinne could leave. They'd have the rest of their lives together, while she was seeing the last of hers. "I will go. Mrs. Bishop was one of my early supporters. She always told me what she thought, whether I wanted to hear it or not."

Mrs. Gowan gave him a commiserating smile. "She's always told all of us what she thinks."

"By the way, *is* Amanda here?" Will asked. "I needed a moment with her."

"She'll be liking that," Mrs. Gowan said. "But what is it you wish to speak to her about?"

Will was not about to say his true intention.

"A small matter," he said. "A misunderstanding between us."

"Does this have anything to do with her making calf's eyes at you all the time?"

"A bit," he hedged.

"Let it be," her mother advised. "Joshua and I are encouraging Peter Clemson to court her. The lad's very shy, but he's had an eye on her for a long time. She'll be leaving you alone once she is married, which we pray will be very soon."

"That would be a good match," Will agreed, but his mind was churning over where Amanda could be. If she wasn't here, then where?

"I don't know why she didn't pass the message to you. She practically knocked her father out of the way in her urgency to deliver it for me."

"Yes," he replied, distracted. "Please tell her I'm looking for her."

"Is anything the matter, Mr. Norwich?" Mrs. Gowan's earlier ease was replaced by a mother's sense that all was not as it should have been.

"It's fine," he assured her. "I'm certain there is a good reason why she didn't deliver the message, but now I know what you wished to say, and I thank you for it. Mother Bishop has always been most kind to me. I'd best be on my way." He began walking toward the church.

Amanda had not run to her home. Where could she have been?

Old Andrew, working on pruning the winter wood off the roses in the graveyard, hadn't seen her either.

Will did come across two boys playing in the woods. They were both Clemson's grandsons. One said he didn't know Amanda Gowan, but the other did and either way, no girl had crossed their path.

Will stood at the edge of the great oaks. Amanda's disappearance was a mystery—yet weren't young girls famous for running off to be alone with their problems?

He returned to the rectory for Corinne's advice. "I don't know where she could be," she said. "But probably she's searched out friends. I'm certain your name is being blackened. I'm teasing," she hastily added when she saw how seriously he was taking this matter. "Will, the girl needs some time alone. That's how I would be. I know this is hard, but I sense we need to leave, with or without talking to her. I won't feel at ease until we are away from Lord Bossley."

"Yes, yes," he agreed, distracted, "but before we leave, I must pay my respects to Mother Bishop. Her approval was important to me when

I first arrived in Ferris. I don't know how poorly she is doing, but the family has requested my presence. She is a local character, full of vinegar. She's been ill for some time."

"Of course," Corinne said. She'd already packed what little they owned. They'd take his clothes, but he'd leave his books and other items behind. She reached up and placed a hand on the side of his jaw. "You take care of everyone," she said, her voice warm with loving concern. "You act more like some clan chief than their clergy."

"I know I am being ridiculous. Mother Bishop probably won't even know I'm there—"

"You are not being ridiculous," she answered. "This concern is part of your character. You can't deny it, and I love you all the more for it. I wondered if I'd ever meet a man I could respect and admire. Will, I'm yours, forever. I love you and wouldn't have you any other way than how you are."

No one had ever expressed such faith in him. Or had understood the responsibility he felt for the people in this parish. They had become his family.

But Corinne was his future, his life. He was no longer alone.

He felt torn.

Turning his head, Will pressed a kiss in her hand. "My love for you knows no bounds."

There was a pause. "We don't have to leave," she offered. "I'll face the scandal. Sail through it, in fact. My family will disown me, but that is a small price to pay. My aunt Catherine paid it once, and I know she has no regrets. On the positive side, Freddie won't want me. I'll be of no value to him."

"You are worth more than any fortune to me," Will answered. "And we must leave here. We need a clean start."

She nodded, her lips pressed together as if she bit back doubts, worries.

"We are going to have a wonderful life together," he said. "I have no regrets leaving."

Corinne smiled, nodded again. He sensed she wasn't convinced. There was only one way he could prove his conviction, and that was to live it. "Roman and I shall be back in three hours' time—"

"Roman," she said with dismay. "What shall we do with Roman? Will, we can't leave him."

"We can. I'll talk to Gowan. He'll take him in. After all I've put Roman through these past months, spending the rest of his life grazing the moors will be a blessing."

"I shall miss him."

Will would, too. "He'll be fine. I'll see to it." He pressed a kiss on her forehead. He would do whatever it took to keep her safe. "I'll return soon." He went to the kitchen door but hesitated, turned back to her. "I love you."

"I love you, too." She smiled her encouragement, and yet she seemed uncertain. *It's all going to be well*, he told himself. *I'll see to it.*

Then he went to saddle Roman.

Corinne walked from room to room after Will left. Up the stairs, then down.

She should have been happier than she'd ever been before in her life. She could still taste him, smell him, feel him inside her . . . and yet she couldn't shake the sense that things were not right.

Leaving Ferris was going to be hard for Will. She was surprised to realize it was going to be hard for herself as well. She liked the people here and felt as if she belonged. This would be a good place to raise children.

Her parents had not been fond of the country and she'd not spent a tremendous amount of time there, but she liked Ferris. She preferred it over all the attractions of London. Life was filled not with busyness but with purpose. Gazing out the window, she realized she'd never see the patch of garden Andrew plowed come to life or the cherries the blossoms on the cherry tree promised.

She told herself she was so happy to be in Will's arms that it was human nature to fear something would take him away. If anything happened to him, she would not be able to go. Not alone.

Corinne reminded herself that a good, caring God would not have let them find each other only to be parted. Perhaps not for her sake, since she was not particularly religious, but certainly for Will's. He believed. He acted on his conscience. He did good things for others. God could not betray a servant such as Will . . . could He?

Religious or not, Corinne found herself crossing the graveyard to the church. There was the smell of rain in the air. A wind was tossing the cherry blossoms in the huge tree that guarded the church-yard, sending them down to the ground.

Corinne slipped inside the peaceful quiet of the church and walked into the sanctuary. She was alone. She sat in one of the pews toward the middle of the church and pulled out its needle-point kneeler. She looked up at the carving of the knight battling the lion.

"Just a prayer," she whispered. "One wish. Please keep Will safe. Don't let anything happen to him." There, that was her fear, the heart of her restless uneasiness.

A footfall came from the back of the sanctuary. Corinne turned, half expecting the other person to be Will.

She was wrong. Lord Bossley stood there.

He'd removed his hat and wore a black caped greatcoat. Everything about him bespoke Quality.

Lord Bossley smiled at her, as if he'd expected to find her here.

Instead of panic, Corinne discovered a remarkable calmness. This was what she'd feared. She recognized it immediately, and now, faced with the worst, she was ready to do battle.

He walked up the aisle and took a seat beside her. "Hello, my lady."

"Good afternoon, my lord." She did not move from her place on the kneeling bench. She also did not take her eyes off of him.

"Very clever, I must say, hiding right beneath my nose," he observed. "And the villagers?" He sighed in disappointment. "They kept your presence a secret."

"I beg your pardon, do I appear as if I am hiding?"

Temper flashed in his eye at her impertinence, but his voice, when he spoke, was patience, long-suffering. "Yes, well, we've struggled to keep your disappearance quiet. It's been difficult," he said. "There are so many who want to fete the bride-to-be before her wedding day. I believe the story we put out was that you have been terribly ill. I sent my son to London to be at your side. He assures me there is so much concern on your behalf."

She pretended to consider a moment, then shook her head. "I doubt if Freddie could keep a ruse up like that. You know, the one about being the lovesick swain. I'm certain he is enjoying London."

Lord Bossley appeared momentarily flummoxed before he tipped back his head and laughed with genuine amusement. "You are an original," he said, wiping tears from his eyes. "Yes, it has been a challenge to keep my son looking concerned when there is so much to see and do in London."

"And he doesn't care for me at all."

"Oh, he cares," Lord Bossley assured her. "He knows what is at stake."

"What exactly is at stake, my lord? Why do you need me?"

"For appearances, my lovely. For connections. You see, years ago I returned from Barbados not knowing anyone of importance. My predecessors had all been rustics without interest in politics. So much wasted on those who didn't care."

"All doors are open to you, my lord. You have made your own fortune."

His gaze sharpened on those words. He was waiting, as if there was something more he expected her to say.

Suddenly, Corinne realized she might *not* know what game was being played. And if she had a part, it was a very small role—but Will's wasn't.

At her silence, Lord Bossley seemed to relax, a forced emotion if ever there was one. "You know the *ton*," he said lightly. "There are those who accept everyone—scoundrels, brigands, insurrectionists—and those whose vaulted opinions of themselves rule out even the choicest of company. The duke of Banfield's lineage allows him access to those who are discriminating."

"And you have ambition?"

He turned modest. "I did not seek it, but I am not afraid to serve my country and my king if asked to do so. Can you imagine? Prime minister. I am honored."

"Of course, the Whigs must regain power, and that might not be easy," Corinne replied.

"I knew you were the right woman for my son," Lord Bossley said approvingly. "Freddie doesn't understand any of this. He's not a deep thinker." His smile turned grim. "Make no mistake, my lady. I have only one son and I cherish him. He's not going to struggle in life the way I did."

"You struggled, Lord Bossley? What struggle did you have?"

A change came over him at her challenge. "That attitude," Lord Bossley said. "That attitude can't be bought. That's why I wanted *you,* Lady Corinne, for my son. The Unattainable . . . because you are the best. Others may say whatever they wish about you, but you choose life on your terms. Such a rare quality in an Englishman, let alone an Englishwoman. From the moment I first observed you, I knew you were the one. And I must say, Frederick has been envied by many men."

"Then they are all as shallow as he is. I'm not the one," she informed him smartly. "A marriage between Lord Sherwin and myself will not work."

"I know Freddie has been cow-handed—"

"Crude, obnoxious, ridiculous," she interjected. "I could think of a hundred such adjectives to describe him."

"You go too far," he warned.

"I don't go far enough," she answered. "I will not marry him. I vowed not to and I have honored that vow by falling in love with a man of substance. A man I respect and admire enough to give myself to him without reservation. I've chosen another, Lord Bossley," she said, proud of herself, because here were the words that would free her of her betrothal. "I am Reverend Norwich's lover and have agreed to be his wife."

To her surprise, Lord Bossley did not appear offended. Instead, he *tsk*ed, chiding her, "It is not your virginity I wanted, my lady. And whatever arrangements you and Freddie make are not my business. You *will* marry my son."

"I will *not*."

She lifted her chin as she said those words. There was nothing this man or any other, including her father, could say or do to alter her determination.

"It's not by happenstance that I am here today," Lord Bossley said, looking around the sanctuary with the idleness of a visitor. "I had an interesting discussion with a young lady, child actually, although she feels very grown up, about my foster son and yourself. I knew you were lovers. Miss Amanda Gowan made that clear."

Corinne warned herself not to panic.

"A woman will follow a man to his grave," Lord Bossley was saying, "unless she feels herself scorned. And then she will dig the grave for the man. It's not an attractive part of the female character, but there it is."

"So she confirmed what I said," Corinne answered, deciding to brazen it out.

"And much more," Lord Bossley returned, pinning her with his gaze.

He knew.

His smile widened. "Yes, Miss Gowan feels so ill-used, she did let slip that she knew who the Thorn was. Frankly, I am startled by her information. It's not that I believed Will would be loyal. I don't expect that from any human, man or woman. However, I did underestimate his daring. I thought him a bookish sort, as passive as his father."

"You knew his father?"

Lord Bossley blinked, as if her question made him realize what he'd inadvertently revealed. He scowled, cut the air dismissively with his hand. "No, never. But I know the sort of man he must have been. The docks are full of that type."

And here was where Will had gained the idea his father had been a sailor.

Annoyance changed Lord Bossley. Hardened him. "You are going to marry my son," he said. "And now you are going to make him a model wife . . . because you don't want to see Will hang."

"No, I don't," she echoed.

He stood. "Return with me now, Lady Corinne. Your cooperation for Will's life. It is a good bargain, no? I'm leaving for London tomorrow. You shall accompany me."

"What of my parents?"

"They assumed you had gone off to London by one way or the other. We were all quite concerned. You could have met with foul play."

So, Major Ashcroft had not mentioned shooting her.

"They've been very worried," Lord Bossley said.

Corinne stood. She had no choice but to go with Lord Bossley. "You will not harm Will?"

"If you do as I suggest, why should I? After all, his being an outlaw could taint my own career. However, Lady Corinne, he is not blood kin. If you value his life, his well-being, you will break off all ties to him as of this moment."

"You killed Simon Porledge," she said with sudden understanding.

"Not I . . . but someone did for me." His matter-of-fact statement put a chill in her heart.

"If anything happens to him, I shall denounce you," she threatened.

"If you are a good wife to my son, if you bear my grandchildren, my heirs, then why should anything happen to Will?"

Hell, she was turning herself over to hell, and she would willingly if it meant protecting the man she loved. "You are right," she said, her throat tight with anger. "You will have no concerns."

"You are very reasonable, Lady Corinne. Now, shall we go? I have a coach waiting outside."

"I need a moment to pen a note to Will," she insisted.

"That is not necessary. I shall deliver the news."

Once again, she sensed there was more at play here than she knew. "Just a note," she begged.

"Regrettably, no." He swept the path before him with a wave of his hand. "After you, my lady."

She hesitated . . . but in the end, she had no choice.

Corinne left the church with Lord Bossley.

Chapter Fifteen

By the time Will reached Mother Bishop's bedside, she was already on the mend. "Did they tell you I was about to breathe my last?" she demanded. She was a stubborn, opinionated woman with steel-gray hair and an unlined face for her age. "Well, they are wrong, Mr. Norwich. I shall recover. I promise."

"They are concerned for you," Will answered diplomatically.

She cackled in triumph. "I know, I know, but I'm not leaving yet, and you can return to Ferris village and tell them as much. My granddaughters take good care of me. Far better than my son does!"

"Well, I can't wait for you to be able to tell them yourself when you come to Sunday service," Will said before realizing he wouldn't be there.

The thought hit him with great sadness, but such was the price of his love for Corinne.

It was late afternoon of an increasingly cloudy day by the time he and Roman returned to the rectory. Will was not unhappy with the lateness of the hour. Corinne and he should leave after dark so as not to attract notice.

The hardest of their going would be leaving Roman. Will ran his hand along the animal's back, then scratched him under the chin the way he liked. "You are a good man. I shall miss you."

He was going to miss everyone.

Roman's response was to push the feed bucket with his nose, a reminder to Will that as long as the horse was well cared for, the beast wouldn't necessarily miss his master. And Will's parishioners would also carry on—Seth the miller and his family would manage, Broxter would do well for his son, the couple he'd married last Saturday would be happy.

Chores done, Will walked to the rectory. Lamplight glowed from the kitchen window. He could picture how impatient Corinne would be. She didn't like to wait.

He opened the door—

Lord Bossley sat at his kitchen table.

Will glanced around the room. Corinne wasn't there. Nor was there sound of her movement in the house.

"You are right," Bossley confirmed. "She is not here. I had her taken to Glenhoward."

"You may bring her back," Will answered.

"I won't," came the reply. "She doesn't want to stay. She's decided she doesn't want you, Will. She came to her senses."

The words were aimed at Will's every doubt. For a second, he couldn't think. *Corinne had changed her mind?*

Well, of course. Bossley was right—she wouldn't want him. He had nothing . . .

He had nothing . . . *but her love.* A woman with a heart as valiant as Corinne's would not turn her back so abruptly on him. She loved him. She wouldn't have given herself to him otherwise.

"You are lying," Will said. "And I'm going to Glenhoward to fetch her."

"Before you go, I must share the information that I passed word to Major Ashcroft that you are the Thorn. After his last encounter with you, I'm certain he'll be tying the noose himself around your neck."

Will shut the door. "I don't know what you are talking about."

"Brazening it out." Bossley shook his head. "I sadly underestimated you, Will. If only Frederick had your ingenuity."

"You didn't go to Ashcroft," Will said. "Because before I'm hanged, you'd be afraid of what I may say about a certain chest of gold coins."

Bossley laughed. "Not any longer. I've given it up for a loss. I hold all the cards, Will. Truly, I do."

Will didn't think so, and he knew enough of his foster father's character to doubt if the man would walk away from that much money. "I'm willing to test your words, sir."

Bossley stood, still chuckling softly. "Bold. You are so bold. But," he said, drawing a deep breath as if needing to sober himself, "I'm ahead of you. I'm no fool. I know when the game needs to be changed, and I'm not as greedy for gold as you may believe I am when it comes to saving my own neck. I sent a letter to Whitehall, to the duke of Banfield, in fact, explaining that I feared the foster son I had taken to my bosom had turned out to be a viper. I wrote that the chest is yours, Will. The messenger has already gone to London."

"And do you have the chest?" Will dared him.

"No, you do. Unfortunate turn of events. The reason Major Ashcroft is not here at this moment is that he and his men are tearing up a . . . what would one call it? Hideaway? That abandoned cottage that the Thorn claimed for his lair? I'm certain it is there. You wouldn't dare bring something so dangerously incriminating here."

Will relied on steel nerves. "I will testify against you and the good major. You can't convince me he didn't know what he carried when he acted as a courier for you."

"He didn't," Bossley said. "Will, not everyone has your determination. Ashcroft never questions me. He's young and handsome and a sheep. He does as ordered. I thought you were the same. As for testifying against me," he continued, "it will be your word against the earl of Bossley's. I shall win, Will. I have friends in valuable places. They would not think me a traitor. Whereas a rogue clergyman who has been waylaying his benefactors—well, he's ripe for all sorts of tales about him. Run, Will. Go. I don't want your death on my hands."

"Why not? You weren't bothered with Porledge's."

Bossley's face fell into hard lines. "Porledge

meant nothing to anyone. And you tempt me
too far. Oh, God, Will, if you knew the truth of
things, you'd understand the nature of my soul.
Should I have done away with you? Could I?" He
shook his head. "No, 'tis better you die by your
hand, by your own deed."

The earl walked past Will to the door. "Go
wherever you must, Will, but don't return to
England."

"I won't go anywhere without Corinne."

"She's taken the choice from you. She's traded
her life for yours. She's gone to you, man. Don't
let her sacrifice be in vain." He opened the door.
"Ashcroft will be here at any moment, depending
on how quickly he finds the gold. You don't want
to be here when the soldiers arrive. As for us, I'll
look forward to our meeting again in hell."

But before he walked out the door, the earl
paused. "One question. The horse you rode, the
one they said snorted fire, where did you find
him?"

"He's Roman," Will answered. "I always said
you underestimated him."

"So I did," Bossley replied. "So I did." He
placed his hat upon his head before assuring
Will, "I shall mend my ways." He left.

Will watched as his foster father strode to the

church, where a groom and horses waited for him. The earl mounted and was gone.

Will shut the kitchen door. Corinne had bargained herself for him. No one had ever loved him enough to place his interests ahead of theirs. Even Bossley, who had rescued him from the streets, had not done so just out of charity. What Will didn't understand was, why? Why had a man so obviously self-serving put himself out for a child?

It didn't make sense.

If you knew the truth of things, you'd understand the nature of my soul. Bossley's words. He'd never spoken to Will this way before . . . and there was a mystery here, one larger than a stash of French coin.

But Will's immediate concern was Cory. He wasn't going to let her sacrifice her life for his.

Their plans would not change. They would leave tonight, as soon as he went for her. Will would tear the walls down from Bossley's estate for her.

The few things around the rectory she owned were gone. Will gathered a change of clothes and his grooming kit and headed outside to saddle Roman. The mighty steed and he were not yet done with each other.

He had no doubt Ashcroft would be coming for him.

Someone had betrayed Will. He didn't believe it was Cory. She was made of sterner stuff and would never have given away the location of the hut. Even if she had, he could understand. She would expect Bossley to honor their exchange of Will's life for her agreeing to marry Freddie.

Perhaps Bossley had just been guessing about the gold. Maybe he wasn't certain he knew where it was. No one else knew where Will had hidden it.

Roman nickered a greeting and moved to the back of the stall. He was not ready to travel again this day, but that was too bad. Will reached for the saddle when he heard a woman weeping.

"Corinne?"

No answer.

He followed the sound to the garden shed located against the back of Roman's stall. The door was slightly ajar. Old Andrew would never have left it that way.

"Hello?"

The weeping stopped. He waited. "Mr. Norwich?" a feeble voice he recognized as Mandy's came from the other side of the door. "Please. I need you."

She did not sound like her young, confident self.

Will pushed open the door. Mandy was huddled in a corner, her face swollen and red from crying. She held up her right hand. The fingers were twisted unnaturally.

A hundred questions sprang to his mind. "What happened? Where are your parents? Are they all right? Who did this?"

"My parents don't know." Mandy started crying.

Will pulled her forward, needing to look at the hand in the light. The index and middle fingers were obviously broken, and the way the others had swollen indicated they might have been as well. "How did this happen?" Will asked. He untied the preaching bands around his neck and started wrapping her fingers together.

Mandy cried out in pain, sniveled some more, then confessed, "I went to Lord Bossley. I told him about the Thorn, about the reiver's hut."

"You knew about the hut?" Will asked, surprised.

"I followed you once or twice. I found it myself when I realized where you always went." Her eyes were troubled, as if she feared his anger.

She should have.

"Amanda," he said, "what did you tell Lord Bossley?"

"I was jealous. You don't love me. You love *her*," she said, as if that explained anything.

"Go on," Will ordered, keeping his temper in check.

"I heard you ask Miss Rosemont to marry you. I saw you kissing."

"We saw you looking in the window."

"My mother sent me with a message, but I wanted to talk to you . . . alone. My parents want me to consider marrying Peter Clemson, as if he or anyone could take the place of you." She sounded hurt, petulant, and so very young. "I wanted to tell you how I felt because you need to know. I love you. I've loved you forever."

"Amanda, we haven't known each other forever. I'm too old for you, way too old."

"That's not how I feel."

He should have discussed this with her earlier. Then perhaps they could have avoided these tragic circumstances.

"Tell me about your fingers," he said, knowing he could talk sense into her now.

"She's not your cousin, is she?"

"No," Will said.

Amanda's gaze slid away from his. Her lower

lip quivered slightly. "I was angry. Everyone thinks you are perfect, but when I saw you kiss her, I knew you weren't. You were playing a hoax on us. Making us think you were holy—"

"I am not *holy*—"

"*I* thought you were." She paused, as if she expected Will to apologize.

He wasn't going to. He couldn't.

"I thought you were perfect. Completely perfect," she whispered. "And then I saw you this morning. It hurt. I hurt."

"What did you tell him, Mandy?" Will pressed.

"I told him that you were living with a woman in the rectory. I thought Lord Bossley should know. I thought he would tell you to stop."

"Instead, what did he do?"

"He asked what Miss Rosemont looked like, and when he heard her name, he was very excited. He was nice. I guess I told him I knew lots of things and he asked me what more I could share. I realized then that maybe I'd said too much. So I wanted to go, but he wouldn't let me leave. He said something about my being the blacksmith's daughter—about the soldiers taking my father. They wondered if one of the things I knew was who the Thorn was. I didn't mean to give you away." She was crying again. "I wanted to leave but he said he needed to know if I told the truth and then he called a man, a servant, and that man broke my fingers."

Will swore under his breath. This girl was no match for Bossley.

"I didn't tell," Amanda insisted. "Even after he broke two I kept quiet, but then he snapped them all and reached for my other hand."

"Was he a tall, thin man with a hooked nose?" Will asked.

"Yes," she said.

The man was Bossley's butler, Dalton. The two of them had been together for as long as Will could remember.

"I told Lord Bossley everything then," Amanda confessed. "They sent me home. They ordered me to leave Ferris. But this is where I live. Where else could I go?" She grabbed Will's jacket, the fingers on her good hand like claws. "I don't know what to do."

"You are going home," Will said. "This afternoon. And you will tell your parents everything. You will also say that I believe you should visit a relative, someone outside the parish."

"I must leave?"

"For now. Amanda, you must be very brave. You are not to say anything of this to anyone but your parents and make them promise to keep this in strictest confidence—"

"Can you please go with me?" she begged. "They will be furious with me."

"I can't," he said sadly. "The soldiers are coming for me. Your fingers will heal." He also knew they'd be crooked, a memento of this time. "I must leave."

"Will you return?"

"I don't know."

She looked more horrified at that thought than she was even at her own pain. "And Miss Rosemont? Will they hurt her too?"

"Not if I have anything to do with it." Will helped her up off the dirt floor. "Now hurry home and be brave, Amanda."

"Yes." She took a step toward the door but whirled to throw her arms around him. "I am so sorry." This hug was not that of a girl attempting to hold on to calf-love but that of someone frightened and alone.

"I know, I know," Will said, softening his voice and giving her the comfort she needed to hear. "Peter Clemson is not a bad sort."

"He's not as brave as you."

"He might surprise you." Will pulled her arms away from him. "Now, go, Amanda. *Go.*"

322   *Cathy Maxwell*

She obeyed him then, dashing out of the garden shed.

Will stood quiet a long moment. After all he'd done for her, including rescuing her father the other night, she had turned on him. He tried to remember that she was young, that her father wouldn't have been in danger if not for him . . . but he found forgiveness hard to master.

"It doesn't seem right, Lord. You allow those like Bossley to thrive while good people suffer."

His studies had taught him not to question the will of God—but those teachings seemed false now. There was only one way to find justice, and it wasn't waiting for it.

Bossley could have the gold. He could betray England. Will didn't care. He wanted Corinne. She was the one good thing in his life.

He left the shed and pulled Roman from his stall. Within minutes he was in the saddle and heading for Glenhoward.

Will sat in the woods surrounding Glenhoward as the hour grew later. His focus was on all the comings and goings in the house.

Major Ashcroft had arrived and left, presumably after reporting that he had not captured Will. Soldiers stood guard. They didn't scare Will away, but he did have a major challenge—he had no idea which room in the cavernous mansion was Corinne's.

All the windows were dark, as if the inhabitants slept well in their beds.

The guards, two at the front door and two at the back garden door, sat on stools and, by the tilt of their heads, might have fallen asleep.

Will had tethered Roman to a small tree a quarter of a mile from the house. He was not worried about finding a way into the house. He and Freddie had played games here, running around every crook and corner of the place. Will had once even climbed up the rainspout to the second floor.

But once inside, how would he find Corinne?

He circled the building two or three times, staying in the shadows of the tree line. The increasing cloudiness of the night worked in his favor.

Just when he was deciding that he must enter the house and run the risk of going from room to room, a light shone from the back left corner window. A figure passed in front of the light. A woman's figure. And she was pacing.

It had to have been Corinne.

Will prepared to spring across the lawn, but

then the window went black. She'd either blown
out the lamp or had left the room. His safest
course was to go to that room. He circled the
house again, looking for the best way to approach it, but then he remembered what Corinne
did whenever she couldn't sleep. She read.

She wasn't in her room. He knew it.

She'd gone to the earl's library. Will grinned.
There was always a library window open. After
all, he'd been the one to break the latch almost
fifteen years ago, and it had never been fixed.

Chapter Sixteen

Corinne had wanted to eat dinner in her room, but Lord Bossley had insisted on her company. He'd informed her they would leave at first light in the morning.

He was also the one who had brought up the topic of Will. He expected to see him before they left and seemed confident Will would show himself this night.

Corinne prayed Will wouldn't. She wanted him safe.

Of course when she did retire for the night, she had trouble falling asleep. She didn't bother to undress. Who knew what would happen this night? Her mind was exhausted with worry, but fear kept her awake.

At one point she dozed a bit, but that sleep was plagued by dreams. Nightmares, actually. They were of her wedding to Freddie, or a figure she assumed was him. In the dream, she couldn't make out the face of the man beside her, but she did know that Will watched. Her dream self caught a glimpse of him in the vestibule. She wanted to run to him, but a power so strong she couldn't fight it pulled her toward the altar. The other dream image still strong in her mind was of flowers. Colorful, exotic flowers. Someone kept repeating, "Botanicals of Barbados."

With that phrase echoing in her mind, Corinne came awake with a start. She knew she could not return to sleep. If that dream wasn't enough to keep a woman awake, she didn't know one that was.

And that nonsense about plants, what in the world could that mean . . . ?

She remembered the book down in the library with that same title. There was something in that book, a sheet of paper that she'd only glanced at, but she now found it was stuck in her memory. A sheet of recordings.

Restless, she lit a candle, threw on a dressing

gown, and left her room. All of the clothes she'd brought to Glenhoward weeks ago were still in the wardrobe, as if waiting for her return. A maid had been assigned to her. When awake, the muscular woman had dogged Corinne's every step. However, asleep in the attached servant's room, the woman's snores were so loud that they threatened to disturb the whole house.

Corinne picked up the lamp and went downstairs with the vague purpose of searching out the book that haunted her dream.

Lord Bossley's butler sat in the front hall. He came to the stairs as she reached the last one.

"My lady, is there something I may do for you?"

"I can't sleep. I'm going to the library for a book."

"I shall accompany you," the servant said respectfully, but firmly. Corinne nodded. What else could she have done?

Of course she was incensed. She'd given Lord Bossley her word of honor she wouldn't run away, but the man was taking no chances. He didn't realize she loved Will more than her own freedom, more than her own future. She said she would marry Freddie if he let Will be free, and so she would.

However, if Freddie thought he'd beget an heir by her, he was wrong.

She'd thought long and hard about it over dinner. She was no fool. Freddie would force himself on her, but women talked to each other. She'd overheard her sister and mother speaking. There was a way to prevent children. Corinne would use any means at her disposal, and that thought alone had allowed her to eat in Lord Bossley's company and not gag.

"I resent being watched," Corinne said when they reached the library. "You may stay out here while I choose my book."

"Leave the door open, my lady," the butler said, again with that respectful authority.

Her response was to go into the library and shut the door.

He opened it.

She made as if to slam it again, but then smiled and shut it three-quarters of the way. A compromise. The butler took a step back and stood guard.

Corinne crossed over to the area of the library she'd investigated the evening of the dinner party. The curtain she'd hid behind was to her left. She wished she could pull it back and discover Will hiding there now. She longed to have his arms around her. She needed to hear him say all would be well.

The book on the botanical life of Barbados appeared as if it hadn't been moved since she'd returned it to the shelf. She pulled it down and took the few steps over to the reading desk by the window.

Her hands shook as she opened the book and found the paper she'd carelessly stuffed back in it. She spread the sheet out on the desk and studied it a moment.

The document was what she'd first thought—a page torn from a recording book, probably from a church. The list included births, deaths, and marriages, with a bit of detail on each.

But what had caught her eye that night, without her consciously realizing it, had been Lord Bossley's name—and the name William.

Corinne drew the lamp closer to better study the entry:

Baptism, May 18, 1782 William Dunleavy Sherwin, son of James Dunleavy Sherwin, sixth earl of Bossley and his wife, Lady Aimée Bossley. Date of birth, April 14, 1782. Godparents—Major General James Cunninghame, HM Governor of Barbados and Lady Lucinda Belmont. First male child and heir.

This William would have been of the same age as her William. But this William was Lord Bossley's heir?

She frowned, trying to make sense of it. Lord Bossley's wife was not named Aimée, and what did it mean to have the French spelling? Perhaps he'd been married before . . . ?

The paneling on the far side of the wall from the desk opened.

Startled, Corinne pushed the paper under the book, hiding it. She could not let it be taken from her, not now that she'd discovered it.

And then to her joy, Will stepped inside the room. He was smiling at her. *He'd come,* her heart joyously wanted to cry—and Bossley was expecting him. Corinne was certain of it.

She quickly put one finger to her lips, a warning for him to be quiet. She pointed to the partially open hallway door.

He nodded his understanding. He was aware the whole house was being guarded.

She picked up the book and took the precaution of placing it back on the bookshelf before offering the torn record page to him.

Will ignored the paper, preferring to take her in his arms instead, and she happily let him.

He felt so good, so solid. She buried her face in his neck, inhaling the scent of him, reveling in the feel of his body next to hers. They kissed, kissed again. Silent kisses this time. Furtive ones. They reminded her that they might not have much time.

"Will, you must see this," she said in as quiet a tone as she could. She handed him the record page and pointed to the name William. "I found this hidden in the pages of a book on botanicals in Barbados," she said.

Will had to turn toward the light to read the faded writing and frowned as he digested what was written. "1782 would be the year I was born."

"Was Lord Bossley married to another? Could *he* be your father?"

Will shook his head. "I don't know. We look nothing alike."

"This is the key," Corinne said. She placed a hand on Will's arm. "Freddie might not be his heir. But I don't understand why he would deny him. Everyone knows Bossley dotes on his son. Will, you must learn the story behind this page."

"Let's go to Barbados," he said. "We'll find

the story there. Come." He started to pull her toward the secret doorway.

Corinne held back. "We can't both go, Will. If we do, Lord Bossley will track you down."

"We'll outrun him."

"He'll take his temper out on the people of Ferris," she said.

"It was Amanda," he said. "Amanda gave me up."

Immediately she understood the situation. "She was jealous."

"I'm done, Cory. We were betrayed out of jealousy and spite. From now on, I'm thinking of myself and you. We are all that is important. Let's leave now."

He took her hand, but she didn't move.

Still keeping her voice very quiet, she said, "Innocent people will suffer. Lord Bossley will think nothing of herding anyone he wishes and accusing him of being the Thorn. You are the one who told me how bad things were before you became the Thorn."

"I don't care."

"She's just a girl, Will. A child, really, Will."

"It's time to think of myself."

Corinne took a step back. "You've lost your faith, haven't you?"

"What?" He shook his head, as if denying her words.

"You've lost it just when I've found mine. Will, who you are, what you've done for the people in this parish has given me courage. Before I met you, I wondered if life meant anything. We live, we breed, we die—such a waste. That's because I had nothing of meaning in my life. But being with you, watching you give your faith, your courage, your kindness to others, well, I saw how meaningful life could be. I don't know what you were like before the Thorn, but now you are a man who has the power to bring people together. Who makes them understand that each and every one of us is important. You can't run away."

"I can't lose you."

"You will, though. At some point when we are running around the Continent or America or wherever we go to hide, you will lose me. We'll have nothing between us. We won't stand for anything. Just like my parents. Or Lord and Lady Bossley. We'll be empty."

"Cory, you are asking me to give up loving you."

"No, I'm asking you to have faith in that love."

And the moment she said those words, she realized they were true. "I had this jumbled, confused dream about my wedding. I couldn't see the face of the man I would marry, but I knew you were there—and I remembered seeing the record page." She looked down at the paper still in his hand. "There's a riddle here, Will. One that can change our lives."

"You are being superstitious—"

"I have a feeling—"

"*No*, Corinne. No more feelings, no more giving to others, no more being patient or believing. I want you, here and now, and if I must defy God—"

She shut him up with a kiss. A deep, full-throated kiss.

For a long, sweet moment, they savored their love.

Corinne pulled away first. "You still have faith," she accused lightly. "Our lives are here, Will. I know it and I'm asking you to trust my instinct."

He made an impatient sound and looked down at the paper she'd thrust upon him. "You would have me go to Barbados? Can I return before you marry?"

"There must be a way to find an answer here," she said. "Someone must know what this means . . ." Her voice broke off as inspiration struck her. "Tarrington. Lord Tarrington. Lord Bossley was sending the chest to him. I heard him say that the night we first met in the library."

Will tucked the paper in his pocket. "Whatever you wish, Corinne, just come with me now—"

The hallway door opened. Lord Bossley and the butler entered the room. His lordship was fully dressed, as if he had anticipated this moment. Corinne gave a cry of alarm and Will stepped in front of her, protecting her from harm.

"Surprised to see us, Will?" Lord Bossley said. "I'm happy to report Major Ashcroft proved himself useful and found the chest. He's on the hunt for you. Of course, now that I have Lady Corinne what I don't need . . . is you."

The butler held up a pistol.

"No," Corinne yelled, but Will was faster.

He shoved her to the ground, leaping over at the same time and disappearing behind the paneled door leading to the next room. The bullet bounced off the wood harmlessly.

"Catch him," Lord Bossley ordered his butler, who was already giving chase.

His lordship walked over to Corinne and yanked her to her feet. "Don't kill him," she pleaded. "I didn't go with him. I'm honoring our bargain."

There was the sound of a scuffle in the next room. A man grunted and then a weight dropped to the floor, followed by the crashing of a window.

Lord Bossley dragged Corinne over to the door. In the wan light from the lamp in the other room, they could see the butler on the floor. He attempted to rise. Blood streamed from his face. "He hit me," the servant told Lord Bossley. He reached up, dabbed at the wound. "He jumped out the window. I lost him."

"Call those useless guards," Lord Bossley said. "Have them start beating the woods for him."

The butler scrambled to his feet. Ignoring his wound, he hurried to do his lordship's bidding. Within seconds, the halls filled with the shouting of orders.

Lord Bossley frowned at her. "Don't smile," he advised her. "He is gone to you. Major Ashcroft found a chest of French gold in Will's hideaway. We have him for treason now. He'll be brought to justice. I promise you that."

"You promised me his life for my cooperation."

"I pray you don't forget that, my lady. I am a powerful man. Will's fate is in my hands."

"If you catch him."

The earl's response was to jerk her around and march her out of the room. She spent the rest of the night heavily guarded.

The next morning, an irritated Lord Bossley took her to London, their coach surrounded by a full company of outriders—a sign if there ever was one that Will was still free.

Chapter Seventeen

Upon returning to London, Corinne quickly discovered that everyone had assumed she'd been visiting friends in the country. Even her sister and brothers believed the story her parents had circulated.

Her parents' reception was decidedly cool. She discovered she'd lost any goodwill her father had had toward her. She was no longer his pet. He had expected her to obey and she hadn't.

Neither parent asked where she'd been. Her mother, of course, continued on as if nothing had happened, but sometimes Corinne felt her father watching her closely.

She had surprised him. The thought amused her, since her will was as strong as his own.

Of course, the servants had also been instructed to keep a careful eye on her. There were four days until her wedding. Days filled with fittings, details, and last-minute dinner parties to celebrate the coming nuptials, occasions that forced her to sit beside Freddie.

Corinne would have played her part. After all, she was waiting for Will. She would have been docile and obedient until that time, but Freddie couldn't leave well enough alone.

He brooded. If she had been enamored with him before—and she certainly hadn't been—his brooding would have put her off him completely. And he would stand by her side as tenaciously as a dog guarding his bone. His hand would wander to her shoulder, her arm, her waist.

Corinne was becoming quite adept at avoiding his touch. She would step forward, step sideways—and always wearing a smile.

He tried to take her aside, inviting her out on the terrace or cornering her during soirees. Corinne managed to put him off. After all, if she stood her ground, he couldn't force her to do anything, short of picking her up and carrying her out of the room, which he wouldn't do in front of all society.

That didn't stop him from making promises. Every chance he could, he'd whisper, "You will be mine, and then no one can stop me from doing what I wish with you."

Corinne kept the smile on her face, her belief in Will unshakeable . . . until Lady Rumsman's luncheon.

Lady Rumsman was a distant family connection who held a weekly salon where many of the great Whig thinkers of the day gathered and impressed each other with their wit.

Although Lady Rumsman and the duke of Banfield shared the same political persuasion, she'd never been particularly fond of him. However, she was a great admirer of Lord Bossley, and for that reason had insisted on honoring Corinne with a luncheon the day before the wedding.

Lady Rumsman had little regard for the duchess of Banfield's intelligence and assumed Corinne was equally guilty by association. Corinne's sister, Belinda, had known the affair would be a bore and had suddenly come down with a headache.

Corinne tried to have a "headache" as well, but her mother forced her to carry on. The two of them sat side by side at the luncheon table, being talked over by the other gentlewomen, all of them bluestockings and many of them bores. When addressing a comment to Corinne, they spoke slowly and overexplained matters.

However, over creme tarts, Corinne learned that the earl of Bossley's foster son had been named a traitor and a price had been set on his head by the Crown.

The Crown. There would be no safe place for Will.

For a frightening second, Corinne feared she would swoon. "He's not," she heard herself say.

The two women who'd had their heads together looked up in surprise. "I beg your pardon?" one asked.

"The Reverend Norwich," Corinne said. "He's not a traitor. In fact, I doubt if you could find a more honorable gentleman—" She broke off. Felt her mother frown. Knew these women would not give Will quarter.

"Lord Bossley has charged Mr. Norwich himself," one of the ladies replied. "Singled him out. Very embarrassing for the family, but most honorable of Lord Bossley."

"Well, no good deed goes unrewarded," Lady Rumsman opined crisply. She was wearing a dress of puce silk, a silly color that truly was giving Corinne a headache every time she looked at the woman. "Bossley found his foster son begging in the streets of Barbados, starving to death, and this is how his lordship's kindness is repaid. That is why I refuse to give so much as a penny to the urchins. Thankless creatures."

"He's not a traitor," Corinne insisted. She had to be true to Will. She had to be. And Lord Bossley had reneged on their bargain. He wanted Will gone. Turning him over to the authorities was against what they'd agreed.

"You would counter the sworn statement of such a prestigious nobleman as Lord Bossley?" a woman across from her asked.

"I would," Corinne answered. "Oh, yes, I would," she reiterated as her temper started to mount.

"Corinne," her mother said in warning. She shifted uncomfortably in her seat. "The weather is quite nice—"

"Give her her head, Your Grace," Lady Rumsman said, cutting Corinne's mother off. "What do you know about Bossley's foster son?"

But before Corinne could defend the man she loved, a servant entered the room bearing a note on a silver tray.

"What is this?" Lady Rumsman demanded and took the note. She set her spectacles on the end of her nose. "Ah ha," she announced after a quick perusal. "Our conversation is timely."

Lady Rumsman lowered the note and looked around the table, her gaze settling on Corinne. "I have intelligence here from Lord Bossley himself. Lady Corinne and anyone else who cares to plead the case for this ungrateful cur of a foster son may do so on the morrow. That is when he'll go before the Magistrate." She held up the note. "You see, my lady, the traitor Norwich has already confessed."

"Confessed?" Corinne repeated in disbelief.

"That's what Lord Bossley informs me," came the reply. "Turned himself in—oh, wait, you wouldn't be able to defend his reputation, since you will wisely be marrying Lord Sherwin tomorrow."

Corinne went very silent. Will had given up? There must have been more. There had to be.

And how was he going to come for her before she married Freddie? He couldn't do anything if he was in the gaol.

"We are all foolish when we are young," Lady Rumsman said to no one in particular. "It's wise of you, Your Grace, to be marrying your daughter off to Lord Sherwin. He'll teach her some sense. And when his father leads our goverent, we'll all have the benefit of that good sense. Sense and civility. That is what we need in this country. Lord Bossley understands the importance of rank and privilege."

Corinne could not wait to leave. She needed time alone, to think. Did no one see through Lord Bossley? Did they all assume he was the image he wished to convey? Or were they hiding fatal flaws as well?

Of course, Lord Bossley thought he had the best of her, but he was wrong. If his lordship stood before her, she would tear out his evil heart with her bare hands . . . and do the same for his lying tongue.

Out on the street in front of Lady Rumsman's house, Corinne decided she had to run. She had to see Will, to do what she could for him.

She started off walking down the street at a brisk pace. Her decision was so abrupt that the footmen who seemed to dog her every step were caught off guard—and she was free.

"*Corinne,*" her mother called.

There was no stopping. Corinne could turn her back on everyone for Will.

But then her father's footmen caught up with her. They surrounded her, blocking her path.

"My lady, you need to return home with us," one of them said.

"I don't wish to," she replied with a sinking heart.

"You must."

Her mother slipped past them. She put her hands around Corinne's shoulders. "Please, Corinne. No scenes, no scandal. Not here."

"He's in prison," Corinne said to her mother. "I love him."

Her mother looked around as if fearing someone could overhear them on the street. "Yes, dear. Yes, yes, now climb in the coach. You will accomplish nothing by running through the streets of London like a madwoman."

She was right.

Corinne was silent on the drive home and quickly escaped to her room. Perhaps there was a way she could leave the house unnoticed? Unfortunately, her new maid—Hattie was her name—would not leave her alone. And footmen lingered in the hall and patrolled the street and small garden of the town house.

She was trapped. Caught.

Lord Bossley had won . . . and she was going to marry Freddie.

For a frightening moment, she contemplated

taking her own life . . . and realized she couldn't. Will would have been disappointed in her if she had.

But her courage was beginning to fail.

That night after dinner, when the family shared a moment in the sitting room, her father singled her out. "Is everything as it should be?" He'd been watching her closely, even with his paper in front of him.

Here was her opportunity to tell her father the truth of what had happened, to warn him of what sort of man Lord Bossley was.

At the same time, her inner sense of things warned her to be cautious. Will had confessed and he shouldn't have. It didn't make sense.

What if he needed her silence?

"It is." She ducked her head, hiding behind the pile of correspondence conveying well wishes. Her hands shook. She tried to keep them steady. "All is good."

Belinda and her children were entertaining the rest of the family. No one seemed to be paying attention to Corinne and her father—and yet she knew everyone watched.

"You have changed while you were gone from us," the duke said.

"The people of Ferris were kind to me." She

shuffled the letters around, attempting to look busy. "I became quite"—she paused, searching for the right word—"involved in their daily lives."

"You did not become involved with Bossley's foster son, I hope."

There it was, the source of her parents' fears. Corinne had assumed they'd known about herself and Will. They didn't . . . or were they pretending? She didn't trust anyone.

"I'm surprised you ask," she challenged.

Her father studied her a moment. "Bossley spoke to me—in confidence," he said as if to reassure her. "He fears his foster son was not the gentleman, or clergyman, he would have wished."

It had been on the tip of Corinne's tongue to proudly announce that Will was her lover, or was that what Lord Bossley wanted? So many intrigues . . .

"He's wrong. Mr. Norwich is the most noble, amazing gentleman of my acquaintance."

"So he had you," her father surmised.

Corinne shot him a sharp look. Guilt brought heat to her cheeks. She should have steered him away from thinking the worst of Will.

He nodded as if to confirm her conclusions.

"I am your sire," he said. "Of all my children, you alone insist on going your own way . . . but I am here to protect you, Corinne. I would not want you to embarrass our family. I know you are set against this marriage, although I chose Sherwin because I believe he affords you great opportunities—"

"Also for yourself." She couldn't resist speaking out.

"Yes, for myself as well," her father agreed. "However, you are my blood. And in spite of being a woman, you have a good sense of things. There are times when you have understood what the rest of us failed to perceive."

"I am like my grandmother," she stated as confirmation.

He leaned away from her. He had never admitted to his mother's gift of "knowing." "Possibly," he said, the best concession she would ever receive from him.

"Then listen to me when I say this, Father—you must keep your distance from Lord Bossley," Corinne warned. "He is not what he seems."

"Is that what Norwich told you?"

She pinned her father with her gaze. "It is what I know."

"It's too late to change the wedding. It must be done."

Corinne leaned forward. "You fear his reaction if we cry off," she said.

"Of course. I'm a man of honor," he said.

"He's not," she warned.

The words lingered in the air between them.

Her father rose. He placed his hand on her shoulder, but he walked away.

Like the Greeks of old who ignored Cassandra, her father would not listen to her.

Corinne went up to her room, where she worried and paced, finally falling asleep in the hour before dawn.

"I can't believe you slept so late," Belinda chastised. She was a bit taller than Corinne, and childbirth had added roundness to her figure, but other than that, the sisters appeared very much alike. "There is so much to be done. I've ordered a bath, and Delora and Hattie will see to your toilette. Mother is busy with all the details. You know how she is when she must host anything . . ." Her voice trailed off. "Are you feeling quite the thing?"

"I don't want to marry Lord Sherwin," Corinne said.

Belinda made a dismissive sound. "We all know that and don't understand why. I find him rather attractive."

"You've never seen his white buttocks," Corinne snapped and was surprised when Delora laughed. So, at least she had one ally in this house.

For the next two hours, she was surrounded by people. The wedding would be held at St. George's Hanover Square, with the wedding breakfast to follow here at the house. The smells of cooking food mingled with that of perfume and powder.

Corinne barely lifted a finger to help. They pampered and preened over her without needing one thought or action from her—and at last it was time to leave for the church.

She went downstairs and wasn't surprised to see her mother completely scatterbrained. The duchess stopped at the sight of her daughter. "You look exquisite," she said with approval. "Belinda, well done. Now, come, girls, we mustn't be late."

"Where is Father?" Corinne asked, not seeing him in the hall. Belinda's husband and children were there, along with two of her aunts.

Her mother made an exasperated sound. "He

left earlier. Said he would see us at the church. Some messenger came, and before I knew it, your father sent word he had to leave the house on an important matter. The man has his finger in everything, but I would have thought he'd make his daughter's wedding a priority. I just pray he arrives before Lord Bossley. We don't want him offended."

"I wouldn't mind offending him," Corinne said brightly. It was her wedding day. This might have been the last time she could express her mind.

"Enough of that, missy," the duchess scolded and then started herding everyone into the coaches waiting at the curb to drive them to Mayfair.

Corinne moved with a sense of detachment. Her mother and sister rode with her. Her brother-in-law and the children were in the coach behind them. Her brothers and their wives would meet them at the church.

Alone with the women in her family, Corinne asked, "Are you happy, Belinda?"

Her sister frowned. "Happy, Cory? 'Happy' is such a funny word. Everyone says it and no one knows what it means."

"You called me Cory," Corinne said.

"I beg your pardon?" Belinda questioned.

"You've never used that pet name before," Corinne answered.

"Cory?" Belinda shrugged. "I don't know why I used it now. Do you not like it?"

"I do like it."

"Well," her sister said, as if confused by the whole conversation, "I shall call you that again."

"I believe it sounds silly," their mother chimed in. "And here we are at the church. Where is Banfield?" The door to the coach opened, and Her Grace was the first to climb out.

Corinne held back, realizing her future awaited—and here she was, placing attachment to any signs she could find that God had not abandoned her. That included her sister's use of her nickname.

"Come along," Belinda prodded. "This is what we do. What we are expected to do."

The day was a good one for a wedding. Spring was in the air and huge, lazy clouds moved swiftly across a blue sky.

A crowd of the populace had gathered to witness the bridal party going into the church. They'd already watched the guests, including the Prince of Wales, arrive. They crowded the coach, Banfield footmen working to keep them at a distance, ready to gossip about the bride.

There were *ooh*'s and *ahh*'s at the sight of Corinne's fine muslin dress trimmed in French lace. She carried her family Bible in one hand and held her train in the other. Delora had swept her hair up into a design of smooth curls held in place by white rosebuds and pearl clips.

Will would come for her. He had to.

St. George's Hanover Square was one of the most important churches in London, albeit plain in decoration. It had a wide aisle with high box pews on either side. Those pews were already packed with everyone of importance.

Lord Bossley met them in the vestibule. He greeted the duchess warmly, gave a pat on the head to Belinda's son, and shook her husband's hand. His gaze met Corinne's and he smiled, as if he knew that everything he wanted was within his grasp.

Glancing around, Corinne asked, "Where's Father?"

"I don't know," Her Grace answered.

"He's not with you?" Lord Bossley questioned. He frowned. "He hasn't been here."

"He left early this morning, summoned for something at Whitehall," the duchess said. "The messenger said it was urgent. I answered that his daughter's marriage was urgent, but no one listens to me."

Lord Bossley grunted a response.

Reverend Hodgson, the church rector, came down the aisle to make inquiries. Upon learning that the duke was not present, he whispered to a guest or two and the word spread.

Corinne was not unhappy with the delay. Up in front of the altar, with its dramatic painting of the Last Supper, Freddie looked like he was asleep on his feet. For the first time, the thought crossed Corinne's mind that mayhap he didn't want to marry her any more than she did him.

She noticed her uncle Banker Montross and her aunt Catherine. Her cousin Abby was not attending because she now lived in the north with her new husband. Lady Rumsman was seated not far from them. She was noticeable because she carried a beribboned staff such as a shepherdess would carry. The ribbons matched the ones in the bonnet on her head. It was a frivolous chapeau and made Corinne wonder why a woman who prided herself on intelligence didn't know how to dress properly.

On the other side of the aisle, Corinne saw Lady Landsdowne whisper to her husband.

Suddenly, Lord Bossley exploded. "I am *not* cooling my heels here. If Banfield does not wish to be present for his daughter's wedding, then that is his choice. Let us be on with it."

"Lord Bossley," the duchess insisted in a conciliatory tone, "he shall be here shortly."

"He should have been here a half an hour ago," his lordship countered. "Reverend, let us start the service." He went marching up the aisle with the authority of a greatly affronted man. He took a place to stand beside his son.

Corinne seized upon the opportunity to delay the wedding. "I shall not marry without my father present."

"Of course, of course," her mother agreed, but with a worried look in her eye. She suddenly perked up. "There's your father."

The duke of Banfield surprised them all by making his appearance at the front of the church. He must have walked in from another entrance. Nor was he alone. He had several soldiers with him—and he had Will.

Will was not in his clerical garb; instead, he looked incredibly dashing in shining Hessian boots, riding breeches, and a bottle-green jacket. He was every inch the fashionable gentleman and appeared nothing like a prisoner.

Of course, he could have walked in in sackcloth and Corinne would have been just as happy. She started up the aisle toward him.

"What is happening here?" Lord Bossley

shouted. He backed halfway down the aisle, almost into Corinne's arms. But then he pulled up short when he recognized Will. "What are you doing here?"

Will moved to face him. "I had some business in London between myself and Newman Knowlys, Esq. You know him, don't you, my lord?" Will gestured toward a man wearing a powdered wig designating the authority of his office, who stood beside the duke of Banfield. "He's the Common Sergeant of London. I'm certain your paths have crossed." The Common Sergeant was an important judge in London's courts and second only to the Recorder in power.

Lord Bossley made an impatient sound. He looked to the Prince of Wales. "I beg your pardon, Your Highness. This is my foster son, the one I saved from the streets of Barbados and took to my bosom. He has turned out to be a viper. Did you know he turned himself over to the magistrate, confessing he was a traitor?"

"Actually, that's not what I did," Will said. "That's the story we put out so that we could have time to prepare other accusations against you."

A murmur of surprise went through the crowd.

"Against me?" Lord Bossley looked to the

Common Sergeant. "What lies is he accusing me of this time, Mr. Knowlys? What half-truths and innuendos?"

"It's not him accusing you, sir," Mr. Knowlys said, "but the Crown. *You* are an impostor, and I'm here this day to charge you with the murder of James Dunleavy Sherwin, *true* sixth earl of Bossley, and his wife, Aimée."

There was a moment of shocked silence from everyone in the church. Corinne filled the void with a decidedly unladylike *"Yes!"*

She lifted her petticoats and skirt, shoved Bossley out of the way, and went running for Will.

Chapter Eighteen

Pandemonium broke out around Corinne as she raced to Will. People were standing, asking questions, shouting denials.

She didn't care. Will was here and he was safe. She threw herself into his arms with such force that she almost knocked the two of them over, but he caught her, he held her.

Tears burned her eyes. He tightened his hold. He felt the same way she did.

"*This is a lie,*" Lord Bossley was shouting. "I never murdered anyone, and I am quite obviously alive. My wife is alive as well." He nodded toward Lady Bossley, who, dressed in her finery, had the look of a doe in a hunter's sights. She smiled, nodded, and fainted back into her seat.

Newman Knowlys, Esq., shouted back that the facts spoke for themselves.

Lord Bossley's friends insisted this was all a Tory plot. The Tories in the crowd denied their charges but crowed they were heartily glad of the turn of events.

In the end, it was the duke of Banfield who restored order. He reached for Lady Rumsman's shepherd's staff, the one festooned with ribbons and flowers, and pounded it on the floor until all fell silent. "Let us hear the charges against Lord Bossley," he said.

"Yes, I would like to hear them," the Prince of Wales agreed.

At the reminder of royal presence, the guests dutifully shuffled back into their seats.

The prince sat and nodded to Mr. Knowlys. "The charges, sir?"

Mr. Knowlys, a political animal if ever there was one, preened at such public attention. Everyone he could wish to impress was here, including the Lord Mayor of London.

He cleared his throat and said, "First, let me tell you what we do know. Lord Bossley was colluding with the French."

Again voices raised questions. The shock of betrayal was loud and clear.

"I am *not* a traitor," Lord Bossley announced, moving to the step of the altar to make himself seen. "However, the Reverend Norwich is a known criminal who had in his possession gold from the French. He confessed—"

Once more, the duke of Banfield banged the staff on the stone floor for order.

"The evidence does not support your position, Lord Bossley," Mr. Knowlys said. "The confession story is one we put out to throw you and your cohorts off the scent and to keep the Reverend Norwich safe. I spoke to Lord Tarrington this morning—a very minor lord, a greedy one, ripe for the plucking—who has been quite forthcoming with information once he realized he'd been found out."

Those who had supported Lord Bossley seconds ago now eyed him with suspicion. Corinne couldn't help tossing a superior glance in Lady Rumsman's direction.

"Go on," the Prince of Wales ordered. "What of the murder charges?" He leaned over the railing of his box with interest.

Mr. Knowlys turned to Will. "Do you wish to tell this?"

"I do." Will addressed his comments to the audience, but his gaze never left Lord Bossley. "Lord Bossley is actually Kenneth Moore, the younger son of an Irish nobleman, who plotted rebellion against England. He was tried here in London and found guilty. He was sent to Barbados to serve out his life as an indentured servant—*my father's* servant. My father was James Dunleavy Sherwin."

"What a pathetic, ridiculous lie," Lord Bossley said.

"Is it?" Mr. Knowlys countered. "I admit I was skeptical until I researched the archives and found the date of your sentencing. I'd wager there is a rebel's brand on your side."

Lady Bossley had started to regain her senses from her earlier swoon. "A brand? *The* brand?" She now fainted dead away again. Damning evidence if there ever was any.

"My father was a physician in Barbados," Will said, giving Corinne a squeeze to acknowledge how right she'd been. "He preferred the island to England, especially since he'd married a French woman, an octoroon whom they said he loved deeply. She had no desire to come here. She was happy where she was."

"Who said this?" Lord Bossley demanded. "Who speaks against me?"

"The dowager Lady Bossley," Mr. Knowlys answered. "She is not well and isn't here, but she gave her account before witnesses, including the duke of Banfield."

"She's too frail to remember anything," Lord Bossley countered. "She rarely remembers her name."

"But I am not," an accented voice said amongst the other side of the soldiers. A short, black man with close-cropped gray hair pushed his way to the front of the company. "I am Henri Biron. I also served the physician Lord Bossley as a free black man. Do you remember me, Kenneth? I thought never to see you again. I searched for you, but you had disappeared."

"No, not disappeared, Mr. Biron," Mr. Knowlys claimed triumphantly. "Kenneth Moore, the servant, murdered his master, Lord Bossley, and claimed his identity. He has been playing us all for fools for almost three decades."

Silence reigned in the church.

Corinne herself was shocked.

Bossley—Kenneth—changed before their eyes. He lost his bluster, his pride. He seemed to shrink and age.

"Mr. Biron reported the murder years ago," Mr. Knowlys continued. "He has been living in

London from time to time with the hope that Moore would someday show himself."

"I never thought he would take Lord Sherwin's identity—*and his son*," Mr. Biron said. "I never thought even he could be so cruel."

"I didn't murder Lord Bossley," Kenneth Moore said. "We were waylaid." He looked to Will, to the others who had been his friends, his acquaintances. To them, he pled his case. "Lord Sherwin was a fool. He had all of this waiting for him in England and he preferred spending his life nursing and healing the poor in Barbados. I could not understand it, except that he felt his wife was happier there."

"She was," Henri Biron confirmed. "I was very close to your mother"—he addressed this to Will—"from the time of my youth. She was beautiful, your mother was."

"Yes," Kenneth Moore agreed. "Lovely." A great sadness seemed to weigh him down. He continued.

"The day of his death, your father took me with him as protection when he called upon patients with the fever. Lady Sherwin also traveled with us. She did that from time to time. She cared for the ill. Myself? I hated going to the poorest sections of Bridgetown. We risked catching the fever. I argued, but your father was insistent. He needed me to guard the two of them and wanted me to assist him. As we were returning home, we were set upon. They killed Lord and Lady Sherwin for his watch."

"But you were unharmed," Henri pointed out. "You say brigands attacked, and you did what? Hide?"

"I was harmed," Moore said in his defense. "They struck me in the head. I told Lord Sherwin to give them the watch. He wouldn't do it. It had been a gift from his father . . . the earl of Bossley. He would not give it up."

Henri Biron looked to the crowd. "I don't believe his story. If I had fought to protect my master, I would have had more than a bump on the head to show for it. The authorities did not know what to think. They decided to believe him because they always believe a white man. They even tasked Moore to escort Lord Sherwin's heir back to England. The lad was no more than three years of age. But on the trip, the two of them disappeared. I followed to see to the welfare of the son. It was the least I owed my patron—but it was as if they had disappeared."

"I say Kenneth Moore plotted this all along," Mr. Knowlys said, taking back control of the testimony. "He realized he had the opportunity to assume Lord Sherwin's identity. Kenneth Moore took on the title of Lord Bossley and robbed the true Lord Sherwin of his birthright," he finished, nodding to Will.

"Because *I* was *robbed* of my birthright," Kenneth Moore lashed out. "I was a young man when I plotted rebellion. It was a lark. A game. The sentence was harsh. Unfair. I was no threat to the Crown."

"But since that time you have become a threat." This comment came from the Prince of Wales.

His words hung in the air.

And Moore had no defense.

"I should have been Lord Clare," Moore said stiffly. "You wish loyalty after you take *my* very identity from me?"

The Prince of Wales rose. "And so you gained the idea of taking Lord Bossley's from him."

Moore nodded, the lines of his face set deep. "Yes. Yes, I took what the man did not want. And look what I did with it. Imagine my surprise when I discovered that all the wealth I thought Bossley had was a myth. His estate was crumbling, his crofters were robbing him blind, he had no influence. I rescued that title. I *saved* that inheritance."

"Yes, you attempted to sell this country to her enemies," the Prince of Wales answered. "You made a mockery of that title. Take him from here," he said to Mr. Knowlys. "Try him for the traitor, and, yes, *murderer* I believe him to be."

"Wait," Will said. "Moore, why didn't you rid yourself of me? You had numerous chances. Certainly you knew there was always the risk of your true identity being discovered, especially with me close at hand."

"Because I am no murderer," Moore repeated. "I could not stop what happened to your parents, you must believe me. As for claiming the title, while taking you back to England, people assumed I was your father. And when I arrived in Ferris, people thought I was the lord. It was foisted upon me. I had little choice."

"You had a choice," Will said. "We all have choices."

Moore snorted. "You've met the dowager Lady Bossley. Would you have preferred to have been raised by her? Your father never thought well of her. All I had to do was increase her living allowance and she became a complicit ally in the deception."

"Yes, but if you had been truthful, you could have had an honest life," Will replied, "instead

of living in the shadows of lies and all of the
machinations to which you resorted to keep
your secrets safe." He turned to Mr. Knowlys.
"You may want to investigate what hand Moore
played in the death of one Simon Porledge, late
of Ferris."

"I shall, Reverend," Mr. Knowlys said. "Mr.
Moore, accompany us." He nodded for the soldiers to take control of their prisoner.

Freddie took a step forward. "Father?"

It wasn't until he spoke that Corinne even
thought about him . . . and then she almost felt
sorry for him. He'd been caught in his father's
lies as well.

"Don't worry, son," Moore said. "See to your
mother."

Moving like a man who had just witnessed
his world being destroyed, Freddie, no longer
Lord Sherwin, did as instructed. His mother had
started sobbing bitterly. Freddie offered his arm.
She took it, and the two of them walked down
the aisle and out of the church.

The officer in charge of the soldiers took
Moore's arm to escort him out the side entrance.
Lady Rumsman hissed like a goose as he was led
away, an odd sound. A cruel one.

Corinne's father approached her and Will.

"Well," he said in the ensuing silence. "That was eventful."

Several of the wedding guests gave nervous laughs at his understatement.

"Suffice it to say," the duke continued, addressing the guests, "there will be no wedding this day—"

"I beg your pardon, Your Grace," Will spoke up. "I wish to marry your daughter, and I shall do it here and now."

Interest buzzed through the church.

"I am not averse to your suggestion," the duke of Banfield said. "It might even save the scandal this day has created. However, there is no license."

"Was it not made out to Lord Sherwin? Am I not he now?" Will looked to the Prince of Wales, who conferred with a raised eyebrow amongst several of his well-placed friends.

"By Moore's own confession, apparently he is," the prince confirmed. "Although this must all be clarified and taken through proper channels for confirmation. Parliament must have their say."

"That could take weeks. Months even since Will's case is unusual. I will not wait for all that," Corinne said. "I love him. I must be with him."

Will faced the duke. "Your Grace, I wish to

marry your daughter and I want to do it here and now."

"Oh, dear," her mother said weakly. "The scandal of this," she whispered to her husband. "Can we not wait? You know, give this all time to, um, be forgotten?"

"My good duchess," the Prince of Wales said, "this wedding will live on in our memories forever. But I have a question—" He turned to Corinne. "Does it matter to you, my lady, if your beloved has a title or not?"

"No, Your Highness. I would marry marry the Reverend Norwich even if he was a rat-catcher."

"Hopefully our clergy hasn't sunk that low," the prince replied, a comment met with smirks and giggles from the elegant wedding guests. "I say they should marry." His decision was met with the applause of approval.

The duke of Banfield referred to the rector. "Reverend Hodgson?"

"The marriage documents have not been signed yet," Reverend Hodgson said. "A change could be made to the special license—" He turned toward those gathered, singling out one of the members of the prince's friends. His dress was elegant although of more subdued cloth and color than the others. "Bishop Randolph, as Bishop of

London, will you make the proper changes to the documents?" Reverend Hodgson asked.

"Of course I will," the bishop said

"Good man," the Prince of Wales replied, beaming his approval. "Ink and parchment for the bishop," he called. "I came for a wedding and a wedding I shall see." A suggestion that was quickly seconded by all assembled.

Will turned to Henri Biron. "Sir, will you stand by me?"

"I would be honored, my lord," Mr. Biron said with a bow.

"And perhaps later you can tell me of my father and mother."

"I have much to share," Mr. Biron said. "They were the best people. I sense their son is very much like them."

In short order, the special license was changed. No one seemed particular about the details, and Corinne found herself standing before the altar with the man she loved.

She had yet to let go of him but held his hand tight. And she continued to hold it as he pledged his troth in the words of the Book of Common Prayer. Her eyes never left his face.

Her husband. Her wonderful, noble husband.

They would be together through sickness and

through health, through good and bad, until death they did part.

Afterward, they walked down the aisle together toward a new life. And as her father's footmen hurried to open the church doors upon a waiting crowd anxious to cheer the new couple, Corinne leaned close to this man she loved and said, "I knew I wasn't going to marry Freddie Sherwin."

Her husband laughed and, to the delight of the waiting Londoners, swept her up into a kiss that set the crowd roaring with approval.

Epilogue

Love conquers all.
Virgil

1812

Word of what had happened at the duke of Banfield's daughter's wedding quickly spread. It would become the affair of the year, of the last ten years even, because of the scandal. And everyone who attended thought him or herself most fortunate. They could speak with authority on what they'd witnessed, something Lady Rumsman did quite often. Yes, indeed, she dined very well on the story.

The trial of Kenneth Moore took a good six

months. He was found guilty of treason. He could have hanged, but his sentence was changed to a life in exile. He was deported to His Majesty's colony in Australia.

Will thought it fitting justice.

As for himself, he was pardoned for his offenses committed as the Thorn. He wanted that formality because he wanted his conscience clear.

Freddie, now using the surname Moore, came to Will shortly after his father was imprisoned and asked for Will's help in purchasing his colors. Will thought it a capital idea that Freddie wished to serve his country and perhaps make up a bit for the wrong his father had attempted. He happily paid for Freddie's commission in the Horse Guard, as well as settling an income on both him and his mother.

There were other matters to be considered as well. Moore had rebuilt the Bossley estates, but he had done so by using a harsh hand. Will saw to it that what had been taken wrongfully was returned. His decision left Glenhoward in tight circumstances, but by the end of the year, the lands were more profitable than ever before.

Corinne opined that was because his parishioners were happy, and he believed she was right.

Amanda Gowan married Peter Clemson, and

the two of them moved to Carlisle. Will saw her from time to time, and her parents assured him she was very happy.

As for himself, he was blessed.

As a clergyman, he had spoken of miracles. Loaves of bread, fishes, good works, and the like.

But his wife was the one who taught him, the scholar, that the true miracle—the one God wanted him to witness—was that of love.

Corinne's love transformed him. He felt whole and at peace.

And just when he thought he knew love, that he loved all he could, she gave him the gift of a child. With his daughter in his arms, Will at last understood a parent's boundless love. It was all encompassing. Not only did he marvel in the child's perfection but he was also amazed that one such as his imperfect self had played a hand in her creation.

Aimee Dunleavy Sherwin yawned and rubbed her eyes with a newborn's innocence, and any hardness left in Will's heart melted. She had her mother's face, right down to her stubborn chin.

What a lucky man he was, blessed more times over than he could ever have imagined. His feet were rooted in Glenhoward's ground, his heart in his wife's soul, and his future in this small human.

Yes, love was a miracle.

Avon Books is proud to support the Ovarian Cancer National Alliance.

September is National Ovarian Cancer Awareness month, and Avon Books is urging our authors and readers to learn about the symptoms of ovarian cancer, and to help spread the "**K.I.S.S. and Teal**" message to friends and family.

Ovarian cancer was long thought to be a silent killer, but now we know it isn't silent at all. The Ovarian Cancer National Alliance works to spread a life-affirming message that this disease doesn't have to be fatal if women **K**now the **I**mportant **S**igns and **S**ymptoms.

Avon Books has made an initial donation of $25,000 to the Alliance. And—with your help—Avon Books has also committed to donating 25¢ from the sale of each book, physical and e-book, in the "K.I.S.S. and Teal" promotion between 8/30/2011 and 2/28/2012, up to an additional $25,000 toward programs that support ovarian cancer patients and their families.

So, help us spread the word and reach our goal of **$50,000**, which will benefit all the women in our lives.

Log on to *www.kissandteal.com* to learn how you can further help the cause and donate.

A portion of the sales from each of these September 2011 titles will be donated to the

Ovarian Cancer National Alliance:

Viscount Breckenridge to the Rescue
Stephanie Laurens

The Seduction of Scandal
Cathy Maxwell

The Deed
Lynsay Sands

A Night to Surrender
Tessa Dare

In the Arms of a Marquess
Katharine Ashe

One Night in London
Caroline Linden

Star Crossed Seduction
Jenny Brown

AVON

An imprint of HarperCollins *Publishers*

www.avonromance.com

www.ovariancancer.org

KT2 0911

This September,
the Ovarian
Cancer National
Alliance and Avon
Books urge you to
K.I.S.S. and Teal:

Know the Important Signs and Symptoms

Ovarian cancer is the deadliest gynecologic cancer and a leading cause of cancer deaths for women.

There is no early detection test, but women with the disease have the following symptoms:

- **Bloating**
- **Pelvic and abdominal pain**
- **Difficulty eating or feeling full quickly**
- **Urinary symptoms (urgency or frequency)**

Learn the symptoms and tell other women about them!

Log on to ***www.kissandteal.com*** for a downloadable teal ribbon—teal is the color for ovarian cancer awareness.

The Ovarian Cancer National Alliance
is the foremost advocate for women with ovarian
cancer in the United States.

Learn more at www.ovariancancer.org

KT3 0911